Avernus

Book One

by Steven Webb

@Steven Webb. All rights reserved. No portion of this book may be reproduced, stored in a retrieval system, or transmitted in any form or by any means—electronic, mechanical, photocopy, recording, scanning, or other—except for brief quotations in critical reviews or articles, without the prior written permission of the publisher.

ISBN: 9781733419758
Library of Congress: 2020910604

Acknowledgment

Tara Click (who knew that a birthday could bring one of the best friends I've ever had). Meeting you during the class photo because of our birthdays being one day apart, led to one of the greatest friendships I've ever had. When I was going through one of the toughest times of my life, you helped me push through. After I left the hospital, you were there to take me home. And now to have you help me with this book just reminds me of how much of a great friend you truly are.

They say that after leaving high school, you don't stay friends with most of the people you've met. Chris Stein, you proved the opposite. After coming home from college, it was as if I'd never left. Considering how crazy I was in high school; this meant the world to me. You helped me achieve peace of mind through the gym and having you to help me bounce ideas around for the book helped bring this project to fruition.

Of course, I could never forget my amazing friend, Katherine Woolley. From dating my best friend in high school to being one of my go-to friends, you always got my strange humor and never judged me. I'm so thankful that you were willing to read and comment on my first draft. I know it was rough but you stuck through it.

Debra Jastrow, I know I haven't known you long but I feel like we have been friends forever. I can always count on you for a smile on a hard day. Your smile and positive energy are so infectious. Knowing that you enjoyed my book helped to reassure me that this wasn't a waste of time. And I can't forget that it's because of you that I was able to get this book published.

Eva Rasmussen, you were the best coworker I could ever ask for. Work would have been boring without you. On top of that you've become like a second mom to me. I know it didn't always seem like it, but your opinions on my book really did get taken to heart.

To the two best teachers I ever had. Mrs. Marianne Perry and Mrs. Nancy Hushek. Without the two of you, I never would have succeeded in life. You both brought endless encouragement to me. Thank you.

I would also like to give a shout out to all my other friends for standing by me and just being wonderful friends. I wouldn't give any of you up for the world. And to my family who has been a huge support throughout my life and this entire project. I can always count on you guys. I love you all.

Carrie Severson, thank you for guiding me through the final product and helping me to get this book published. Here's hoping for many more partnerships in the future.

Book 1

Taylor

The room was large, with seating for three hundred, though this particular class hosted a mere thirty students all vying for doctorates in their respective fields. With that few people in the room, the smallest noise was amplified. Towards the back of the room, one of the students shifted in her seat causing the desk to rattle and creak. This slight movement was enough to startle the entire class. All attention shifted from the doctor to her. The lights, only half on, provided a clear view of each face yet kept any one person's face from standing out. The same faces that Taylor would have committed to memory within a week and would be forgotten a month after the semester's end.

"Throughout the existence of humanity, a fascination with how life, as we know it, came to be, has been at the forefront of our endeavors. Radical theories have been proposed by every culture throughout history in an attempt to explain this bizarre existence. We've looked at theories of aliens bringing humans to Earth and supreme beings creating life from nothing. Only recently in our existence have we begun to see the picture clearly. Evolution is the driving mechanism that has led every living thing to where they are today. Earth is riddled with creatures of all shapes and sizes that have been molded by their environments to survive even the harshest of conditions. We know there are species that can survive the cold emptiness of space. We have studied animals and microorganisms thriving around thermal vents at the bottom of the ocean and bacteria living amongst the clouds. Yet, for all our efforts, only one planet has been found to support the complexities of life. There is only one way to understand this mystery; by studying how biology allows living beings to prosper where they shouldn't."

Doctor Taylor Mantin found the lectures to be his favorite part of his job. Opening the minds of future generations to the possibilities that lay before them. He adjusted his glasses and scanned the room and continued his speech. "As we delve into this semester, I encourage you to ask questions. Challenge me."

Taylor woke up his laptop, revealing the day's slideshow. "Now, since we're all here today, let's start with a simple question to get your minds working. Why do we perceive tardigrades to be, for all intents and purposes, indestructible?" He stepped out from behind the podium and walked towards the front row. "Please take a few minutes to discuss among yourselves why you think this is." Papers began shuffling, and chatter filled the air. This group of students portrayed a refreshing air of curiosity for the class. He made his way around, listening to the discussions at hand. Teaching was about more than just lectures. The discussions he brought up were meant to help expand and broaden their views. The classroom was simply a lab used to test the capability of the mind rather than just fill it with random and easily forgettable facts.

"Okay, let's discuss what you came up with." Taylor now stood in front of the screen. He pointed to a young lady three rows up. "Tell me what conclusions you came to."

She sat fidgeting in her chair, pencil clicking against the desk. "Well, I brought up the fact that they can produce large amounts of offspring both sexually and asexually. This means that even if some are lost, the population can regenerate quickly."

As if he already knew what she was going to say before she spoke, he had a response. "I like where you are going with that. That is absolutely correct. It also means that any defects can easily be bred out. Who else has an answer they would like to share?" A hand shot up directly in front of him. "Ah, yes. This eager gentleman. What's your name?"

"Terri."

"Well, Terri, why don't you share what you came up with."

"I was thinking that their ability to survive in space helped contribute to their classification as near indestructible."

"Now we're getting to the root of it. These little suckers can enter cryptobiosis while floating in the vacuum of space. They have the ability to dehydrate themselves reducing the need to feed. They also produce a protein that protects their DNA from radiation. This means that should nuclear war ever break out tardigrades would be able to survive."

As if the Universe itself was in on some joke, a loud boom shook the walls of the classroom. "Well either we just had a nuclear war break out or the more likely option is an experiment gone awry." The fire alarm let out its irritating response. "Looks like the latter. Everyone, feel free to head home and we'll pick this discussion up tomorrow. No point in you guys standing outside in the snow."

The classroom emptied of students as Taylor packed up his laptop and threw on his jacket; the blaring squeal of the alarm ringing out around him. He headed out of the lecture hall. A blast of icy air struck his face sending a chill down his body. The cold air fogged up his glasses as he stepped outside. *Damn glasses*, he thought, taking them off and removing the moisture from his lenses. The snow crunched under his boots. As he made his way across the campus, a ray of sun broke through the light gray clouds that covered the sky. *It's like a false hope of warmth.* Despite being cold, he loved being outside in the snow. It brought with it a quietness that seemed to calm the world, with the exception of the alarm coming from behind the door. The trees were covered in fresh powder, leaving snow-free patch marks under the shade of the branches. The path towards his lab was half shoveled to expose a thin sheet of smoothed ice. Either side of the path was littered with footprints of people who found it easier to track along than struggle across the ice. This was Taylor's same thought.

By the time he reached his lab, the snow was caked onto his pants and encompassed his shoes. The door scraped against the ice coming to a stop halfway upon its pivot. Taylor entered the long hall and headed towards his lab. An afterimage remained on the floor comprised of small muddy puddles that vaguely resembled the shoes that created them. His steps echoed through the hall. There was no sign of anyone to be seen or heard. The keys chimed as he removed them from his pocket and opened the door to his lab. Inside, the bulbs flickered before springing to life. The roaches and mice scurried through their cages in search of shelter. His notes were spread out across the table, a mess, but somehow organized in his mind. Directly in front of him his office door sat open which came across as odd. He peeked his head inside the office. A small figure laid curled up on the couch gently snoring. Brunette hair covered her face. Shoes and a lab coat sat in the chair. Gently, and with the intent of a parent waking their child, he placed his hand on her shoulder and spoke softly, "Carrie, wakie, eggs, and bakie."

The figure rolled over. Her soft brown eyes were barely open. "Sorry it got so late and I wanted to avoid the storm." she shifted her body weight, throwing her feet off the couch to propel her upright.

Taylor handed her the shoes she had left in the chair. "No worries. How did the lab tests go last night?"

"No unexpected results from the mice." Carrie stood up and threw on her lab coat, missing the first two buttonholes. "The control group and test group B for the cockroaches are standard. However--"

She walked over to the windowless door connected to the lab and turned the handle. As she opened it the light shone with the brightness of midday. Large Terrariums lined the walls and a shelf divided up the room. On the left sat the mice and on the right cockroaches. The ones in the middle of the room were currently unused. "...Tank eighteen B."

"Everything looks normal," he bent over to have a closer look. The log at the front of the cage suddenly shifted and dozens of full-sized cockroaches streamed out followed by hundreds of hatchlings. "Holy shit! The combination of shortened light cycles and substance HF seems to have triggered a large-scale increase despite the cold temperatures."

"Already recorded and the observational write up is on your desk," Carrie said seeming to have read Taylor's mind.

"Well, then it seems you've done all the leg work for me," he continued staring at the unbelievable results. His mind seemed unable to fully grasp that such an impact could be achieved.

"Head on home. You've got the rest of the day off."

His voice was infused with tones of giddiness. It took everything he had not to jump out of exhilaration. He heard the door leading out of the lab open. A blur of white fur caught his attention. It quickly scurried across Taylor's foot and into the lab. The figure, which he failed to recognize at first, was one of the mice rushing for the door. "Quick don't let it out."

"Let what out?" Her response came too late. It had made it past her and into the hall.

"You head home and leave it to me," he rushed past her and down the hall and around the corner.

The mouse was losing ground. Taylor reached his hand out readying himself to close the gap. Without warning, his foot hit a puddle, launching him into the air. The ground stopped him with a thud. He stared at the ceiling, motionless, while cold water soaked through his clothes. "Ugh," he moaned. He tried to catch his breath. He noticed the wet patches along the floor when he regained his footing and stood back up. "Stupid janitor." His eyes caught sight of the mouse once again. It sat outside the door to the department head's office. He walked towards it hoping it would remain in place. The pain in his back was distracting him from the task at hand. Finally, the mouse was within distance. As if accepting its fate, it sat still, allowing him to close his hands around it.

"Taylor, please come in," a voice said from behind the door.

One glance into the room brought sight of an old friend of Taylor's, he was sitting in the office talking with Shay, the head of the biology department, a briefcase containing a stack of documents sat on the desk between them. The official NASA logo on the guest's jacket meant business, not pleasure. In a blur, the man leaped out of the chair sending the briefcase flying.

"Frank, what the hell brings you all the way home?" he asked in excitement. Forgetting the mouse in his hand, Taylor embraced his childhood friend.

"Always the hugger," Frank said, the wind being squeezed out of him. His glasses nearly fell off his face but his large nose held them in place. "How've you been?"

"It's going great. I was actually planning to call you. I'm supposed to be getting an engagement ring for Megan soon." Taylor still stood in disbelief that Frank was actually here.

"Congrats Curly. On that note, you'll want to plan the wedding in the next year."

"I don't even know how long it's been since I heard that nickname." Taylor's curly hair earned him that nickname in elementary school and Frank apparently never forgot it. "What do you mean in the next year?"

Shay jumped in. "Actually that's got something to do with the conversation we were just having. But first, could you put the mouse in the cage over there?" Taylor knew the routine. The cage had been brought into the office because of Taylor. Mice from his lab were constantly escaping, and since he wasn't in his lab much, once caught the mice were brought to the department head.

The cage clicked shut with the mouse inside. Taylor turned and faced his friend. "So, what are you two conspiring about behind my back?"

"As you know NASA has been working to send a manned mission to Mars." Frank handed a stack of papers from his briefcase marked classified. "What you don't know is that scientists believe they have discovered a possible hotbed for bacterial activity."

"You mean they think they found life on Mars?"

"Exactly. But we can't know for sure unless we send a group up to collect samples. I put your name in as one of the candidates. You've been accepted. The only problem is you have to go through training in the next year"

Shay said leaning forward. "That's why we've been talking. I agreed to let you go on paid leave for the training and the mission as an extension of your research."

He sat down in shock. "Wow, I can't believe it. This is every kid's dream. I would need time to check with Megan. Plus, who would take over my lab and class for me?"

"I was going to offer your position to your intern if you think she's up to the challenge."

He sat in astonishment. "I have no words. It's just… I mean … Holy Shit."

"This is a once in a lifetime opportunity. Take some time, look over the information, and get back to me." Frank closed his suitcase and started to head out.

"If you're in town tonight would you like to come over for dinner? Maybe explain things in more detail? Meet Megan?"

"I would love to but I have to visit another recruit tonight. If you agree to come out, we can catch up in Florida."

"I'll call you once I've decided." Taylor watched Frank leave. He grabbed the papers and headed for the door.

Shay stopped him. "If you need to talk this over, let me know. Oh, and don't forget your mouse."

The whole trip back was a blur. His mind spun in circles trying to figure out how to explain this to Megan. *I don't understand why I'm so nervous about telling her. I know she would tell me to jump on this opportunity.* His nerves were making him jittery. News this big could not be taken lightly. *What if she doesn't want to join me? What if NASA decides to change their minds? No, I've got this.* He found himself back in the lab, the mouse still struggling to escape from his hand. He placed it in a temporary cage and sat down. With the lab quiet, he began reading over the documents.

The cover had the NASA logo printed on it. Below the logo were the words **Mission: Phoenix VII**. A giant red *Classified* was stamped across the page along with the date, January 12th, 2056. He flipped open the document and began reading:

On March 15th, 2024, an unmanned probe discovered a pocket of methane gas located at the base of a crater on the surface of Mars. The Crater F114, or Gorgon Crater, has shown signs of water. Researchers believe the Crater was formed when a comet struck the surface of the planet. It is unknown at this time whether the methane was produced by the Comet or life forms already living on the planet. Mission Phoenix VII will rely upon a specialized Spaceship designed for multiple trips to and from Mars. It will feature state of the art equipment to determine the possibility of life on Mars. Until the mission is complete, we request, under penalty of perjury, that no details contained within this file are to be discussed without permission from NASA.

Taylor flipped through the pages, amazed at all the information. The possibility of finding life on another planet was stunning, but to be one of the few people to be given the chance to possibly study it was unfathomable. Realizing he had managed to read away the afternoon, he gathered the documents and fought his way through the slush to his car.

Snow-covered roads slowed Taylor's travel home. The extra twenty minutes it added onto the commute stretched on forever. The anticipation of bringing this up to Megan both excited and terrified him. Growing up in different states, he never truly grew attached to any one place. The same could not be said for Megan whose entire life had been spent in Denver. Her closeness with her family and their inclusion of him was integral to their way of life. He pulled into the driveway, snapping out of his distractive thoughts.

Megan's voice greeted him when he entered the house. "Hey Darling. I hope you don't mind. I ate without you."

Crap, Taylor thought, *there goes the whole telling her over dinner plan.*

Megan continued talking, seemingly oblivious to her boyfriend entering the room. "I just ate leftovers. I think there might be some chicken in the fridge. Three minutes in the microwave oughta cover it."

Taylor placed his arms over her shoulders, brushing the hair away from her neck. He leaned in, caressing her skin with his lips. Her body wavered under his kiss. She turned her head and pulled Taylor's lips up to meet hers. "How was work, Hun?" she said, pulling the headset from her ears.

Taylor took off his jacket and tossed it across the room. "It was pretty much just like every other day. The class went smoothly. One of the mice escaped and I didn't get any lab work done. Oh, and Frank stopped by the school."

"Frank? Is Frank one of your old lab workers?" Her nonchalant tone revealed how long it had been since Frank had come to visit.

"He's my childhood friend. We lived on the same street as kids. I swear I told you about him."

"Doesn't sound familiar."

"You know, the story of how I broke my arm as a kid when we were playing destruction derby with our bikes?"

"Nope, not ringing any bells."

"The guy who went to work for NASA?"

"Oh, Frank Bruner."

"Yeah, that one." The nervousness returned once the purpose of Frank's visit returned to the forefront of his thoughts.

"What brought him up from Florida?"

"That's what I wanted to talk to you about." He fidgeted, suddenly unable to find a comfortable way in which to hold his hands. "He offered me the chance of a lifetime. The opportunity to travel."

"Do you mean as an Astronaut? You would be going into space?" Her countenance changed as the idea hit her.

"Yeah. Not just space but a chance to be one of the first men…." He hesitated, unable to believe what he was about to say. "…on Mars."

Megan flew out of her seat, throwing her arms around him and screaming with joy.

"The only issue is we would have to move to Florida while I get trained."

"Well, that doesn't sound so bad." She squeezed Taylor in her arms. Her reassuring voice calming his nerves. "So, tell me about the mission. What do they want you to do?"

"I was asked to study potential life on Mars. To do that NASA has decided to send us to set up a space station in orbit around the planet. Apparently, we'll be using that as a place to study the planet in real-time from space and travel to and from the surface."

The conversation drifted along for hours. Before long, Taylor found himself lying in bed, Megan next to him. Taylor glanced out the window at the rising sun. Realizing they had talked all night. He felt as energized as a child awaiting Christmas morning unable to sleep. He turned on his side and stared at Megan. He was ready. Ring or no ring, there was no better moment than this. The two of them connected, joined in agreement. "Megan." He spoke up breaking the only silence that night had held. "I know I'm not prepared for this but, with us moving to Florida… and with us being together for four years…." He sat up in bed, placed her hand between his. "Will you do me the honor of marrying me?" He couldn't believe how surprisingly calm he felt despite the slight hesitation.

Taylor watched Megan's big golden eyes fill up with tears. "Of course, I will," she squealed with excitement.

Taylor saw a bright future ahead of him. Within a year he would be married and flying off to his place in the history books as a leader in the future of scientific advancement. And soon he would no longer be just a professor.

Zea

Today, training for the Phoenix VII mission would officially commence. Zea's night had been long and sleepless, instead filled with Internet surfing and early morning reruns of TV shows from the 20s. The oldies always intrigued her more than modern programming. She reveled in their campiness and originality. Being born at the end of the decade she had missed it completely. It helped pass the time. Pure adrenaline born from excitement flowed through her veins, turning two hours of sleep into eight. Nothing could maintain her interest at this point. *Early is better than on time* she thought to herself heading out to her car. In her excitement, she dropped her keys. A penny sat heads up next to her keys. "Looks like it's my lucky day," she said, picking up the penny along with her keys.

Warm air blew in through the open car windows carrying along with it the scent of the ocean, A reminder that the training was more than just a dream. Zea loved this smell. Being from Montana she rarely got the experience of coastal life, until now. Her brown locks whipped around in a frenzy but rather than tie it up, she allowed it to move freely. Thoughts of a world with no people crept through her mind as she watched the endless empty road ahead. Images of a barren city easily imagined. The clouds glowed ruby and golden orange above the rising sun. This drive was the only time her new home state ever felt at rest. It was a drive she would take daily from now on. Zea decided to capture the moment. Pulling up to the first security gate, she stopped short and reached for her phone to record this moment. She spoke to the camera: "Beginning of a long adventure," aiming the device towards the NASA Building ahead of her. The phone awaited her order to share it with the world, a moment that would become a part of history upon her return to Earth. The message sent into cyberspace, Zea jumped in her car and continued past the raised security arm.

A reserved parking spot sat right in front of the building she would spend most of her time in. Security ran heavy along the exterior of the building. Being a curious soul, Zea drove around the facility. Her wide eyes took in every detail of the large buildings. She drove along reaching the entrance that led to the infamous launch pad of Cape Canaveral. The gate was locked up but she knew her time was coming. Looking at her clock she realized the time for the meeting was almost upon her. She turned around and returned to the main facility.

Once inside Zea was led down a long hallway lined with images of the past. The entire history of the space program sprawled across the walls. The further she traveled the more progress was made toward the ultimate goal of mastering the universe. Buzz Aldrin and Neil Armstrong stood on the surface of the moon. Sally Ride, the first female American astronaut. Scott Kelly aboard the ISS in orbit. Phoenix II and the first humans to travel beyond the Moon's orbit and return. For the first time she felt truly humbled to be counted amongst her heroes.

Zea reached a conference room sitting at the end of the hall. Frank addressed her directly. "Morning Zea, have some breakfast, and take a seat. We're just waiting on a few more people."

Two people stood next to the breakfast bar dressed in uniform discussing what could only be some previous military encounter. Attempting not to interrupt their apparent bonding time, Zea crept past them towards the breakfast burritos, but the two left their discussion on hold to greet her. The Woman stretched out an open hand. "Captain Addison Somers, I'll be the Captain of this mission."

Zea met the hand with hesitation. Looking away she uttered softly, "I'm Zea Charbonneau."

"Lovely name. And this man next to me is General Rocco Blanche. We've known each other for what, seven years now?"

"Sounds about right," Rocco replied. He stood tall and confident like a puppet being held up on strings. A short tight military cut gave him that tough battle-ready look. "Glad to have you on the team Zea."

"Thank you both," she said, her voice quaking.

"It's alright to be nervous. Do you like cats?" Captain Somers pulled a wallet out of her pants. She opened it, revealing a picture of a black and white cat sitting on top of an orange cat. The lower one's mouth was agape in panic and legs blurry from moving during the shot. The top one staring at the ceiling. "These are my baby's Astro and Sam."

Zea found herself unable to contain the laughter. A small snort squeezed out triggering a chain reaction of laughter. Feeling out of control she quickly reigned it in and caught her breath. "They're adorable," she said over belated breaths.

"Thanks, I love them dearly. I'm sitting along the back table if you want to sit next to me. And feel free to call me Addison. No need for formalities."

"Ok." Zea finished grabbing breakfast and headed to the table. She looked around the room getting a feel for the people she would be with for the next several years when Addison came and sat down next to her.

"Let me introduce you to the others. Sitting at the table on your left you have Joseph Cullen, he's one of the geniuses who helped design the Phoenix VII."

Joseph looked up at Zea. "Nice to meet you." His gaze returned to his phone.

Addison continued, "And sitting at the table on the right you've got Trent Blaum."

"Math Wizard Blaum thank you very much," Trent chuckled.

"And I'm Hugh Jass," the man next to him quipped.

"Shut up Taylor," the girl with straight jet-black hair interrupted. "Just ignore these two. They're harmless really. His name is Taylor Mantin, and I'm Sophie. I'm a planetary geologist. Come sit next to me." She pushed Taylor, forcing him to move over.

"I appreciate it, but would it be alright if I stayed here?"

"Sure." Sophie went back to chatting with the two guys.

Zea began poking at her breakfast in front of her while she flipped through the packets on the table. As she was glimpsing over the mission safety detail, in walked the lady responsible for her psych eval, Nova Lenus. Her dark skin and fit build were unmistakable.

Nova waved at the group. "Hi everyone. Good to see you all again." Despite being the shortest crew member, she carried herself with such grace and confidence. Under her left arm, she bore a stack of files. she gestured at the seat next to Zea. "Mind if I sit here?"

"All yours." Zea slid her plate back in front of her to make room for Nova's papers.

Frank's voice interrupted their conversation. "Ah, perfect, Nova's here. And it looks like our last two folks just arrived. Come on in Diego, Carl. Everyone, this is Diego Ramone, our IT guy and Programmer for this mission. And this gentleman is Carl Weiss, an Atmospheric Scientist. Have a seat so we can get started." Once everyone had settled down, he continued. "Welcome to NASA. As was mentioned in the packets I gave you, in 2024 NASA discovered what we believed to be a chance of life on Mars. This information has been kept secret along with the mission we are preparing to send you on."

Zea's attention drifted in and out as she listened to Frank drone on. She couldn't take him seriously. His shirt was half-tucked into his baggy oversized khakis pants, with a mustard stain on the front. The little hair he had on his head stuck up everywhere.

"Finally finished building a specialized space station that you will be setting into orbit around Mars. Think of it as a working research station and port for travel down to the surface."

Zea began doodling on the pages around her to kill the boredom. She already knew all of this. Between the first meeting, debriefings, and forms she had to sign, this was the seventh time this info had been relayed to her.

"You'll be traveling aboard the Phoenix VII, a detachable ship that will be used to carry the Mars Orbital Station and return you guys to earth. During the flight out and back, you will each have a personal stasis pod to make the journey easier."

The meeting seemed to never end. Zea took notes while keeping an eye on the clock. Eventually, the hand reached 5 p.m. and the day was over. But she found that the slowness with which the day passed didn't apply to the rest of the training. Days flew by and she grew closer and closer to the crew.

Underwater simulations became her favorite day. It felt like being in space but less dangerous. Zea adjusted quickly to the different ways of working with tools and moving inside the spacesuit. These days were followed by emergency simulations. They seemed to have thought of everything from running low on food to half the ship being torn asunder by space debris.

As if without notice, the day of the shuttle launch had finally arrived. The crew prepared themselves in their rooms on base. Zea walked through her morning preparations, Florence and the Machine playing in the background. She danced around the room to the fluid beat of the music. Each time the chorus came on she would stop to sing along. A knock came at the door.

Addison stood outside, "Ready to go?"

Zea looked out the door to see the rest of the crew waiting by the van. "Sorry, I got a bit distracted." She turned off the speakers and grabbed her phone. As she walked out the door a man walked in and grabbed her bags. "Okay, let's go." She headed over to join everyone else. "Oh shit, I forgot my ring on the sink." Zea ran back into her room. She searched high and low with no luck. The bedding flew through the air as she shook it around hoping the ring would drop out of it. She ran into the bathroom and scoured the cabinet. Still no luck. Panic overwhelmed her. The only thought she could hold onto was that she had lost her mother's ring. It was the only thing she took after her mother died. She retraced all of her steps, all the while getting angrier with herself, yet she couldn't remember the last time the ring had been on her finger.

Addison walked into the door. "You alright?"

"No, I can't find my mom's ring."

"What did it look like?"

"It's silver with a ruby on it. Me and my mother's birthstone." She continued to look under every piece of furniture. "I hope it's not at my house."

"This one?" Addison said holding up the ring.

"Oh my God! Thank you." Zea wrapped her arms around her, tears filling her eyes.

"Let's get going," Addison said, patting Zea on the back. Zea followed Addison to the waiting van and helped her load the van.

The ride was loud. Excitement flowed through the van. The atmosphere was electric. It felt like a trip to Disneyland as a child. They could see the shuttle sitting on the launch pad and the crowd on the far side of the lake watching the countdown clock. She had never seen so many people gathered in one place, not even outside a sporting event. The brilliant sun reflected off the calm lake. Its glass-like surface free from any imperfections. Seagulls called overhead, landing amongst the crowd in hopes of dropped food.

The van pulled up to the launch building, letting the soon-to-be astronauts out. The crew headed inside with Zea following closely behind. Once inside the waiting room, each crew member put on their spacesuits. Their cumbersome nature made walking difficult and unseemly. Moving around required shifting several extra pounds. Once everyone was suited up, Frank came in to give one final pep talk.

"Today you are preparing to venture further than any human before you ever have. Every move you make will be watched with wide eyes by children and adults alike. Stay focused on your goal and remember your mission. You are a family first and foremost. Take care of each other. Don't forget you could very well be the first humans to see life outside our planet. You are the future. You are our journey forward. Good luck."

Zea walked out and headed through the maze leading to a metal bridge connecting to the shuttle. The craft was the size of a bus with two large engines attached to each wing. The wings loomed large over the platform at four times the size of the ship's length. The Gen Space's logo had been plastered across the body. It had become common knowledge that NASA no longer built the crafts but looked to private corporations to produce them.

Zea headed to her seat inside the ship and buckled up. The G force simulator had made her throw up the first five times but she quickly found herself adjusting. She hoped that the actual launch wouldn't get to her. She closed her eyes.

Frank's voice came over the speakerphone. "Launch in t-minus ten minutes. Phoenix VII crew please, check in."

Zea pressed her button, eyes still shut tight.

"Everyone's set. Check systems and make sure all programs are running for self-launch."

"Systems check out," Joseph's voice said.

The ship began to shake. A loud roaring filled the cockpit deafening Zea. She could barely make out Frank's voice.

"Ignition. Launch in ten...nine...eight...seven...six..."

Zea felt the seat shaking her entire body. Her vice grip on the seat managed to gain strength.

"Three...two...one...lift-off."

The seat absorbed Zea's body as gravity attempted to hold her down to Earth. Her head felt like a brick unable to move. As the speed increased, her vision began to blur. The left side of the ship began to jerk violently.

Addison shouted out, "NASA, we have a problem. The left engine is coming loose."

"Hang on tight, it should hold up," Frank reassured the crew.

A creaking sound echoed throughout the room. Bolts whined under the stress. A loud cracking sound hit Zea's ears. The entire ship jerked to the left.

Rocco screamed over the roar of the remaining engines, "Our leftmost engine just detached early, everyone, hold on tight. Ground control, we have a problem."

"It'll be okay. The other three engines should have enough power to get you out of the atmosphere. Actually, the fourth engine should be attaching right about..." A series of pops signaled the engine's release. "...And there we go. Should be smooth sailing from here."

The engine noise died down. Zea breathed a sigh of relief but had forgotten that the second set of engines would be kicking in. This time it was as if a bomb had gone off within the cockpit. The ship belted forward.

"You'll be out of the stratosphere and in orbit in three...two...one..."

The engine roar was gone, silenced by space. Zea no longer felt attached to her chair. She watched Carl unbuckle himself and float into the air. *Guess I should follow suit*, she thought, releasing her restraints.

"NASA, we've cleared the atmosphere successfully," Joseph said. "Despite the engine situation the ship appears to be alright. We're in orbit."

Addison turned and faced the crew. "At 17,000 miles per hour, we should be able to dock with the CAPS within six hours." After the ISS had been deemed nonfunctional, the CAPS, or Cosmic Analysis Planetary Station, had been created to continue space research. It functioned much like the original but with a few variations. The space station rotated to create artificial gravity. This made longer trips more feasible. The size had also increased to include separate sections for each nation which now sat at thirteen. It now also hosted a garden for experiments on plant life.

Zea enjoyed playing in the zero gravity: Spinning around, pushing off walls, and drifting uncontrollably. The experience was indescribably beautiful. It felt like she was flying like superman. Her hair danced around with no real purpose. She looked towards Nova who managed to tie her hair back in a braid. Zea pushed herself towards Nova. A slight miscalculation threw her directly towards a chair. There was nothing around to grab ahold of. In an act of self-defense, she stretched out her arms hoping to grab ahold of the chair. She managed to latch onto the arm and pulled herself over to where Nova floated. "Can I borrow a hair tie?" Nova pulled one from her wrist and handed it off. It took a few tries to wrangle all the loose hairs in, but every time she thought the hairband was in successfully, a loose bunch would float past her face.

"Here, let me help you out." Nova's hands wrangled Zea's hair up. "Do you want your hair up in a bun?"

"Actually, I really like the way you did yours."

"I think I can handle that." There was something relaxing about the way she worked the braid. As she got lost in the moment, the ship came around and the sun began to rise through the window. Zea and Nova both stopped to stare out at this spectacular view. The earth below them rotated slowly. She could see storms rolling across the sky and lights shining from cities in the night. CAPS lied just ahead. Attached to it were the MOS station and Phoenix VII ship hybrid.

The gateway to the stars now stood before her. "There, all done. You know, it actually suits you more than me."

The only response Zea could muster was to blush. She quickly diverted her attention away from Nova and back out the window. The space station was now overtaking the view.

The docking process was relatively quick. The capsule pulled alongside the station, matching both speed and spin. As it did, a small amount of gravity returned to Zea's body. Her stomach dropped. It reminded her of hitting the bottom of a rollercoaster. The familiar adrenaline rush consumed her. In all her wildest dreams, nothing could compare to this. Riding on a giant, standing atop the world.

When the airlock opened, an unfamiliar woman awaited them. "Welcome aboard the CAPS. My name is Andrea. Over the next few days, I'll be helping you familiarize yourself with your new home. Let's start with a tour."

As they wandered endless corridors, Zea found herself lost in the wonder of the ship. *To think a ship like this exists.* The halls were well-lit, with strings of blue light running along the floor. The ceilings provided plenty of overhead clearance for even the tallest member of the crew. That was unexpected based on the outside of the ship. There were people wandering the walls acting as if they were in a regular building back on Earth. Their chatter brought the place to life. Massive steel doors with the room names on them lined the halls. She placed her hand against one of the cold steel ribs used to give structure to the hall. In all her excitement, the realization that outside the ship was an empty cold void hadn't hit her. She stood in awe, trying to take in everything.

"Zea, please keep up." Andrea's voice broke out, attempting to steal away the beauty of the moment Zea was having. She stood a bit longer before catching back up to the group.

Andrea handed each of them a plate. "Here is the dining hall." She walked over to a large machine against the wall, pushed a button and, in minutes, out popped a rectangular chunk of what could only be described as a mud cake. "Everyone, please take some time and eat. We have a long day ahead of us yet."

The machine whirred around producing all sorts of strange shapes. When Zea approached, Captain Somers stood next to her and pointed at one of the buttons. "I suggest you try this one."

Zea had grown to trust the Captain so she figured why not go along with it. The machine left a murky grey sphere on her plate along with three small disks. She headed to the bench and grabbed a fork from the table. Beginning with the ball of goo, she began poking around. The substance held up well. She placed a sample in her mouth. The taste was phenomenal. Somehow everything told her she was consuming honey roasted pork. Everything, that is, except the texture which was creamy like frosting. Not that it bothered her. Lunch was followed by a trip to the main deck of the phoenix ship. And then dismissal to get familiar with their personal quarters.

The quarters were small but cozy. Zea placed her lucky penny inside the top drawer and buried it beneath clothes. It seemed silly, but if there was a chance that the luck would rub off onto her clothes, it was a risk worth taking. After getting her things arranged, it was time to wander the ship on her own.

Days passed learning the ins and out of the Phoenix VII. Zea had learned every nook and cranny, making sure to have emergency supplies stored around the ship. You never knew when you would run into trouble and getting back to the med station could become a life or death situation. With all preparations complete they were ready to ship out.

Zea stood amongst the crew as the bay door closed on the MOS. The people beside her were now her only means of interaction. They headed towards the bridge to begin mankind's most epic voyage. The first trip to another planet, a possibility for life, and the farthest space flight to date would all change the course of humanity regardless of the mission's outcome. The ship roared to life, and from the bridge Zea watched the Earth begin to slowly shrink into the distance, followed by the sight of the moon filling their window into space. Once the ship was safely out of Earth's orbit, Zea followed Captain Somers into the Stasis pod room. When she awoke the god of war would be there to greet her. His face smiling at her like a parent watching, waiting for them to open their eyes, prepared to teach them all that they know. Opening them up to a whirlwind of new information and knowledge.

Sophie

The destination hung in the emptiness of space before the ship. Sophie had been awake for the past week, at least that's what the onboard clock indicated. It was the only means of tracking time without the regular cycling of the sun, making time all blur into one long day. Her focus for the week was on observing geological features of the red planet's surface visible from space. From atop this perch, one could view the entirety of Olympus Mons, the highest peak on Mars at two and a half times the height of Everest, unaided. Seeing a volcano this large with the naked eye was unlike anything she had been witness to in her life. Not only was the height impressive but the expanse over which the volcano stretched was remarkably large. She wanted nothing more than to reach the surface and dig her fingers into the red soil. The area around what was being called the Gorgon Crater seemed to have different geological features from the surrounding surface.

Sophie had been working closely with Taylor to designate the best locations for sampling. Tomorrow the lander would be taken down for the first time and a research base would be established within a short distance of the desired area. She stood next to Taylor staring at the map of Gorgon Crater.

Taylor pointed at the center of the map. "If anything, the floor of the impact crater should be our biggest goal. That seems like the best place for life to survive. Air could potentially get trapped down there."

She ran her finger over a swath of darkened land just outside the crater. "That is true but look here. This is what we call microbially-induced sedimentary structures. The only way these could be produced in this quantity would be through some form of ancient bacterial life. Here it looks just like ancient fossilized microbial life sites in an ancient floodplain." A picture popped up on the display alongside the map. "From what I can tell, the meteor probably crashed into the ground, but life was most likely already there. And here along the crater's edge, those are unmistakable signs of recurring slope lineage. Water must be coming from somewhere to produce these; my guess is an underwater source right around here." She pointed to one of the seven different red circles she had drawn earlier. "You know as well as I do that the odds of bacteria being able to survive on the surface are astronomical at best."

"So, our best bet seems to be setting the base camp up here," Taylor placed a miniature model of the habitat along a midpoint in the north sector.

Knowing her theory held the most weight, she moved the model over towards the clusters she circled in red. "If we want the best chance, the base needs to be here."

"No," Taylor said, pulled the model back to its original location without even a second glance at Sophie. "This spot is ideal. It has a nice open flat patch for the lander and sits between a large grouping of possible testing sites. Plus, it's closer to the easiest entrance to the crater."

Sophie was getting fed up. "I'm telling you, that's plain wrong. Why not set down here and we can test out my theory on the way to the crater." *If I were a man, he would listen to me, guaranteed.* At that very moment, Joseph walked in the door. He would help her for sure. She made her way over to him and stood there looking forlorn, attempting to receive his pity. If this was the game she had to play, she could manage it. Being the top geologist, she had become an expert at dealing with men not believing her.

"Joseph, come settle an argument Taylor and I are having."

The perplexed look on his face meant she had to try harder. Sophie walked over to the table keeping Joseph in tow.

"I think the station should go here but Taylor wants to put it here." She gestured to the two opposing locations. She knew her spot was right but her opinion wasn't getting through. She had to make Joseph side with her to prove Taylor wrong. It was now a matter of principle. "Tell him, Joseph. Tell him I'm right."

"I have no idea," he said, attempting to walk away.

"Come on. I mean, look at these beautiful sediments here. And don't tell me these pictures don't look alike." Sophie said, trying to urge him into agreeing with her. His demeanor still hadn't changed. She had to try harder. "Come on, who you gonna trust, someone who was able to prove life started over three billions ago, or a guy who plays with rats for fun."

Taylor stood back and rolled his eyes. "Listen, I don't know why we're arguing about this. You know as well as I do this is the best spot."

Joseph pulled back. "I guess I'm going to have to agree with Taylor. Can I leave now?"

Are you shitting me? She had to keep her cool. This was a pivotal moment everything hinged on it. "What could it hurt to put the base here. I mean, just think how much extra time we would have to waste driving all the way back here and then back to the base when we could make it all one trip."

"Whatever," Taylor sighed. "We'll just go with your option."

"Good." Sophie grinned. She knew she had won. "So, it's settled. Tomorrow we'll land here and set up base camp."

"Can I go now?" Joseph asked hesitantly.

"Yeah, sure." Sophie waved him off. She was too focused on the fact that she had succeeded. "Taylor, let the Captain know I figured out where to go." She left the room, walking with confidence. The ship was her domain.

Now it was time to meet up with Nova for a girls' movie night. But first, she wanted to stop by her room to change. The specially designed jumpsuit was fine for regular use but she could never really relax in it, for that she opted for her special robe. A sensual piece whose short length exposed her long slender legs, driving boys crazy. The robe graced her body in a silken cloth that fluttered when she moved. The left shoulder often slipped down her arm. Its low cut made her feel irresistible, though she'd had some trouble getting any attention from the men aboard the ship. Despite that, she enjoyed wandering the long halls wrapped in its soft if not revealing presence. After being treated like an idiot, now more than ever, she needed to feel confident in herself. Fully prepared for the movie, she exited her quarters.

From down the hall, Diego was headed towards her. *This is my chance*, Sophie thought, throwing a seductive smile his way. She made sure to grace his arm as their paths crossed, letting him feel the smooth edge of the robe. His visage stopped and turned in her periphery. *I've still got it.* With an air of confidence, she began swaying her hips as if they were waves on the ocean attempting to pull Diego out to sea. She took slow, deliberate steps, and walked on the balls of her feet to accentuate her features. A short turn left her facing her onlooker. "Oh, hey Diego, I didn't realize you were there."

He stared at her completely flummoxed. His unwavering gaze locked on Sophie. "Where...where you off to?"

Sophie began twirling her long black hair. "Just a movie with Nova. Some chick flicks."

"Sounds kind of boring."

"Yeah it'll probably be really sappy, but Nova likes 'em so I don't mind." She locked eyes with him and pushed out her exposed chest. "You could join us. Might make it more fun." A bright red color overtook Diego's generally pale face.

"I...I... I," words seemed incapable of escaping Diego's mouth. "I have to finish programming for tomorrow." Despite a sense of urgency in his voice, he remained where he stood.

Sophie could feel the cold recycled air brushing against her skin. Having all the rooms just within earshot, she knew their conversation could be interrupted at any moment. Not to mention, standing there in the barren metallic hallway beneath the fluorescent lights was less than an ideal location for this conversation. Needing to get things moving, she touched his arm, "Come on, don't be a party pooper. The movie's not that long. You'll have plenty of time after. I went through so much work to make all the snacks. It was hard pushing the button. You wouldn't want it to go to waste." She watched him, hoping for some response. A hint as to what he was thinking. "You're working too hard. I know what'll motivate you." She leaned forward and planted a kiss on his lips. "Is that more convincing?" In an instant, Diego was following her down the hall.

"Are you sure Nova's gonna be okay with this?"

"She won't mind. We do this several times a week. We've had a hard time convincing the others to join us though."

The room appeared ready for the "night's" activity. Trays of gelatinous snacks littered the table, a mystery grab bag of flavors. The movie's menu displayed across the back wall lit up the room. Nova laid spread across the arms of a large chair with her legs hanging over the edge.

"Oh, there you are Sophie," Nova said sitting up. Her disheveled hair clinging to the chair. "Hi Diego. Are you joining us?"

"It would appear that way, yeah."

"Well don't let me stop you guys from sitting down." Nova reached for one of the mystery blobs. "We've made a little game out of the snacks. Five of them are horrible but we have no idea which one."

Sophie reached for her own snack and bit in. "Apple pie, you've got to try this one." She passed the treat off to Nova.

"Mmm, that's delicious." Nova garbled through her mouth full of food. "Nice seeing you take a break from work Diego. Guess you finally took my advice."

"Yep."

Going out of turn, Diego grabbed a snack and took a bite, presumably to get out of the awkward conversation.

"Oh, God." He spit the food out from his mouth and began retching. His hands frantically swiping at his tongue.

Sophie burst out laughing, tears streaming from her eyes.

"It tastes like spicy rotten fruit mixed with garlic."

Sophie's guffaw grew ever louder as she struggled to catch her breath. It was nice to finally see someone else other than her get the nastiest flavor. "That was…" she struggled to breathe amidst the laughter. "…the funniest shit…" she huffed. "I've ever seen."

A greenish-blue sphere flew past Sophie and towards Diego. Nova chortled, "Try that one. It's mint chocolate chip, I promise. I use it as a palette cleanser of sorts."

The night dragged on with Sophie cuddling up against her newfound Paramore. Only bits and pieces of the movie caught her attention. If asked about the plot the only response would have been a jumbled mess of words. On the other hand, her attention on Diego grew sharper. His cologne filled her senses, yet to this point it was not something she recalled him ever wearing. Maybe it was just her imagination. As the movie ended, Nova got up and turned on the lights blinding the unsuspecting duo.

"Really Nova," Sophie screamed out, slapping her hands over her eyes in a futile attempt to block out the light.

"Hey, I had to let you two know the movie was over somehow. This just seemed like the more humane option. Besides, I'm off to bed. We're launching in ten hours and I need all the sleep I can get."

With Nova finally out of the way, Sophie was free to pursue Diego. In one smooth motion, her body twisted around, positioning herself atop his lap. His muscular body beneath her legs came as a surprise. The subtle scent of cologne continued to pierce her nose. What started off as an attempt at getting some attention was turning into something more. A feeling of true desire. Longing to feel his presence all through the night. She leaned her body towards his, her head hanging over top of him. Their eyes met. Her dangling soft black hair shut out the rest of the world. Time slowed as she inched her lips towards his. Eyes closed; she felt his warm breath. Endorphins pumped through Sophie's veins when their lips touched, triggering her innate desires. She placed his hands around her waist and then her hands on either side of Diego's face. The kiss was passion incarnate.

Before either one knew it, an hour had passed. "Come with me," Sophie muttered, staring her partner in the eyes. Instinct kicked in and she stood up and grabbed Diego's hand. She led him down the hall, lost in the moment of pure ecstasy. The moment the door to her room opened, she threw Diego on the bed. Before the door managed to close, she was on top of him, leaning in for the most passionate kiss of her life.

His hands gripped her hair and pulled her head back, forcing a small moan from her mouth. She let her lips grace his one more time before sitting up. His gaze was mesmerizing. Slowly, but deliberately, she gripped the top of her nighty and pulled it down, exposing her breasts to him. His breaths grew shallower. Between her legs, she could tell he was getting excited. That was all the encouragement she needed.

Sophie pressed her hips down into his and rubbed against him in slow circles. His hands reached back and rubbed against her exposed back. The passion grew, and before she knew it, they found themselves intertwined in bed. His chest was covered in scratches and her hair was a mess. They fell asleep briefly only to awaken to return to their escapades. Finally, exhaustion caused Sophie to pass out.

Waking up to the sound of gentle snoring, Sophie dug the side of her face into the warm body under her. She opened her eyes to see Diego fast asleep. This was a moment she didn't want to end. His breathing was rhythmic and soothing, his heartbeat faint but steady. With her eyes closed, she took in the moment. *We should probably get up now* she told herself but not truly believing it. This was where she wanted to stay. Despite her desire to remain in the moment, Sophie lifted herself up and began kissing Diego's chest. His body shifted under her. Her lips moved along his muscular chest, working their way towards his neck and then on to his lips.

"Morning," Diego moaned with a raspy voice.

"Oh good, you're awake." Sophie planted another kiss on his lips. "We should probably get cleaned up and go eat before launch." She climbed out of bed and headed towards the bathroom. The air was cold against her naked body. Stopping in the doorway to glance over her shoulder, she beckoned Diego, "Well, are you coming?"

The surface mission drew closer as the two struggled in the cramped space provided by the shower walls, to clean the mementos left by their night of passion. Sophie's mind began to feel the reality behind what was about to happen. This was to be the first human contact in an alien world. Surfaces never seen through human eyes. Sand painted red by rust, reflecting light from the distant setting sun. She lost focus. *What was I supposed to be doing again?* She asked herself, attempting to get back on track. *Crap that's right, I haven't eaten breakfast yet.* With the water still running, Sophie left Diego to fend for himself, but not before turning and giving him one more passionate kiss. A quick pat down with the towel was all she needed to get her suit on. Her wet hair left behind beads of moisture glistening on the jumper. As quickly as she had left the shower, Sophie was out the door to go grab food.

The excitement was too much for Sophie to handle. A few bites were all she could muster. *I'm not really hungry.* She looked around the room. *I'll just grab some travel rations for later.* The cabinet presented an array of freeze-dried and dehydrated snacks. The jerky packs looked the most appetizing. With her pockets full, Sophie scooted off towards the launch bay to await the surface trip with the rest of the crew.

The launch deck was bustling with activity, as the crew fumbled with their spacesuits. The wall was lined with lockers filled with multiple suits. Should something happen to one, back-ups would be available. Sophie opened the panel with her name on it and removed the neon green suit. The color had been decided as a way to spot each other against the stark red background. NASA's emblem adorned the front left breast, leaving the rest of the suit to be covered in monitors, knobs, pouches, tool straps, an air supply, carbon scrubber, and a quick escape flap. Sitting on the bench she struggled to slide her feet into the boots. Once completed she was able to squirm the rest of her body in through the neck.

Captain Summers stood, helmet in hand, near the entrance. "Everyone, please begin boarding the lander. We'll be running a system check and launching in just a few minutes."

Despite scanning every face, Diego was nowhere to be found. "Aren't we missing someone?" Sophie asked, attempting to appear nonchalant.

"He decided to stay back for the first trip to make sure everything runs smoothly from up here."

Sophie's face quickly turned to disappointment. "Well if he stays, I want to stay too," she huffed. Her feelings were no longer hidden behind the veil.

Captain Summers turned her back to Sophie. "Everyone on the lander; No exceptions."

"Yes, Captain." Her head hung in dejection, Sophie took her seat and buckled up. Without a role in landing the shuttle, she resigned herself to sitting in silence, watching the others click away at the machines. Out of boredom, she picked up her helmet and fiddled with its smooth surface. This was the first time she had ever really looked at it. The strange oblong shape of the dome with the protective carbon plating around the back. Intricate patterns helped strengthen its structure. Her interest in it waned quickly. Soon enough she found herself dozing off, the sound of clicking buttons fading away.

Violent tremors tore through Sophie's body, causing her to awake in a panic. Her hands dug into the arms of her seat, leaving them a ghostly white. For a moment she had forgotten where she was. "What the fuck!" She attempted to scream but her words seemed nonexistent amidst the engine roars. It all began coming back to her. Through the front window, the outline of Mars filled her view. Its surface cloaked in darkness. A sliver of red appeared on the horizon. As the ship continued its journey, daylight took over.

"Hold on everyone, we're about to enter Mars's lower atmosphere," Carl said. "Once we hit it the ship is going to drop rapidly."

Captain Somers jumped in, "That means we need to make sure our suits are working before we start falling."

Sophie checked her gauges from the arm of her suit. It had a setting to monitor not only the suit but external conditions as well. Everything seemed good. Like dropping from the top of a roller coaster, the ship began its downward descent. She grabbed her helmet and attempted to put it on. The locking mechanism refused to cooperate. A pair of hands reached around the front of the helmet, twisting it in place. The rumbling sound was gone, replaced by a hissing noise accompanied by a gentle breeze of cold air filling the suit. A chill ran down Sophie's spine. She shuttered before turning on the speaker system. "Thanks for the assist."

"Anytime," Nova's voice came back.

The surface was approaching quickly. The flat plain gave way to a pockmarked landscape. Mountains and sand dunes took shape. Her sensor showed the temperature inside the ship was rising.

"Hit the rockets now." It was Diego's soothing voice. The ship began to slow as it approached the landing pad, which had been sent down along with the rovers four hours prior. The engines threw up a cloud of dust hiding the metal platform. "Looks like you're right on target. Just a few more meters."

Gears whirred and squealed. The hydraulics could be heard pounding away.

"Landing gear down," Joseph shouted, trying to still yell over the roar of the engines. "No technical failures. The worst part is over."

Sophie was pissed. "For the love of God, stop yelling. We can hear you just fine. Well, could. Now I can't hear anything."

"Sophie, I need to be able to hear Joseph." Captain Somers's voice broke in. "If you need to turn off your communicator, for now, that's fine. But if something happens one of us will tap your shoulder to let you know to tune back in. Deal?"

"Yes, ma'am." Sophie went silent. She listened as the crew shouted back and forth in preparation for landing. How they managed to make her feel so useless now, she wasn't sure. *You've got this. They are just doing their job. You're sleep deprived so everything seems worse than it is. They're not mad at you.* She took a few deep breaths and tried to enjoy the moment.

The ship rocked back and forth until finally touching down onto the Martian surface. The engine shut off. The entire crew heaved a huge sigh of relief. "Nasa we've made contact." Diego was now talking to both Nasa and the Phoenix crew. "I repeat, the first humans have landed on Mars. The new age of man has begun."

The entire crew began whooping and hollering, even Sophie found herself feeling swept up in the moment. All her frustration disappeared under the great feat they had accomplished. The pod door opened onto the surface of the red beast. In the muted light Sophie glanced around expecting to see clouds covering the sky, to her amazement though not even one was to be seen. She pulled the camera and land surveyor unit from her pack to snap a few photos.

"Get one of me jumping," Trent said, leaping past her camera. Busy snapping photos, she watched Captain Somers, Rocco, Zea, and Joseph working tirelessly to get the base camp set up.

"Let's take the rovers for a spin," Taylor said breathlessly, running towards the two large vehicles. They sat 100 yards away soaking up sunlight and keeping their batteries charged. They sat roughly four feet off the ground, propped up by eight large wheels that appeared to be mesh. Their green metallic bodies glistened in the low light. On both sides of the vehicle, a large door hinged on a beam at the center of the roof. Large windows decorated the front and sides. She made her way towards the rover yelling, "I call driver," yet by the time she arrived both driver and passenger seats had been taken.

"You get next round," Taylor said, his voice laced with enthusiasm.

The next hour was spent driving around the nearby dunes and around the edge of the crater. Soft dirt gave way under the tires. It was slow going but still faster than walking.

"Stop here." Sophie tried opening the door to no avail. "I need to sample the soil."

"Need or want? Because if it's 'wanted' we're not stopping."

"It's 'needs" Joseph. Those are stromatolites. I'm sure of it. I'm telling you, there's bacteria there. Just pull over."

"Too late now. I've got the throttle all the way down."

"Dude, seriously? This is part of my job you know. You'll have the rest of the day to go play with your toy."

"We'll circle back around."

Sophie couldn't believe her ears. This jackass was taking over.

Nova interrupted them, "Just stop for her Joseph. She'll be quick. Won't you Sophie?"

"It's going to take a while to get several samples."

Joseph continued pushing the vehicle at full speed. "Come on, just do it later. It's not like the dirt's going anywhere. There's nothing for me to do while I wait. No, screw that."

"Sophie, can't you just take a quick sample?" Nova's voice switched to a soft motherly tone. "We'll even mark it for you so we can come back."

"I'll take whatever time I can get." Sophie felt hopeful that she'd soon be discovering what no one had studied before. Under her breath, she muttered, "so sick of these jackasses." It really was the effects of sleep deprivation getting to her but she didn't care right now.

"A Jackass huh. Well in that case," Joseph turned and started heading away from the crater.

"Joseph, turn back around," Nova said with a gentle voice.

"Not after she called me a bastard."

Nova's tone switched from soft to stern and determined. "You two need to get it together. Joseph, you're going to turn around and stop at the edge of the crater. Sophie, you're going to apologize to Joseph and then take a quick sample and get back in. Otherwise, you two are going to be stuck in the office with me for two hours together."

"Fine," Joseph grumbled as the vehicle abruptly turned back towards the crater. Sophie was quiet as they approached the edge once again. "If she doesn't say it, I'm not stopping."

"I'm sorry," Sophie moaned, unable to hide her discontent. "You're a great crewmate and I respect you and what you do. I promise to be quick. Now can we please stop." On command, the vehicle whined to a stop.

She threw the door open and rushed outside. *Should I go deep or shallow*, she pondered reaching behind her for the soil sample tool or SST. Without hesitation, she went for a deep sample. The SST began boring into the soil throwing dust everywhere. The hole disappeared. All measurements of depth would have to be guesswork on the budgeted time she had. If she stopped to let the dust settle, as she should, it would be close to an hour. Within minutes a four-foot hole had been bored out. A quick jerk pulled out a long, solid core to be studied later. The sample slid into the metal canister and she screwed down the lid. Only after throwing the sample into the chest did a moment of realization hit her, *I can grab a surface sample real quick*. A small scoop made easy work of the sample. With the new sample in a separate metal canister she screwed the lid on, headed back to the rover, and jumped in.

"Twenty minutes lost. Real quick." Joseph sounded pissed, but at this point, Sophie couldn't care less. In her hands, she held the sign of victory.

Nova

Team Assessment:

The crew of the Phoenix VII Mission appears to have bonded immensely since the induction of the trip. While Captain Somers remains the leader of the mission overall, individuals have stepped up to take control of sub-projects. After a month on the surface of Mars, progress is being made. Diego made it down to the surface leaving the ship in the hands of NASA. His hesitancy to join was concerning and appeared to be cause for alarm but was quickly remedied upon seeing Sophie. Some tensions remain between Sophie and Joseph prior to the incident mentioned earlier. The rest of the crew remain in good standing. I have pushed for extended bonding time via movies and game breaks. Also, each crew member is required to meet with me monthly. Joseph appears the most reluctant to meet resulting in short meetings. No cause for worry. Zea has opened to me revealing a talkative side I haven't seen till now. Everyone else's meetings remain routine. (see individual notes)

Psychological effects from being isolated to small quarters are offset by surface excursions for testing and data collection. No long-term effects appear to have been caused by time spent in stasis.

"Nova, we're heading out in five." Carl's voice broke her train of thought.

"I'll be there in just a minute." Nova shut down her tablet. *Is it really that late already?* The women's bunk room seemed even starker than any room aboard the Phoenix VII. Four beds lined the walls. Underneath each cot laid a bag of clothes, some overflowing with clothes that seemed to dwarf the space inside the bag, some opened with folded laundry neatly set inside. Nova's was of the latter type. She found a clean space equated to a clear mind. From out in the common room the familiar hiss of the airlock sounded. *The crew's heading out. Guess I need to get out there.* Wandering through the habitat, an uneasiness swept over Nova. It happened every time the place sat empty. An eerie silence surrounded her. No clanking metal, or engines from the ship. Not a single bird chirping, nor leaves rustling. The absolute quiet was unnerving. Her heartbeat echoed out. At that moment the air scrubber kicked on, a welcome noise to be sure.

Nova shuffled off to the airlock to find her Exo suit waiting. A few minutes of squirming and the body portion was on. She fastened the helmet and watched the glass fog up. The air system made fast work of it. She entered the airlock and wandered out to the surface of Mars once again.

She stepped onto the same soft red dirt, and her feet sunk in just like every other time before. The faint red sky above her no longer had the same luster it had when she had first looked upon it. In the distance, mountains towered over the landscape, but now they were just another piece of dirt along the horizon. When she arrived, it was like being a child exploring the stories of a book. Everything was new and exciting. That had all passed on, leaving her feeling like it was no major ordeal to be standing on another planet. "I need to come up with a way for us all to regain our awe of the situation."

"What was that?" Carl asked.

"Oh, sorry I was talking to myself."

A few short steps and she was at the bright green rover with its doors opened skyward, awaiting the crew. The massive windows allowed her to easily peer at all the flashing control inside. Its massive mesh wheels designed to mold around rocks always made it a struggle for her to climb into the vehicle with her short stature but even that had just become a regular part of her day. "Where's everyone else?"

Carl sat in the driver's seat awaiting her presence. "A few went on ahead and the rest are testing samples in the lab."

"Probably shouldn't keep them waiting then." Nova leaped into the open rover with ease and closed the door. "What are we waiting for?"

Nothing," he said, kicking the vehicle into gear. "This one's gonna be a long one. We're heading into the crater." The gear let out a grinding noise as Carl attempted to shift.

Nova removed her helmet and took a deep breath. "Don't need this for a while then. Ah, recycled air. Come on Carl, join me. No sense in trying to drive for an hour with that on." He slowed the vehicle down and removed his helmet revealing his caked down blonde hair peeking out from the head sock.

"Okay, let's go." The vehicle resumed gliding along the sand. "You know, I can't believe God created something this amazing and we're only just getting to enjoy it."

"Well, hopefully, we're the first of many. It's a big planet with lots to tell. Think we'll find any life out there?"

"I don't think life exists outside of Earth. God created life specifically for Earth."

"Interesting, so what made you want to come on this mission?"

"Just the opportunity to study Mars' atmosphere in person. It's a fascinating possibility. Who knows, maybe one day my discoveries will help humans live here. Call it a pipe dream but I think it'll happen."

His positivity always seemed to stem from an unending source. It was amazing. Even his brown eyes seemed to have a glow to them. Hope resonated with his words.

"Well, I think the odds of that are pretty good."

The drive went on as the sun rose higher in the Martian sky. The longest part of the trip would be descending into the crater. Steep slopes necessitated a crawling pace. They could make out the other team's rover sitting in the middle supposedly making headway. Nova watched Carl praying under his breath as they descended. One wrong turn would lead to an inevitable disaster and this seemed to be his coping mechanism. She kept quiet so as not to disturb his focus. The vehicle swayed across the path clearing swaths of dirt. The slope to the left hung, at moments, mere inches from the tires. On the right hung a wall of dirt mixed with black streaks of minerals. After ages, they finally reached the bottom of the crater.

"You're pretty good at driving this rig around." Complimenting Carl's work had proven to get the best response out of him.

"And I got us here really quick. Shaved fifteen minutes off the drive easily." The stress from the drive down, dissipated from his countenance.

"My numb butt thanks you. You'd think they would have put better seats in these things. But I guess it does… oh look I can see the other team."

"Could you start activating the device? I need it up and running as soon as possible."

"Sure," Nova released her restraints and made her way to the back. "Okay just tell me what to do."

"Flip the battery power switch on. You should see a green light come on."

"Got it. It's making a beeping noise."

"Good, that means it's getting power. Next, press down the button that says circulate. Hold it for ten seconds."

"Check."

"Now twist the knob to the right of the button from zero to four, this should start turning the cylinder on top."

"Okay, anything else?"

"Just make sure the straps are undone."

"We're all set."

Nova clamored over the seats back to the front and put on her helmet. The rover came to a stop just as air began flowing into her suit. She headed out of the vehicle and opened the back. "Rocco, Trent, could you guys give us a hand pulling this thing out?"

"Ten-four little lady," Trent chuckled over the intercom.

A few tugs found the apparatus free from the compartment. Once set up, it reached ten feet into the air. The whole system began whirring and the numbers on the display started turning over.

"What's this thing's function?" Trent asked, touching the strange piece before him.

"I want to measure air quality, CO_2 levels, air pressure, and wind down here. It's then going to be compared to the readings from the weather balloon Rocco is launching."

"Balloons in the air."

That was quick," Nova muttered in amazement at the setup Carl had prepared. She had only come to observe the crew working together, but her attention had been captured by the impending work. Unsure of their purpose, Nova helped set up devices in a 50-yard perimeter around the device, excited to be able to help. They worked on and off for several hours. Trent sat converting figures for Carl. Rocco monitored the balloon, while Carl kept wandering off randomly.

"This doesn't make any sense." Carl's mumbling over the speakers seemed out of place. "There's...no... check again. This thing broken or something?"

"What are you rambling on about," Trent mockingly replied as if Carl had been having a conversation with him.

"What? Oh sorry, for whatever reason the sensors indicate high levels of Sulfur and Nitrogen accumulating near the crater floor. It doesn't seem present anywhere else. This is probably what they were reading from Earth."

Nova had no idea what the significance of it was. Rather than keep up, she just sat back and kept the crew company. Heavy eyelids presented too much of a challenge to overcome. *I'll close my eyes for a bit, not like I'm doing anything.* Everyone else was so busy they wouldn't notice.

Just then Carl interrupted her attempt to nap, "Guys we've got a large dust storm approaching, let's head back before it hits."

"Hey, I'm going to head back with Rocco if that's alright with everyone. Trent, would you mind riding with Carl?"

"What, are you trying to set me and Carl up? You know these rovers aren't very romantic."

Rocco joined in. "You crack yourself up, don't you Trent? I guess someone had to laugh. Let's get moving. Get in Nova. Carl, how long till the storm hits?"

"Just over an hour. If we leave now, we'll just make it back in time. This looks like it could be a long one." In the distance, a dark red wall climbed high into the sky, the sun struggled to shine through its apex, only managing to appear as a lighter circle of red in the dust. For a moment, lightning flashed inside the cloud, illuminating it from the inside.

"That's what your mom said," Trent began whooping and hollering.

"Nice one bud." Carl's words dripped with sarcasm.

"What about the tower?" The thought of leaving the expensive equipment out there seemed unfathomable to Nova. The massive mountaintop that had been visible over the top of the crater disappeared inside the cloud as she spoke. Soon the tall crater walls would be gone too. There was no future that she could see in which the floor on the crater didn't get buried in dust, and, in turn, the machine along with it.

"Don't worry about it. The winds aren't strong enough to do anything. The sensors will continue to collect data and once the storms clear it can relay it up to the MOS."

"Okay then. See you at the top." Rocco jumped into the rover. "Oh, and one more thing. Try not to get too far ahead."

"Rodger Dodger." That was the last come from Trent before his door shut and Carl took off. Rocco waited patiently for Nova to buckle up before leaving.

The drive out was routine. Nova watched Carl and Trent Disappear over the crater's edge. They soon followed suit and came face to face with a magnificent black wall of dust. The sun turned blood red and then began to fade into darkness. Light evaporated away. The crew became enveloped in a blanket of dust, the headlights shining no more than twenty feet ahead.

"Carl, how far ahead of us are you?" The concern in Rocco's voice was obvious. Broken words amongst static were the only response he got.

"Rocco, you're going to have to get us out of this mess." Nova knew he could do it. She had spent a week reading over his files from the Saudi war. His team had gotten trapped in impossible situations only to blow the odds away. It's why she had chosen him. She knew his problem-solving skills were unparalleled. "You're the best we've got."

"Okay give me a moment to think."

There Nova sat, the only thing she could do was count on Rocco to get all four team members back to the Habitat.

He reached down into a bag next to his seat and threw a strange object Nova's way. "I had Joseph concoct a device designed to pick up a high-frequency pitch being produced by the habitat, on the off chance we got stuck in a storm just like this."

The dials were confusing but Nova watched as the needle bobbed left and right depending on the direction it faced. "Looks like the strongest signal is coming from over there she pointed out to the right." She held the device, impressed that his mind was able to think up such a masterful plan ahead of its need.

"Now you keep pointing that towards the signal and I'll follow the remnants of the other tracks to meet up with Trent and Carl."

Slowly they traveled along in hopes that the other vehicle had remained in place. They searched through the darkness until, finally, their headlights illuminated the unmistakable bright green paint of the other rover.

Nova tested the intercom hoping the range was close enough. "Are you guys there? Can you hear me?"

"You found us, Thank God."

"Don't you mean thank Rocco, that rugged bastard?"

"Really Trent?" Carl retorted in frustration.

Nova hoped she could get them to remain focused on the task at hand. "You guys let's not bicker. Rocco has a plan to get us out of the storm but you have to follow us."

"Lead the way," both men said in unison.

The storm raged around them. Sparks of electricity shot through the dust bringing bursts of light to the otherwise dark world and leaving behind an ear-splitting crack. For a brief second, the wall of dust came to life. Just as quickly as its animation began, its spark died out and blackness overtook the vehicles again. A slow pace ensured the rover found good footing. The signal was getting closer.

Monitoring the device and trying to keep the team company kept Nova busy. "Everyone doing alright?"

"Trent keeps telling me he could drive this rig better than me, but yeah we're good."

"Well, at least everything seems normal on your end," Nova said knowing she was going to have her work cut out for her later. "Rocco, you've been pretty silent. You all right?"

"Yes, ma'am just focused on the mission at hand. it's like driving in Saudi Arabia only with lesser explosives to worry about."

"Can't argue with that one." It was amazing to watch Rocco in his element.

"Research...*hiss*..plea...*shhh*... over."

Answering the line, Nova messaged back to base. "On our way lab. I repeat, on our way lab." They were close.

Finally, the lab could be seen through the cloud of black ahead of them. Its outside was coated in a fine layer of dust. They exited the vehicles and made their way to the door. Nova brushed away the fine powder caked onto the airlock handle. Four people crammed in like sardines. Bursts of air flooded the room, allowing Nova to pull her helmet off. Her dark hair clung to the inside of the helmet and stood on end loaded with static electricity. The door opened.

Before anyone could step foot back inside the habitat, Taylor was waiting to greet them with what could be considered frustrating news. "NASA got ahold of us before the storm hit. We're stuck inside for the next three weeks till the storm lets up. Time to get comfortable."

"At least give us a chance to get in before you crush our spirit," Trent whined from behind Rocco.

"Where's the fun in that? Guess you can help me check dirt samples with Sophie."

"Son of a bitch."

Glancing around the room Nova spoke to everyone, "Guess that leaves me to my notes. I'd like to have a one on one with all of you since we don't have anything better to do." The team was already getting tense. Nova could only imagine what would come of the next few weeks. The crew split and went their separate ways.

That night she enacted her first of many group activities to try and lift their spirits and kill the boredom. A night of charades brought out a lively side of the group. On one team Nova placed Trent, Zea, Joseph, Taylor and herself, and Addison, Sophie, Diego, Carl, and Rocco on the other.

Taylor started the round off by swinging his arms wildly in the air. He then started scratching himself under the arms and banging on his chest. He followed it up by pointing at the ground and making a circle with his hands. The room filled with people shouting out random answers but the timer ran out.

Taylor let out a huff of displeasure. "Planet of the Apes. Man, you guys suck at this."

The next round, Rocco sat down on the ground. His hands pretended to be gripping something as they moved together in circles.

"Rowing!" Sophie shouted out.

In response, Rocco touched his nose with his finger. He then stood tall and raised one foot in the air as if standing on something. As answers of rum and Captain Morgan rang out, he just shook his head and held his position.

From the side of the room Diego could barely be heard talking. "George Washington crossing the Delaware."

Rocco gave an emphatic point in Diego's direction. He then held up two fingers but the timer buzzed.

The game ran on for hours before everyone found themselves worn out from too much laughter. A good thing by Nova's standards. It seemed as if they had all forgotten about the dust storm outside.

With the game over, the group headed back to their duties. Zea followed Nova out of the room. "Mind if I had a chat with you?"

Of course, come on in. Nova led Zea into the girl's bunk room and closed the door. Some classical music helped to set the mood. "What's up? Everything alright?"

"It's just that I don't really feel like I fit in well. I thought it might get better once we were here but the whole age difference is too much to handle. On top of that, I just don't feel like I'm of any actual use here."

Nova touched Zea's knee. "Listen, you're an amazing Doctor. Just because we don't see your work doesn't mean you aren't doing anything. You help maintain the oxygen levels, check our radiation uptake, plus you keep an eye on what we eat and make sure we are exercising. That doesn't sound like nothing to me."

"You're right. I mean Addison gets me. She's been extremely kind. But I have no idea what to talk to the others about."

"You seemed to do a good job tonight during the game. You really came out of your shell."

"Thanks. I'm glad I have you to talk to. You kind of remind me of my mom. It's been five years but I still miss her."

I'm here anytime you need me."

The conversation drifted on for a while before Zea decided she was tired. Nova left the room to let Zea get some sleep. Laptop in hand she headed for the common area to work on her report some more.

Rocco

Weeks had passed since the dust storm settled. Outside the habitat, the surface remained stagnant from one day to the next. Dirt accumulated in fine layers over all the equipment. As part of his morning routine, Rocco found himself outside in his suit brushing off both the solar panels and rovers. No one else was dedicated enough and for him, it brought a certain level of comfort having the stability of repetition to make life in cramped quarters more bearable. It was one of the biggest takeaways from his time spent in Saudi Arabia. Large stretches of time there were spent huddling in vehicles or scouting locations for days at a time. A boring yet necessary job at the time much like his excursion now.

Rocco pulled the duster out from his pack and began making his rounds. Each step sent him bounding through the air. Off in the distance were the first clouds he had seen since reaching the surface. Their consistency was rather thin and wispy, but they were there, nonetheless. The trip came to a brief halt while he stopped to admire the Martian sky with its faint red hue overhead and drifting into blue towards the horizon. High above his head, snowflakes drifted through the atmosphere only to melt away long before reaching the ground. The amazing sight would soon be seen around the world, relayed by the camera built into Rocco's helmet. "Back to the dusting," he told himself, heading to the large panels beside the structure. "God I'm getting sick of sand. Can't wait to get out of here. Huh, never thought I'd say that."

Soon enough the first set of solar panels was cleared. Next on the list were the rovers. Yesterday's trip out resulted in a lighter layer of dust buildup. *This will be a cakewalk, and after today I won't have to...* his thoughts strayed from the task at hand as he found himself tripped up by a rock, his body falling gracefully towards the ground. Reflexes, finely tuned in combat training, kicked in. Without thinking, Rocco brought his left shoulder towards the ground but with the slower fall his body overspun, landing him directly on his back. He pulled himself up in the clunky suit. Directly in front of him was the object of his downfall. The sun glinted off the rock. *The hell is this?* His mind flashed back to the moment his subordinate stepped on a mine. For an instant, the only thing he could see was the smoke, then the unrelenting screams. A shake of his head brought him out of the nightmare. "I'm on Mars." He stared down at the ground then up to the sky. "The dirt was an orangish-brown. The sun was faint in the red sky. The habitat was silver, white and black. The rover bright green…" He took a few deep breaths. "I feel the soft inside of my gloves. The suite is hard against my back and feet. I can feel sweat on my face." He stood up still taking deep breaths. "I can hear my suit's mechanisms running and the generator from the lab. My voice is loud inside the helmet. I smell sweat and recycled air." His head now clear, Rocco returned his focus to the object in the ground.

Rocco's hands dug the dirt away to reveal an unlabeled metallic sample canister. "Where'd this one come from?" He had no recollection of anyone dropping it during the surface outings. In fact, this was the first time he'd seen it during all his outings. "Maybe someone else will know if one's missing." A switch brought the intercom online. "Come in lab, this is Rocco." No response. "Lab please come in. I found something out here." Still complete silence from the other side. He slipped it into his pack and headed back to the lab.

The pressure inside the airlock stabilized and released the inner door latch. Without a word, Rocco removed the canister from its holster and strolled into the lab. "Did anyone misplace a sample?" he inquired of the team, but no one could hear him past the helmet. In a moment of extreme focus on a solitary goal, he had forgotten to exit the suit. Off went the helmet but he left the rest on for now. "Okay now that you can actually hear me, anyone here remember misplacing a sample?"

"Let me see…. No everything's here." Sophie seemed perplexed.

"I found this one outside. It must have fallen before the dust storm hit."

"All my numbers are accounted for. What's the label say?"

Rocco showed off the container. "There isn't one. At least as far as I can tell. Unless you etched something or wrote in invisible ink."

"Let me see that." She grabbed the sample from Rocco and began examining it. "Oh, I remember taking this. It's my sample from when we first took out the rovers. I've got nothing better to do right now and since we're leaving tomorrow, I might as well log it right now." She struggled and strained to remove the lid to no avail. "Hey Mr. Muscles, open this."

The first attempt fell short. "That's really on there." Rocco put his full strength into it. The lid released letting out a soft *pfft*. A sulfur smell filled his nostrils, emanating from the jar. "Why does this smell so bad?" He handed the stink grenade back to Sophie.

Taylor turned away from his notes. "The hell is that smell? Is it coming from that? Holy shit, give it here."

Rocco had never seen anyone this excited about anything, especially dirt that reeked of rotten eggs. Before he had time to process the situation, Taylor had taken the sample from him and was locking it inside a glass box.

Taylor's hands worked furiously through a pair of rubber gloves. After roughly ten minutes of this, he opened the box up and revealed ten glass slides. "Close that box for me would ya."

"Got it." Rocco closed the lid unsure what all the energy was about.

"Nothing…" Taylor tossed the slide aside. "Nothing." Another one flew off the microscope. "Yes! Fuck Yeah. it's…Goddamn! I…I… Can't believe it." His eyes never seemed to leave the lenses despite the yelling.

By this time, the entire team was running over to see what had happened, including Rocco.

"What are you yelling about?" Zea asked, wiping the sleep from her eyes.

"This sample! Cells! We found it!"

Trent spoke up, "But we checked all our samples over and over. Are you telling me we missed something?"

"Actually, I found it outside," Rocco muttered trying not to seem like it was actually his doing. "It's Sophie's sample from when we first got here."

"I took it from somewhere on the edge of the crater. It's from the same place I took the first deep soil sample. Now let me see."

The group bustled over the microscope. Rocco stood back with Captain Somers letting the others have at it. With the initial shock wearing off Rocco managed to get a look at the discovery of a lifetime. Beneath a thin layer of glass sat a dulled yellow oblong cell. Little oar like arms projected from all around the outer edge. This is where the similarities to anything on earth seemed to end. Three large circles lay inside: one a soft orange with dark spots, another clear with dark lines running throughout, connecting to the surface of the sphere, and the third one a cloudy green orb. Spiny little oval-shaped pieces lined the front edge of the cell. Moving around the sample revealed hundreds of them.

"Someone get NASA on the line," Taylor shouted, hands gesturing towards no one in particular.

Joseph replied, "Sounds like a job for you. I mean you know more about it than I do."

"I'm trying to document everything. I'm too busy to make the call."

Rocco figured if he didn't take care of it now it would never get done. The video monitor was already turned on awaiting departure information in the coming hours so Frank was bound to be in. He typed in the call command. The ringing was drowned out by the commotion of the crew behind him, completely oblivious that he'd taken the initiative.

Franks face popped up all pixelated. A staticky voice broke through the speakers, "Phoenix Crew this is NASA, please don't tell me something happened." His face made jerky movements as the signal was adjusted.

"We found life, sir. Small bacteria-like life." Rocco responded. He patiently waited for the signal to reach earth and bounce back with Frank's response.

"Hey, was that Frank?" Taylor jumped in front of the screen. "This is incredible. The most amazing …"

Frank broke in, "Say that again. I thought I heard you say we found love. Your message didn't make sense."

"He said we found life on Mars. Little green men, only they're yellowish, and they're more like individual cells instead of men. Frank this is the most important find in the history of humanity."

Rocco stood aside as Frank and Taylor tried to communicate. He couldn't help but chuckle at the two old friends attempting to communicate through the transmission delay.

"We need to get this back to the labs before we can run any real tests." Taylor ran off from the screen yelling, "I'm sending you pictures and my findings so far."

With the distraction out of the way, Rocco returned to his discussion with Frank. "I think it would be wise to wait until we've had a chance to return to Earth before anything comes out about this." Patiently he awaited the response.

Rather than Frank responding, a strange young redheaded man appeared on the screen. "I'll get a few official statements going that we made some scientific advancements but that we're waiting for you guys to be able to tell everyone about it in person. That should hold off the vultures for a few months."

"Captain Somers what do you think?" Frank asked from behind his understudy.

"I'm in agreement with Rocco. If you need to, you can always just say we found liquid water on Mars. They'll eat it up. The more we wait, the less room there'll be for any wrong info. Until then we'll see about collecting a few more samples to bring back." Her voice carried across the room.

Rocco rubbed the back of his head in frustration. "Well, I'm already suited up so I guess I'm going back out. Sophie let's go. Taylor, Diego, I want you guys to come along too." Out of the corner of his eye, he saw Sophie's face light up, presumably at the mention of Diego going along.

The final surface exploration team of the mission had been formed. They moved out to the rover. Sophie clung to Diego as if they were one person, going so far as to sit on his lap inside the confines of the Rover. Had this been his crew during an army mission their actions would be uncalled for but he figured there was no harm this time. All he wanted was to keep the piece to get this over with as soon as possible.

The GPS location appeared to be close. A twenty-minute drive placed them at the original sample sight. The mouth of the crater opened wide

49

before them, with a steep ledge falling hundreds of feet. Rocco watched the others scurry about taking samples. Sophie scuttled about trying to find the exact spot from before, Diego following her like a lost puppy. Taylor's approach seemed more methodical, following the crater's edge scraping away at the dirt every five steps and placing the tube in his pack.

It took a few minutes of watching the others work for Rocco to configure an optimal strategy. He took a row of three samples spaced out by fifteen feet. A similar row was created fifteen feet above and below forming a box of nine samples. The first two boxes went smoothly and created a Zen-like feeling. He moved on to the next zone. Following the pattern of the last two, he picked a raised mound of dirt to begin digging. The scoop dug in easily enough but quickly encountered a dense patch. *Packed dirt? That's a first.* He pushed the soft dirt away from around where he was working. What greeted him was a brown layer that quivered when disturbed much like a bowl of jello. The soft sand flowed through the fingers of Rocco's glove and closed in around it. As he pulled his hand out, the surface reformed seamlessly. In an instant, he realized exactly what this was. "Everyone get over here. I found something." The team approached as he continued running his fingers through the wet substance.

"What did ya find, water?" Diego asked incredulously.

"Actually yes. Look." He picked up a handful of waterlogged dirt and presented it to the others. "I say we get this back. We need to test it before we launch."

"I brought a microscope. I'm going to take a look." Taylor grabbed a tube from Diego's belt to scoop up some mud.

Rocco filled the rest of his sample vials and met Taylor over by the Rover. The screen sat dark. A flick of the switch from Taylor and suddenly an orange glow filled the view. The hazy image cleared to show individual particles floating around. Several of the particles appeared to be shaking. "You alright? You're shaking quite a bit. Look how much the dirt's moving."

"That's not me, take a look." Taylor threw his hands in the air as if to make his statement clearer.

Upon closer inspection, Rocco saw the small yellow cells from earlier squirming around. Next to them sat small amorphous blobs that seemed to be crawling through the liquid. "What the hell are those?"

"They appear to be like amoeba. But we won't know until I run some tests."

"Fascinating. You're telling me these are just like life on Earth?"

"Not exactly, more like similar design different makeup."

Captain Somers's voice took over the intercom. "Attention crew, our departure window is closing. I need everyone back to help pack up. Before take-off."

"Yes Captain," Diego and Sophie spoke one after the other.

"Gotcha, "Taylor followed suit. "Also, we found water teeming with life. We'll be bringing it back to analyze once we're on the ship."

Packing up a few more samples, the team moved out leaving the planet to cover the precious small collection of water once again. Once they arrived back at base there was no time to relax. The immediacy of the launch was all that mattered now.

Rocco went to work folding up the solar panels he had spent so long taking care of. Once they were all collapsed into small four-foot-wide squares he had to place each one inside the habitat. No reason to let them get buried outside with a perfectly usable shelter around. Next came the samples stored inside a large crate along with their personal effects. It fit snugly inside the lander's compartment. The ship loaded; Rocco stopped to view the red beast one last time before climbing inside. He took his seat behind the controls. "Prepare for launch."

Faint whirring noises grew, giving way to a soft rumbling. The engine kicked in snapping the ship from its slumber. In response, the metal shook with anticipation.

"Main engine online, "Joseph called out.

Trent pointed to his on-screen map, "Trajectory set for intercept course with the MOS."

"Prepare for launch in 10...9...8..." The thrusters roar blurred out any attempt to hear the countdown. Despite the futility of going on, Rocco continued counting. "3...2...1." the ship lurched into the air with minimal effort. It rose swiftly through the atmosphere and into orbit. "MOS dead ahead."

A pair of claws jutted from the Space Station waiting to pull the lander in. Rocco delicately maneuvered the ship into the waiting arms. For one full hour, he adjusted the lander's angle until the ship was fully docked. "Open the door." A loud burst of air rushed into the cabin. The crew stood up and one by one entered the MOS.

It was finally time to head back home. Rocco wanted nothing more than to climb into his stasis pod and wake up to the sight of Earth's blue oceans. Once he was back, he would spend a month at his cabin lake away from everything. A chance to restore his mind after all this time cooped up. Only one thing stood in his way, detaching the Phoenix VII, and setting their course. This task remained easier said than done. Ideally, he imagined a few switches and they would be off. As it turned out they required a team of four to go on a spacewalk in order to release the bonds. Begrudgingly Rocco found himself once again locked inside a spacesuit. For the first time, he began to feel inklings of claustrophobia. He couldn't stand being confined to such a small restrictive piece of equipment. *Focus on the task at hand, you'll be out of this thing faster than you know*, he had to keep reminding himself. Captain Somers decided to take the opportunity to assist Rocco.

The bay door opened into the void of space. No external sounds, no engines, no wind. His suit was the only source of disruption in the calm. The other two members, Trent, and Joseph, traveled to the far side of the ship climbing along the built-in handholds. Rocco and Captain Somers were tasked with unlocking the front of the ship. Coordination between partners was essential. The sleek metal surface made gripping difficult. His pack provided short bursts of momentum to help the travel. Before him stood a large metal brace, secured with bolts. He latched himself in next to the Captain. "I've got the drill if you'll grab the bolts and twist the latches."

"I gotcha," Captain Somers signaled, throwing him a thumbs-up.

The front bolts released easily enough. Rocco worked his way over towards the backside and locked himself back in. Deciding that waiting was pointless and wanting to get out of the suit as quickly as possible, he rushed ahead, undoing the bolts, and catching them as they drifted off. "Only two bolts left."

"Perfect, sorry it took me a while to finish the other side."

"No worries. Let's just get this done." His drill popped out the next two bolts but the latch refused to move. "Goddammit. It won't budge."

"Here. You just need to use a little force." Captain Somers pulled a crowbar from her belt and worked it between the metal joints. "Just...a... little...more." The joint flew open. The ship was now free. "Our end's done, guys. How's your end looking?"

"Well Trent's using the drill to spin in circles, so you tell me," Joseph chuckled.

"We'll meet you back inside. Captain out."

Relief was in sight. Rocco and Captain Somers pulled themselves into the bay. They passed through the airlock and back into the safety of the Phoenix. He threw his suit aside and headed to the bridge to make the final adjustments.

"Trent and Joseph are back."

"Thanks, Zea." All that was left was for Rocco to enter his numbers. "We're all set Captain."

"Diego, take us home."

Yes, Captain."

The ship began pulling away from the now empty station. All that was left to do was get in his pod. They would get the samples back to a lab and be considered legends. He took one last walk around the ship making sure all samples were sealed up. The time had finally come. He stripped down and hooked himself up to life support. The gel was cold but it wouldn't matter. He shut the lid and drifted off to dreamless slumber.

Trent

Trent awoke to the disconcerting sound of what could only be described as a banshee's wail. His ears began to throb as it pierced his skull but, as quickly as it had come, the sound disappeared. He opened his eyes to find himself staring through a clear gel-like substance illuminated by a faint blue light. *Blue light, Blue light,* he thought to himself. *What was that supposed to signal?* He pulled his left hand up through the gel that surrounded his body and placed it against the glass above him. It moved away as if it had read Trent's movement. A hand gripped his and pulled his torso out of the slime. A dark figure that was lurking to the side placed a soft towel in his hands to wipe his face off with.

When his vision cleared, he found himself sitting in a large grayish-black pod made from an advanced polymer that while extremely lightweight, could withstand a small explosion, keeping the person inside safe from impact. This model was designed specifically for the Phoenix VII mission. The gel it contained was a nutrient bath designed to be absorbed slowly through the skin. It remained chilled to help suppress the body's metabolism.

A light shock suddenly caused both of Trent's quadriceps to tense up. He reached into the gel and removed the pads producing the electric pulse. These pads were strategically placed on different parts of the body to help move the muscles while in stasis, preventing muscle atrophy. After all the pads were off, he stood up and removed the rest of the gel from his body.

"How are you feeling?" the figure he came to recognize as Zea inquired. "Are you experiencing any side effects?"

Trent removed the breathing apparatus from around his mouth, followed by a raspy moan.

"Sorry, I forgot that it takes a bit for your voice to return. Just nod your head if everything feels alright."

He nodded his head to reassure her that all was well. The lights slowly came up and the cabin lost its blue hue and instead became flooded with a soft white light. Zea stood shoulder high to Trent, golden-brown hair flowed down to her shoulders. "I assume you noticed the blue light. We got an important message from NASA. Take an hour to get dressed and adjusted to moving around again, then come to the bridge for a debrief," she said, sounding concerned.

Trent sat next to the Stasis Pod from which he had emerged. A row of pods sat on either side of the room and a lit-up path ran down the middle. The curved dark metal walls flowed seamlessly into a low hanging ceiling with color-changing lights. Each color was used to convey a certain message to the crew upon being awoken from stasis: yellow signaled equipment failure, orange indicated fluid or gas leaks, red glowed when in emergency mode, purple light appeared when life support maintenance was needed, green represented an external threat, and blue meant NASA had an urgent message for the crew. The onboard programming would analyze the severity of the situation and deactivate the necessary pods. This prevented any delay in response time in case of an emergency. The other Pods in the room sat empty, *the rest of the crew must be in the mess hall* he thought to himself. *What's so important that Captain Somers decided to wake the entire crew?* After getting his uniform from the floor compartment, Trent got dressed and stumbled off to the mess hall on shaky legs. He felt like an infant attempting to walk to its parents.

By the time Trent entered the mess hall, his steps conveyed a more confident pattern. Being in stasis for four months had left him with quite the appetite. Located next to the door was a small tablet that linked to a machine in the corner of the room. He picked up the tablet and it sprang to life. Holding it at eye level allowed it to clearly identify his face. With the scan complete, the display changed to show a list of most requested meals along with the option to create a new one. "A steak with asparagus sounds delicious," he said, realizing that his voice had finally returned.

"Too bad all you'll get is 3D printed slop," a voice from across the room mocked.

"Better than that Tofu block you're trying to eat," Trent replied, pushing his selection on the screen. The machine in the corner began whirring and ticking. He turned around to see Taylor sitting at the table in the center of the room. He looked like a mountain man, his curly long hair all tangled and frizzy, and his beard so thick it engulfed his mouth. It was customary for male crew members to shave before entering the pod, However, Taylor's tradition was to remain unshaven for the duration of any trip he went on. Trent, on the other hand, preferred to shave not only his face but also his entire head. There was less hair for the gel to stick to that way.

"Man, these last few months haven't been nice to you," Trent quipped. Right as he said it the machine's door opened to reveal his meal. "All Joking aside, do you have any idea why command felt the need to wake the entire crew up?"

"Who the hell knows. With them it's always something." Trent grabbed his meal, took a seat at the bench across from Taylor, and began to scoop the meat-like substance into his mouth. While the system they had designed to assemble the food was capable of succulent flavors, the texture left something to be desired.

"Last time they had to wake up an entire crew they had them attempting to intercept a comet and land a probe on its surface," Taylor continued, "Guess we'll find out soon enough."

Within minutes, Trent cleared his plate and sauntered off towards his room. He wandered into his bedroom and slid the door shut behind him. Manual doors were cheaper to install and removed the need to replace intricate mechanisms, allowing them to be opened even in the absence of power. The bedrooms were, by all accounts, a glorified closet. Against the left wall, the bed sat on top of a platform. The right wall, as well as the bed's platform, housed many cubicles in which to store personal effects. Trent reached into the cubicle at eye level to grab a clean uniform. Upon doing so, his hand touched a cloth doll that laid beside it.

The doll was a gift his daughter had hidden amongst the luggage. It was her most prized possession, and for a three year-old, the greatest gift she could give her dad. Along with the doll, she left a note scribbled out in large crayon letters:

    bere dady,

    LET ganit ceep U saf

    i luv U

    LUCY

The letter was stained with tears of both joy and sorrow. The tears of a father who wanted the world for his little girl. Staring at the mementos, memories of his time with her began to flood his memory. A tiny girl sleeping in his arms as he rocked her to sleep to the sound of lullabies. His wife and daughter are asleep in bed on a spring day. *I can't wait to see you two again* he thought. *So many stories to tell.*

Grabbing up the crisp, clean uniform, Trent headed for the bathroom at the far end of the room. The bathroom contained just enough room to fit a toilet, a sink, and a shower. A half turn on the handle was all it took to get the water flowing. Small fragments of dried gel peeled away like the skin of a molting snake. Once he was sure all remnants were gone, he turned off the water and dried off. Slipping on his clean uniform, Trent headed for the bridge.

Addison

The stars had always fascinated Captain Somers. She had found herself completely engrossed in all matters related to the glowing giants when she was growing up. By age eleven she could name and identify all of the constellations of both the northern and southern hemispheres. Just by looking at the stars through a telescope she knew, with a degree of certainty, which stars were at what stage in their life. She understood how they worked, formed, grew, and even died out. A sense of belonging came just from looking up at the behemoths that populated the night sky, this time however, was different.

She stood on the cold metal bridge, staring through the large glass dome, hoping to find that familiar comfort. She wanted nothing more than to calm her chaotic mind. Nearly twelve hours had passed since the alarm first awoke Captain Somers. Upon hearing the message being delivered, she found herself unable to leave the bridge, even foregoing showering. Bits of dried gel coated her hair. Zea tried many times to get her to eat, but the food remained undisturbed. Her stomach was in knots. Just the thought of eating at a time like this made her nauseous. She replayed the conversation with NASA over and over again. It had been brief but drastic enough that she felt the need to wake the rest of the crew. *I need to get focused, she* told herself. *NASA's call is due any minute*. She walked over to the control panel in the center of the platform and began pressing a series of buttons. Three rods sprouted from the back of the panel. Each rod split in two to reveal the screens hidden inside. Mathematical formulas and graphs popped up on the first display. The screen on the right lit up to show an image of the ship relative to the solar system. It then shifted to reveal the ship's earth-bound trajectory. The center screen remained empty, awaiting the live feed from NASA.

To her left, Joseph sat running through primary function analysis of the ship's systems. Somers had personally selected him, out of all the applicants, to maintain the ship on its voyage. During her time in the Air Force, she had worked alongside him on several missions. In the same room, Zea remained hard at work updating the crew's medical files.

"Zea, anything to report on the status of the crew," Captain Somers inquired. She needed some good news right about now. If the crew was all doing well, then she could focus all her attention on the matter at hand.

"No ma'am, all members are awake, and their vitals look good," she replied.

"Perfect. Joseph, inform the crew that we are ready to begin." For a brief second, she felt her body relax at the news, but her brain immediately returned to the disaster they were facing.

"Yes, Captain," he said, activating the intercom. "Attention all crew, please assemble on the bridge at once. We will begin shortly." His voice echoed through the ship's halls.

A beeping noise arose from the console in front of Captain Somers. Despite knowing what the message was about, she couldn't help but feel herself freaking out as if she was just hearing the news for the first time. Seconds later a large man wearing glasses appeared where a blank screen had been. "Can you hear me, Captain?" he asked. Though she knew it was Frank, she was having a hard time believing it. His face was pale and drawn. Dark bags beneath his eyes relieved his lack of sleep. Daniel and Frank had most likely been working nonstop on this for days.

"Yes, Frank we hear you. We are waiting on one more person. As soon as he arrives, we can begin." *What's taking them all so long?* Perhaps it was the fact that she was still recovering from the stasis pod or the lack of food. Her stomach growled inside her confirming the latter. She hoped no one had heard. She couldn't afford to appear weak at this moment.

As she spoke, Taylor strolled into the room looking disheveled. He walked over and stood next to Carl who sat silently muttering to himself, a necklace bearing a cross gripped in his hand and pressed against his chest.

She continued. "It appears we're ready. One week ago, at o-eight-hundred hours, NASA received intel that unusual solar activity had been spotted. After investigating, they discovered the sun is preparing to emit a massive solar flare. Our ship is directly in its path."

With a single command on the console, the right screen pulled up an image of the sun. It looked so harmless. The swirls on the surface were beautiful. It was like staring at a cosmic dance. "By my estimates, the flare will be emitted within two weeks."

Frank broke into the conversation, "The Phoenix VII has been equipped with a radiation shield. That, coupled with your suits, should absorb enough of the radiation to keep you guys protected. However, as it stands, we are unsure of the effects on the electrical equipment."

"Let's say worst-case scenario, what kind of damage could we be looking at?" Trent asked.

Frank stared down his glasses at the crew. "I'm gonna let Joseph answer that one."

He began fidgeting in his chair. "As Frank was saying, the radiation will be completely harmless to us. The electric lines are a different story. A strong enough wave could short out all electronics and disrupt any radio signals. Essentially we would become a giant rock that we can no longer control."

"We believe that with full cooperation between us and NASA's top scientists we can minimize that damage," Captain Somers suggested. "They are currently running simulations back on Earth."

Frank took over. "The plan is going to involve setting the ship's trajectory just before the flare hits. Our hope is to get you close to Earth and let Earth's gravity do the rest."

Taylor raised his hand as if he were waiting to be given a turn to speak. "And what about the solar sails? Won't those fry too?"

"They will if they remain exposed. I've been working on a plan for that," Joseph said walking over to the console where the Captain stood. Where once his gait was filled with confidence, he now hunched over. His fingers typed furiously at the consoles. Every click rang out through the silence. "The solar sails come attached to long cables. I've been running numbers and we should be able to retract the sail with minimal energy loss to our internal battery system."

"Don't forget what'll happen if we lose life support," Sophie exclaimed, seemingly trying to hide her fear, yet Addison knew better. The twitching eyes, and scratching at her arm were a dead giveaway.

Diego practically jumped from his seat, "We need to make sure we have food and water too." Unlike the others, his energy level seemed to have spiked. The calm and quiet man she was used to seeing, was now a fidgeting mess.

Joseph continued, ignoring both, but became slightly perturbed, "The only catch is it needs to be done as late as possible. Without them we won't have enough speed to reach Earth. The sails will be folded inside the ship. My hope is that the outer layers protect the inner folds. However, it will require a significant portion of our power. To account for this, we will run all essential power from the backup battery. I need all --"

Sophie once again interjected, "But won't that affect power to the air filters? If we don't make it, who cares about the ship."

In all her years of military duty, Addison had always felt in full control of a situation. This managed to pull any team together. This time was different. She knew deep down that success was a long shot and she would be a bystander through most of it. The most she could do was issue commands. These feelings were wearing off onto her crew now. She felt so lost. Out the window, she could see the sun shining so unassumingly in the distance.

Addison had to get the crew to let those who could do something get their ideas out while assuring those who were freaking out that their concerns mattered. If she started with Sophie, maybe that would help. But she had to be commanding. "Sophie, I need you to refrain from any further interruptions. We'll address your concerns soon. Joseph please continue."

"Thank you, Captain. As I was saying. I am going to need all of you to help me prepare the ship's electronic systems. Once the sails are in, we'll be able to disconnect all power sources and run dark through the flare."

Frank then spoke up. "Our team here in Florida is finalizing a few methods to shield the hard drives on the ship's deck. As soon as we figure something out, we will let you all know."

Captain Somers knew it was time to address the concerns gnawing away at everyone about their own survival. "Now to address your concerns, Sophie. Zea, please fill us in on your plan." This was a massive bet she was placing on Zea's shoulders.

She turned her chair to face everyone. "Yes, ma'am. I plan to place vital monitors on each of you," she said cautiously, her soft voice barely audible to the crew. "I also have stores of oxygen to use, as necessary. The uniforms are weaved with lead. It should be enough to shield you from radiation." She turned back around to her computer in silence.

Captain Somers looked at Sophie. "I hope that answers all of your questions. Diego, you asked about food. The ship contains enough dehydrated and freeze-dried rations to last several months. Water can be manually pumped from the reserve tanks." She could tell from the glances of the others that they were gripped by the anxiety of what was to come, the exception to this being Rocco. He stood in the corner stoic and unfazed. His strength at the moment helped to fuel her on.

"These preparations are solely for the worst-case scenario. We expect the ship to make it through just fine. But, do not let this be an excuse to not contribute." She had to remain calm in order to sell her bold lie. The system was ill-equipped to handle a flare of this magnitude. Frank had warned her of this ahead of time. "Your families have been informed of the situation and once communication is restored, they will receive a live feed from us." *That should settle their nerves*, she concluded to herself.

Nova stepped forward. "I would like each of you to take some time and come sit down with me."

"Thank you very much Nova. "Now, unless any of you have any further questions you are all dismissed," Captain Somers ordered. She waited for them to walk out one by one, then turned and stared at Frank with dismay in her eyes. "Joseph, Zea take a break. Go get some food."

She heard Joseph's reply of "Yes Captain," followed by Zea's slightly informal "yes ma'am," response. At twenty-two years old Zea had been the youngest astronaut to make it through the training. Because of this the Captain naturally felt the need to take Zea under her wing. A maternal bond had formed between the two so that when the phrase yes ma'am was utter Somers accepted it with grace despite her usual hatred of being addressed that way. This whole scenario was a lot to handle and with so much responsibility being placed on one girl she knew Zea would need support. On the other hand, Joseph was a competent leader. He had proven himself over and over again.

"Now that we're alone Frank I have to say I don't know that these people will be able to deal with this news."

"They'll be just fine. You wouldn't have selected anyone you deemed subpar. Hold on just a moment." His visage disappeared from the screen. A common effect caused by the distance of communication. A few minutes passed before the image of her husband filled the screen. Tears welled up in Somers's eyes.

"Honey, how you holdin' up?" Daniel's voice was soothing. His brown eyes invited her to tell him every secret, yet the bags under them revealed many sleepless nights.

"I'm worried that we won't be ready when the time comes. I just feel so unprepared," she sobbed softly. "I wish you were here to help me."

"Listen to me, Addison, I know you can do this. I've seen you pilot ships missing wings. There's never been a problem you couldn't figure out. I love you so much and we'll make sure we help get you home safe."

If anyone could be relied on at NASA to figure this out it was her husband. During Addison's time training for her first mission, she met Daniel. He had an uncanny knack for creating the puzzles used during emergency simulations. Addison soon learned exactly why the other technicians had taken to calling him Kobayashi, after the famed Star Trek test. His more elaborate tests were next to impossible. "I spent the last three days running programs to recreate the solar flare. I'll be running a live version to test our theories within two days. Just stay strong Sweetie, I promise you'll do great."

Addison wiped away her tears and took in a long slow deep breath to refocus herself. "Get back to me as soon as possible. I love you." He was her drive. The thought of him awaiting her always provided the force to get her home. Never had she felt more trapped without him.

"I love you too."

The transmission cut out. The room now sat silently waiting for the Captain to disrupt it. This time she had decided to sit and enjoy the silence. The burden was gone. Everyone on board was well aware of where they stood and would be on point. She laid down on the deck staring out the window once again. Thoughts of her future rolled through her head. When she arrived home, she would tell Daniel she was finally ready to take that next step and bring a child into their home. Settling down and retiring from work as an astronaut had long been the subject of their late-night discussions. She slowly closed her eyes. The slight hum of the ship rang through her core, a bedtime lullaby gently ushering her into a deep sleep.

Joseph

"Joe do you have a moment?" Nova's voice inquired over the intercom.

He looked up briefly from his book at the sudden interruption of what had otherwise been a relaxing cycle. *Maybe she'll just go away,* he thought. *Now, where was I.* He ran his finger along the lines searching for a spark to remind him where he had left off.

"I know you're there," the intercom crackled again. Joseph reached over for a pillow, set it in front of the speaker, and laid his back against it in the hopes of blocking out the disturbance. "The Captain is just worried about you," the muffled sound continued. He slammed the book down in frustration. "Please just come down. It won't take long," the voice went on again. Fed up with Nova's barrage of pages, he threw the pillow across the room freeing up the speaker to emit a clear message, "come this one time and I'll leave…"

Joseph pushed the button, cutting off her stream of words. "Fine, I'm coming. Just give me a minute," he responded, trying to hide his frustration. The speaker stayed quiet this time around. No more squawking meant he had staved off the demands for his cooperation. He scooted over to the edge of his bed placing his bare feet on the metal floor, it's cool touch was a stark contrast to his warm bedroom floor. Reluctantly, he stood up and left his room for what he considered an absolute waste of time.

The sound of trickling water emanated from Nova's office. As he drew closer the bird whistles mixed into the background along with the rustling of leaves. Joseph knocked on the open door. Nova glanced at Joseph and closed her laptop.

"Come take a seat," she beckoned, tapping her hand on the chair opposite her.

"If it'll make this end quicker then fine." He sat down and crossed his arms in defiance.

"How are you sleeping?"

"Fine."

"Any feelings of being overwhelmed?"

"Nope."

"Let's try something different. What are your thoughts on the whole solar flare conundrum?"

"I'll be ready when it comes."

Nova scribbled something on her notepad. "Do you think you can get this ship safely back into earth's orbit?"

"What are you writing?"

"Just some notes so I can let the Captain know you're doing alright. Now back to my question."

"Let the Captain know I've got it under control." Joseph started fidgeting in his chair. "I've checked the stats on the ship, she'll be fine."

"Just one more question then you can head out." She leaned forward, placing her elbows on her knees. "What message do you want to send to earth in case things don't go well?"

"Tell the rest of the crew's families I'll make sure they all get home." The chair let out a squeak as Joseph stood up to leave. "We done here?"

"What about your family, don't they deserve to know as well?"

He stopped mid-step, looked over his shoulder, his face contorted with rage, and spoke with a stern commanding tone, "don't bring up my family." He stormed out of the room and down towards the common area, his heavy footsteps echoing his frustration through the halls.

Joseph hated everything about his family. His mother was an abusive alcoholic whose only desire was to come home from work, drink, and pass out in peace. Any interruptions to this routine often left him with bruises. His father had walked out on the family when Joseph was twelve, leaving him to care for his younger sister. Ten years later, his father had attempted to reconnect with Joseph in order to appease his own soul and to introduce his son to the woman he had left them all for. His sister got married to her high school boyfriend. The two of them ran off and severed all ties to the family including Joseph who had raised her. In college, Joseph entered the Air Force ROTC program while studying for a mechanical engineering degree. Upon graduating from college and entering the Air Force, Joseph had gained enough independence to remove his family from his life entirely. They had tried to contact him several times leaving seemingly apologetic voicemails that always ended with them attempting to weasel money out of him.

He found himself at the entrance of the common area, a large open room designed for use during downtime aboard the ship. Games, TVs, radios, computers, and some exercise equipment. The idea had been to keep the crew entertained should the stasis pods not work. Mental stimulation would be paramount to their wellbeing. Sophie, Diego, and Carl sat around a table playing cards.

"Three queens," Diego proclaimed, slamming his cards down. "Victory is mine," he said laughing.

Sophie interrupted his laugh of accomplishment, "No, no, no you didn't win." she revealed her hand with excitement. "Full house. Threes over fives."

"Dammit, every time. You know I'm gonna beat you next hand."

"Dream on, Diego. You won't beat me."

"Glad I folded." Carl flipped his cards over. "An ace and a two. Complete crap."

Diego kicked out the chair across from him. "Joe get your ass over here and join us."

Carl gave the cards a shuffle. "How do you feel about buying a round of drinks? Rules are you bet a round of drinks per hand."

"Don't scare him away Carl, we want him to have to owe Sophie rounds, not us."

"Hey, not my fault you guys suck at this. I'm looking forward to those free rounds when we get back to Earth."

"Deal him in, Carl. Joe looks like he could use the drinks."

Joseph took a seat as cards flew across the table, coming to halt directly in front of him. "Wouldn't you need a drink after talking to Nova?"

"Oh, you poor soul," Sophie said, reassuring him. "I got mine done quickly so she'd leave me alone."

"You just have to make stuff up." Diego traded out a few cards. "I'd never show her my true hand." He let out a little laugh, "Speaking of which, my hand is killer."

Sophie glared at him. "Glad you can amuse yourself."

"Just glad I'm free now," Joe said. "So, which one of you gets the honor of buying me a beer?" he laid his cards down revealing a 7 high straight.

Carl set his cards down. "I'm out. I'm gonna head back to my room for a nap."

"Aww poor baby's tired," Diego mocked. "Don't worry I'll lose enough for both of us." He threw down a pair of twos.

Sophie placed four jacks on the table. "Looks Like you owe me a drink now Joe."

The lights in the room gradually began to glow green, then changed to blue, followed by red. "That can't be good." Joseph pushed himself away from the table.

A beeping sound came out of the speaker system. Captain Somers's voice began to resonate throughout the room, "all crew to the bridge at once. The Solar flare's on its way."

Joseph appeared to be in complete shock. "That can't be. We still had a week to prepare the ship!" He ran down the corridor towards the bridge. Trent and Captain Somers were already on deck working at the ship's controls. "What happened? I thought we had more time?"

Captain Somers was typing furiously at the controls. "We did too but the sun's activity sped up. You jump on life support systems," she yelled as Zea entered the room.

"Where do you want us?" Taylor's voice came from the doorway. Carl, Sophie, and Diego followed behind him.

Joseph bellowed out, "Carl I need you and Sophie shutting down all non-essential systems. Taylor, take Diego and close off as many doors as you can." He pulled up the ship's rocket system and began diverting power. He heard more footsteps approaching and turned around to see Nova and Rocco running up.

"Rocco, I need you to assist Joe. Nova you're with me." Captain Somers pointed at the control panel next to hers. "We need to get the solar sail pulled in."

"Data says we have 10 minutes till the flare," Trent said

"That's not enough time," Captain Somers replied.

Rocco rotated the ship's schematics. "Nothing's secure. Power isn't being shut off quick enough."

"I have an Idea, Captain, but it's going to take all the time we have left."

"I trust your judgment Joseph, just tell us what you need."

"Get everyone back up here and have them seal off the main door to the bridge." Joseph ran over to Captain Somers's control panel. "I need you all to help me maneuver the ship. We're gonna place the solar sail between us and the sun, while maintaining our course" He began powering the wing thrusters. "Rocco, take control of the thrusters on the front of the ship."

"Taylor, Diego, Carl, Sophie return to the bridge." Captain Somers turned to face Joseph. "Once they get here I'm going to seal the door and shut off power to the back of the ship."

"Perfect." Joseph listened to the ship moan as the thrusters came on-line. Then a loud rumbling took over. "Thrusters are up and running. Trent, keep track of our progress."

The four remaining crew returned to the bridge. The heavy door slid shut behind them, releasing a loud clanking sound signifying the lock was engaged. For some reason, this sound was more terrifying than normal.

"Give the left thrusters ten percent power." The stars outside the window rotated slowly, the only indicator that the ship was adjusting its position. "Now increase the right thrusters by forty percent. Rocco, maintain the front at thirty-five percent while gradually adjusting the angle to keep the ship moving forward."

"I need all of you to lock yourselves in," Captain Somers ordered. "We're out of time."

The ship grew silent, except for the engines burning pointlessly in the background. Joseph stared out at the sun and the tiny blue dot in the distance that was Earth. Time had run out. No amount of strategy could help them now. It was all up to his ship to pull them through. Normally he was confident in his work, but this was an entirely different ball game. They were facing a force, even those on Earth were not entirely prepared for. This was true terror like he had never felt before.

A large arc of plasma leaped off the sun's surface towards the Phoenix VII. The light streaked through the empty void of space ahead of them. It was a blinding sight. He had to look away. A wave of radiation flew out hitting the solar sails that halfway obscured its path to the hull, causing the entire ship to lurch. A loud explosion followed. There was no doubt in his mind the engine was going out. The entire ship lost power shutting off all thrusters and confirming his suspicions. Joseph helplessly watched the stars roll in and out of view as the ship continued to rotate uninterrupted with nothing to slow down what they had set in motion. It was like being stuck on one of those spinning bridges at a carnival. His entire body started to waver as though he were drunk. He couldn't tell which direction was up, and which was down. The ship flew dead through the vastness of space left to the will of fate. The momentum of the ship had been used to provide a semblance of gravity on the ship. With the thrust generated to maneuver the ship, and no way to restore proper rotation, all artificial gravity was lost.

He watched the rest of the crew floating helplessly around the bridge. He felt so lost. All hope of returning home had vanished at that moment. His breathing grew more reserved, and his chest quaked as he tried to keep himself from crying. The tars were welling up in his eyes, taunting him, by growing over his eyes, with nowhere to go.

Zia called across the bridge, "Six hours of air remaining."

Joseph stared helplessly at the crew. They had become floating balloons, tied down and forgotten, unable to go anywhere. Silence encapsulated the bridge leaving an uneasy feeling in Joseph's stomach. He wrapped a hand around the bar he was tethered to, pulling himself towards the computer. With his other hand he reached over and pressed the power button hoping that the small light would come on. No luck.

He released his grip to return to his static position in the air. All hope that their circumstance would change was fading.

"I'm going to take Rocco with me and we are going to attempt to jump the backup generator."

Rocco pulled his body to the bar, lifted his feet up placing them on either side of his hands, and slowly spun his body facing his back to the ceiling. Joseph watched and followed suit.

"The ship should still have enough air in it for the two of you to make it safely out and back should something happen," Captain Somers said.

"Got it," Rocco nodded.

Joseph and Rocco angled their bodies towards the bay door and unclipped their safety lines. In unison they pushed themselves away from the bar, flying at the entrance bracing for impact. Joseph grabbed onto the emergency handle with his right hand. Rocco hit the door. Immediately his body began to drift back. Joseph latched onto him with his left hand and jerked his body back to the door. A loud thud echoed through the silence.

"Ugggh," Rocco moaned out in pain.

Joseph twisted the handle of the door. The lock released, creating a small gap between the two panels. "Rocco reach in there with me and help me separate the doors."

Rocco reached his hand into the slit right below Joseph's and the two of them began to move the door. The gap slowly opened enough for Joseph to pull his weightless body through into the hall of the ship. He grabbed onto the other side of the door.

Rocco followed suit. He pointed to an open door halfway down the hall, "they left the door open to the electric room."

"Okay, let's get in there."

The two men pulled themselves along the wall until they reached the entrance. The backup generator was unhooked from the system, its cables floating through the air like snakes preparing to attack. Joseph pushed himself off the wall towards the generator and grabbed the cords mid-flight. He bounced off the opposite wall and headed towards the electric panel. Its shape made for an easy handhold to stop the momentum. A tug at the metal panel covering the extra power input sent it spinning through the air right towards Rocco.

"Look out Rocco!"

Rocco launched himself up towards the ceiling hit it and then bounced down towards the floor missing the metal plate that now bounced around the room. He caught the bar and re steadied himself. "All good."

Joseph chuckled, "God you're clumsy."

"Shut up and fix the power."

He latched the cables onto the electric box. "I got it. Rocco, start the generator."

He stretched out and flipped up the ignition switch. The engine roared to life. The lights began to glow a faint red color. Slowly but surely they grew brighter.

Joseph felt a sense of relief at the returning familiar hum of the ship. Within seconds the gravity was restored, pulling Joseph down to the ground. He landed wobbly on his feet and wavered a bit before regaining his posture. The metal panel let out a loud clanking sound as it hit the floor. He looked over to see Rocco already standing by, waiting for him.

"Look baby's taking his first steps."

"Hahaha." Joseph started walking towards the door. "We need to get back to the bridge."

The door to the bridge still remained partially closed, forcing them to squeeze between the panels once again, in order to rejoin everyone. The computers had started turning back on. The crew's faces colored up blue by their screens.

Diego opened up a window full of hardware diagnostics. "Computers appear to be in working order. I still need to ensure none of the data was corrupted."

"Get on that." The Captain walked up behind Zea, placing her hand on her shoulder. "How are the life support systems?"

"Running at seventy-five percent. It's enough for now."

Joseph listened to the crew run through their emergency checklists. *None of that's gonna matter if the engines can't get up and running.* His fingers glided across the keyboard. A window popped up, displaying the ship's onboard diagnostics. The program ran itself, checking every part of the ship to make sure they weren't compromised. Each section that was completed pulled up a full window of statistics for him to work through. *Hull integrity one hundred percent. Perfect.* He then moved to the solar sails. They had lost seventy percent functionality. The situation wasn't looking good. They only had one remaining engine.

"Joseph, I need an update on the ship." Captain Somers's voice was filled with muted concern. She was trying to hide how scared she was but Joseph had known her long enough that he could read her like an open book.

He pressed several buttons. "Hull's intact. We're running on thirty percent of our solar sails. We have one thruster engine left. Maneuvering thrusters are out completely." He switched screens. "But if we go out there we should be able to get them up and running again. Let me get a suit."

"I'll help guide you from here," Captain Somers said. "Carl and Sophie go help Joseph get out the airlock."

"Yes Captain," Carl replied.

"I'm pretty sure I remember doing it in the simulation," Sophie said. "I just hope it's the same setup."

Carl and Sophie walked out ahead of Joseph. He lagged behind trying to listen to Nova quietly talking to the Captain.

"Listen I understand you're dealing with a lot right now. You have too many other things to worry about, forget the thrusters. Let Joseph and Trent get the ship under control."

"I appreciate that Nova, but please let me do my job."

Their voices trailed off on his walk through the hallway. Joseph wound his way through the ship towards the airlock. Waiting at the entrance for him, Carl held the door next to the airlock open. Behind it was a room filled with the spacesuits. Joseph grabbed his suit. He utterly hated being stuck inside one. There was limited room inside causing the suit to sit tightly against his body. Adding the helmet just piled on to the closed in feeling. To make things worse he had never been on a spacewalk. At least on Mars there was gravity holding him in place, but outside that door there was just empty space. *Remember you're the only one capable of repairing the thrusters.* He slowly zipped himself up in the suit. *It's just like a blanket.* Joseph grabbed the helmet and secured it in place.

"Rrr oou rdee," Sophie's muffled words came through the helmet.

"I can't hear you guys," Joseph yelled, his voice captured inside the glass walls around his head. A wave of his hand grabbed their attention. He pointed to his ears and shook his head. Carl gave a quick thumbs up then mumbled something to Sophie.

The intercom system in his ear let out a quick beep accompanied by the Captain's voice, "okay I'm going to open the airlock door in 10...9...8...7...6."

Carl handed Joseph the tool kit to strap around his waist.

"3...2...1."

A soft whooshing sound made its way past the helmet upon the door opening. He entered the small room and pressed the button to close the door to the ship. In front of him was the exit he would soon be using to leave the safety of the ship.

"Okay, your room is depressurized."

"Let's just get this done with."

The door slid open without a sound. Before his eyes sat millions of stars. The only thing separating him from them was the suit he wore. He walked to the edge of the opening, and reached around the corner. There he grabbed onto the ladder leading to the top of the ship. He gently placed his foot onto the ladder rungs, making sure to not slip. His lower foot lifted with ease, as he stepped up to the next rung. He pulled himself up and almost went flying from the force. The next step he slowed down, locking his arms to counter the momentum. Upon reaching the top, the difficult process of crossing the walkways to the thrusters still remained. The solar sail blocked the sun with its majestic spread of copper and silver panels. The solar system continued to revolve around Joseph and the ship. He closed his eyes and focused his breathing.

"I want you to head along the upper portion of the hull towards the bridge." Captain Somers jerked his focus back to the mission at hand. "Continue forward until you reach the four-way junction."

"Gotcha." The ship had just enough artificial gravity that the effects could be felt on the entire hull of the ship allowing him to stand and walk around. However the slick surface caused him to decide crawling would be a better option. He attached his safety line to the rail and proceeded towards the junction ahead.

"Now head right towards the raised panel."

Out of the corner of his eye, Joseph spotted the surface camera looking up at him. "Nice to know the cameras are working out here." He unlatched his anchor and re-hooked it onto the next rail. Again he crawled to his destination trying to focus on footing and hand placement as a way of distraction from the confines of the suit. Seemingly by magic, his forward motion came to a halt. He looked up at a short wall in front of him.

"You need to climb onto the panel and look for an electric box near the outer edge."

In one steady motion he stood up and pulled his body up onto the platform in front of him. The metal box stuck out of the metal floor. Joseph approached the box and removed the drill from inside his tool pouch. After removing the bolts, the lid opened up revealing a rat's nest of tangled wires. One by one he pulled cords out rearranging some, and cutting and splicing others. "Okay what readout are we getting?"

"Right thrusters fully operational," Rocco's checked in.

"That's what I want to hear!" Joseph exclaimed. "I'm going to head across to the other thrusters." The box resealed easy enough. Joseph walked back to the end of the platform and climbed down. He worked his way back to the junction and crossed over to the other side this time a little quicker, confident he knew what to do this time. Once again he opened the electric box and began messing with wires. A black residue coated the lower wires. "This doesn't look good."

"What's wrong?" Captain Somers sounded confused.

He continued fiddling with the mess of cords that lay before him. "The wires are fried. I don't think I can get it up and running again. I've done all I can. Give me some good news from your end."

"Nothing," Rocco chimed in. "They're dead."

"We need those rockets to stop the ship from spinning."

"So then what should I do Trent?" Joseph stared at the thrusters in disbelief. Without an idea there would be no way to get the ship back on course. "Seriously, any suggestions would be great."

Trent spoke up again, "Hold on, let me run some numbers." Silence filled the intercom. "Can you climb down the backside of the panel where the thrusters are?"

"Looks like it." Joseph faced out into the abyss beyond.

"Position yourself just above the thrusters"

Rivets poking out from the metal provided Joseph with handholds to climb down on. "In position."

"Now I need you to release the governor from your booster pack on the suit. When I say go, turn the power to max and lay into the ship. I'll control the other side."

The governor slipped off with ease and floated off into space. Joseph turned on the pack and suddenly found himself pushed up against the metal siding. "Please tell me this is working."

"Slowly, but yes the spin is slowing."

"How much longer? I feel like I'm being crushed."

"Just a little more."

Joseph began to panic inside the suit. Sweat streamed down his forehead. He closed his eyes and pictured a beautiful beach scene but couldn't get the reality of where he was out of his head.

"That's it. Turn off the pack."

With a strong slap to the upper portion of his arm, Joseph turned off the power releasing his body from the wall. "Uggggh," he sighed with relief.

"Come on back in," Captain Somers said. "We'll make you a nice hot meal."

Joseph climbed back up, took one long look at the stars, thankful he was still on the ship, and headed back to the airlock.

Frank

"I need confirmation that the ship's alright," Frank blustered, trying to grasp the events that had played out. "Allie get all the observatories on the phone. I want to know exactly where the Phoenix is."

"Sir should I try our foreign contacts as well?"

"No, leave that to Randy. Randy team up with Judy and get all our connections in India, Russia, China, and Europe on the Phone. I'll join the Conference call in an hour."

"We'll get right on it." Randy picked up his cell phone and walked out.

Frank turned to face the room. "Caleb, what's our radio communication status?"

"All signals are down. Transmission towers remain fully operational."

The room fell silent. Frank stared out at a sea of panicked faces. It took every ounce of control to remain calm. "Everyone, keep trying to locate and reach the Phoenix VII, we'll get them back home no matter what." He walked out into the hall, only to be greeted by Daniel.

Daniel's red face and bloodshot eyes locked onto Frank, unflinching. The tears were still streaming down his cheeks. "You Bastard!" he screamed. His fist clenched so tight they were losing color. "How the fuck could you lose them. You were supposed to get them home."

"I know, I'm sorry. We should have been ready."

"Sorry? Sorry? That's all you can say?! How about, I swear we'll get your wife back? Should-haves just don't cut it."

"I don't know what to…"

"Shut the fuck up and get out of my way!"

Frank grabbed ahold of Daniel and pulled him in, wrapping his arms around him. "I swear to God I'll get her home no matter the cost."

Daniel's body transformed into a limp weight pushing against him. Frank could feel the rapid compressions of Daniel's chest as he broke down in tears. He felt for his friend. This was all his fault. There was no conceivable way that he could think to fix it. The pain was eating away inside of him, but for the moment he still had to remain strong. The next few hours would be pivotal.

Daniel finally regained enough composure to stand up on his own. "I'm sorry for that," he said with an exasperated breath.

Frank lowered his arms. "It's Ok. I have to get going but if you need anything let me know. We're gonna figure it out." He took one more look at his friend. "Promise me you're going to be okay for the next couple hours."

"Yeah, I'll be fine. I've got to see what help I can be."

"I'll be back soon enough." Frank left hoping that Daniel wouldn't do anything stupid. Now his mind was torn between the lost astronauts and their loved ones. He headed towards the conference room. Accents from all around the world chattered about. The door opened to large faces covering the walls. "Thank you all for taking the time to join us. I promise this will be quick." He walked to the head of the table. Whoever had designed the room had intended for anyone on a video call to appear to be sitting around the table. The front seat of the table was the only screen that remained dark, the seat held for the NASA scientist in charge. The importance of this position wasn't lost on Frank.

"At five am this morning the Phoenix VII Interplanetary Space Ship was hit by a massive solar flare. All communication was lost and the ship is nowhere to be found. As of right now our top scientists are trying to figure out how to restore communication. I need your help tracking down the ship. We need all your available telescopes to help search for their location."

He watched the stoic faces hoping for some sign of understanding. The translation finally kicked in and one by one they began to agree to help.

"Thank you. We won't forget this. Please send word if you find anything." One by one the talking heads disappeared leaving behind black screens.

Now came the hard part. Frank began to feel nauseous. He placed his hand over his mouth and hunched over. *Get ahold of yourself.* It took all the strength he had to ensure the little food he'd had over the last twenty-four hours would stay down. Recouping himself, he dialed up the president's direct line.

President Graham's office secretary asked him to "Please hold."

"Listen, it's of the utmost importance that I talk to the President immediately. Tell him this is the Head of NASA. I need to speak to him."

"Sir, please don't raise your voice to me. It won't make this go any faster. I'm putting you on hold."

"Tango Bravo three four one." He needed to make sure she had heard him. The President had given him special permission to use that code but only for situations of a truly dire nature. It could drag the President out of any meeting. The line remained silent. He held his breath hoping it had worked, knowing it had to work. Word would spread soon and if he wasn't ahead of it, the fallout would be enormous. Seconds dragged on. He knew time was relative but this was just ridiculous. Never before had his perception of it been so acute.

The phone sprang to life. "President Graham here." The apprehension, which had visibly shaken Frank, broke at once.

"They told me there was some kind of emergency. Is this true?"

"Yes sir." Frank struggled to focus his thoughts into a cohesive sentence. The line remained dead.

"Please get on with it. I have urgent matters to get to."

"Oh, yes. Sorry." He adjusted his glasses as if preparing for a well-rehearsed speech. It had become such a force of habit that he did it even when talking on the phone knowing full well the receiving end had no way of seeing what he was doing. "I'll keep it brief. This morning a burst of radiation hit the Phoenix VII earlier than expected. Without proper time to prepare, the ship took a direct hit. The status of the ship and everyone aboard is unknown at this time. I've reached out to our partners around the world and they are helping us to find the ship and get back in touch."

"Tell me what resources you need and I'll get them for you."

"The sooner we can get the press conference out of the way the better."

"Just send me the information and I'll have my Press Secretary get on it."

"Actually sir, I would prefer to do this one myself. It was my mission and I owe it to the world to be the one to tell them."

"If that's what you want we'll make it happen. Give it four hours and everything will be set."

"Thank you, Mr. President." Frank hung up the phone. The queasiness returned with a vengeance. He threw the conference room door open and ran down the hall. It seemed to extend forever. The only thought in his mind was to not throw up in the hallway. After all he had an image to maintain. He fumbled with the door and quickly made his way to the stall and hunched over. Signaled by the sight of porcelain, the contents of his breakfast fled from him, escaping from the agitator they had been confined to. He stood waiting to see if anything would work its way free before he placed the toilet seat down. Frank closed the stall door and sat down on the toilet. All the fear, stress, anger, and sadness came flooding out. Tears poured from his already weary eyes. His muffled sobs echoed off the ceramic walls. *I could just walk out the door right now and never come back*, he thought to himself. *There's no way to get them back. I've failed everyone. I'm a piece of shit. I can't even take care of a pet. Why did they trust me with a mission this big?* His erratic breathing started to normalize. With a loud smack, he hit himself in the face. The jolt of pain brought him back to what he needed to do. *This is my responsibility. I can't stop. Not now. They're counting on me. Get yourself together.* He wiped away the tears and stood up with a regained sense of purpose and walked out of the bathroom, turning around almost instantly, remembering he had just thrown up. A swish of cold water helped to rinse his mouth out and splash to the face helped him feel refreshed. *Time to get my speech ready.* He left the bathroom once again, this time, continuing towards his office.

There he sat in front of his computer unable to formulate a cohesive statement. Each line being reworked over and over again, his brain searching for the words to say. He only got one chance at this. The press would tear apart every word he said. Carefully constructed sentences formed on the paper. After what seemed like forever he hit send. There was no turning back now. He had an hour left to get his speech down.

He left his office practicing his speech and continued practicing as he navigated the empty halls towards the prep room.

Once inside the room, he paced back and forth running through every word one more time. His sweaty palms left the pages of his speech damp. The hour grew to a close, he could feel his heart pounding inside his chest. The thumping rang out in his ears. One sip of water and he was off to the show. Stepping onto the stage of the press room, he was greeted by a sea of faces, illuminated by bright lights shining from every direction. With the revelation would come the agony of seeing the shocked faces of those before him. He took several deep breaths, calming his nerves. Camera lights flashing everywhere. The teleprompter lit up. A small cough allowed him to clear his throat. The time had come.

"At 5:00 a.m. this morning, the sun emitted a massive solar flare. The direction of the burst prevented any effects here on Earth, however, the Phoenix VII ship was directly in its path. The ship was unable to avoid the radiation traveling towards it. Upon being hit, all communication between NASA and the crew was lost. It has yet to be determined the amount of damage they sustained during this incident. We have crews all around the world attempting to reconnect with the team traveling back from Mars. Before today, measurements had shown the solar flare would occur sometime next week, and this information was relayed to the Phoenix VII in hopes that steps could be taken to stop any adverse effects. Our hope is that enough preparation was completed to ensure the safety of everyone on board. As soon as we've established a link, I will release another statement. For now, I will not be taking any questions until we know more." Frank wrapped up his speech amid a flurry of questions. Security escorted him off the stage and through the crowd.

Caleb stood in the hallway, his hands grasping a stack of papers. Not a usual site but nothing struck Frank as out of the ordinary. He turned towards Frank, held up the stack of papers, and spoke up. "We believe we have a plan to regain communication."

"Let's talk in my office." Frank placed his hand on Caleb's back, escorting him to the quiet room. "Stay out here while we talk," he directed the security team. "Keep everyone away while we talk." The door closed and he took a seat behind the desk. Caleb organized the stack of papers in front of him. Numbers and charts covered their surfaces. "Tell me you have a viable solution."

Caleb placed a page in Frank's hand. "It appears that way. We are calling it Deep Space Relay Satellite. Basically, the idea is to send a satellite up that can bridge the gap between us and the path of the Phoenix VII. Theoretically, it would allow us to send messages to and from the ship, bypassing the need for an antenna."

Frank rubbed his head, running over the numbers. "It seems like it could work. What kind of time frame and budget are we looking at?"

"We should be able to get a working model up within a month. Our foreign contacts have agreed to let us launch it aboard one of their rockets."

Let's get a move on it while we see if there are any other options available." A spark of hope returned to Frank's eyes. *This idea actually seems feasible.* Now the only real struggle would be time.

Diego

The ship was cold. Less heat meant less energy wasted. Life support was more essential than the crew's comfort. These conditions were less than ideal for Diego. His fingers struggled to keep up with the speed of his brain. It didn't matter though, computers were the ultimate test of his capabilities. For the first time the puzzle came with more than just a paycheck and a sense of completion. This solution would be the one necessary to ensure the survival of himself and the entire crew. A little cold would hardly hold him back. "We lost all contact with Earth," he said, so focused that his tone would be misconstrued as callous to an outside observer. The crew had grown used to his cold working nature.

"What do you mean we lost all contact?" Somers asked, her voice laced with nervous tension. "Are you suggesting that we have no way to get ahold of NASA?"

Diego's eyes carefully scanned the code on the display, his eyes moving as fast as they could to find the source of the problem. "It's much worse than that. NASA has no way of knowing where we are or sending any information to the ship itself."

Captain Somers approached from the side and stopped to glance at the monitor. "Is the problem something you can fix?"

The clacking of the keyboard was the only response Diego gave. A box in the center of the screen eclipsed the code he had been working on. He closed the box and resumed the task at hand. "It seems all programs are functioning. So no. However, I'm working on a program designed to get us back to Earth."

Somers's demeanor changed. "Fantastic. How long will it take you to get it up and running?"

"Give me 24 hours. Also I need Joseph and Trent at my full disposal."

"I'll make sure they are."

"We're back," Joseph hollered through the hall.

Diego turned around to see Sophie and Carl walking behind Joseph who was still wearing his spacesuit. "Did you happen to see if the satellite was still intact?"

"I was a little too distracted," Joseph said nonchalantly, taking a seat on the bench.

"Well once you're done playing Buzz Lightyear would you like to help me out?"

"Anything for you darling."

"Trent's already up to speed, but basically I need the two of you to help me get the ship on course. I'm working on the program now. Once I finish, I'll need to have you guys put in your numbers and calculation."

Trent walked away from his station and towards the rest of the crew. "The system doesn't appear to know where the ship is located so we'll need to let it run for a bit."

"Okay, everyone make sure you all get some food and rest," Captain Somers ordered. "It's been a busy twelve hours."

A resounding "yes Ma'am," filled the air.

Joseph joined Trent at the computers. They worked hard but the stress of the day was impossible to miss.

Diego realized that Both of them appeared to be running on fumes. He felt bad. His desire to push himself was affecting more than just himself. "You guys should join the others.

"We're good." Joseph let out a yawn. "We don't leave until you do."

You feel the same way Trent?"

Eyes half-closed, he nodded.

If you say so." Diego wasn't one to argue. He fell into the monotony of coding, cutting out the outside world. After a while, the sound of his computer caused him to worry. When it continued despite his actions ceasing, the realization that Joseph was asleep, broke his concentration. "Trent, wake Joseph up and you two go take a break. I'll finish up here and you can pick it up tomorrow."

Without hesitation, he did as Diego recommended.

That left Diego alone on the massive bridge. Line after line of code passed across the screen. The familiar sting he associated with countless hours behind a computer began to set in. He sat admiring the code being produced. For all intents and purposes he was a god creating something from nothing with full control of the outcome. If he willed it, it would come to be. He finished entering the last numbers and started the compiling process. At that moment, the 12 hours that had passed hit him like a ton of bricks. *If I'm going to get this done I better get some sleep.* Diego pushed his chair away from the desk. In a daze of exhaustion, he wandered down the hall still running through every possible piece of information he needed to account for, hoping he hadn't missed anything.

The door to his bedroom was wide open, welcoming him in. He stumbled to his bed and laid down, ready to fall asleep. Warmth radiated from the bed which seemed odd. Typically the rooms were cold, keeping the beds nice and chilled. Rolling over, he found Sophie lying beneath the sheets. Her arm reached across his body. Their lips touched in the dark.

"You're back. Did you finish your work?" Her kisses began slowly descending Diego's neck while she spoke. A warm hand crept up underneath his shirt, rubbing along his stomach.

His breathing was heavy. "I hit a breaking point. Can I get a rain check? I need to get some sleep. I promised Captain I would be done in twenty-four hours and I already used up twelve."

"Of course." She rolled over. "But afterward you're all mine. Love you."

"Love you too." He closed his eyes only to find himself being awoken by his alarm. "Goddammit I just fell asleep." Sophie was still passed out next to him.

Trying not to wake her, Diego hobbled out of bed. The metal frame retching and squealing with each move. Making his way through the dark he found the bathroom sink. A few splashes of warm water to the face were not enough to wake him up. Remnants of the water dripped from his dreary face and into a puddle on the floor. He grabbed a towel, wiped off his face, and headed back to the bridge. The entire trip down the hallway felt as if he were in a dream.

By the time Diego reached his desk the haze had gone but trying to keep his eyes open seemed impossible.

"Hey you look like you could use this," a nearby voice said.

Not realizing anyone else was in the room, Diego jumped in his chair. He looked around the room to see where the disembodied voice came from. Carl stood next to the drink holder on the bridge. The only thing it really held was energy drinks and water, but when you're trying to fly a ship anything else is just unnecessary. He threw a purple pouch towards Diego. Instinct kicked in, causing his hand to shoot up and catch the flying pouch.

The drink consisted of a special formula that included caffeine, ginseng, and taurine. Nasa provided four different flavors that all equated to cough medicine, and no one had yet been able to distinguish any difference. The effects however could last a full day due to a slow uptake agent added in the mix. Diego was now drinking the "guava" flavored one. "Fuck these things are nasty. Why did we finish all the good ones on the flight out? I would kill for a strawberry daiquiri one. Slightly more bearable."

"Just be glad we still have some."

"You know I am, considering I drank most of 'em." Diego's hand squeezed the pouch accidentally forcing the gel-like substance to ooze out, and run down the side of the pouch. He raised it to his mouth, lapping up the precious liquid off the container, being sure not to let a single drop go to waste. "Program's finished! Time to test it. Carl could you help me run some trials?"

"I don't know what I'm doing. You don't want me touching it."

"Precisely why I asked you to help. I want to see how it handles shit data. Oh and if it's easy to use." Diego walked over to a desk on the other side of the bridge, grabbing a thin packet, placing it in front of Carl. "Here, this should give you the numbers you need. Pick two sets of coordinates and try 'em out."

"Okay can do."

Diego sat back down at his station. The program appeared to be running smoothly with no major errors. Clicking on each page, he scanned everything to see if the functionality was fully present. *Man I made one hell of a program given the time window. It's weird actually wanting to hit the deadline. Good thing my boss isn't here to see this hehe. At least at work, I got to eat real food. And listened to music while I worked. That always made the time go quickly. Maybe I should go play some video games after I get done here. Not like I ever really stop working up here. I could use a hard drink.* A sudden shaking of his shoulder followed by Carl's voice snapped him back to reality.

"Any chance we're ready to get things going?"

"Yeah, of course. Do you wanna get Trent up here?"

Carl pushed the button on the intercom. "Trent, Diego says he's ready for you."

"I guess I could have done that myself huh. Oh well too late now."

"Seeing as we'll be back on course soon, what are you gonna do with all the fame?"

"I didn't do anything. I was just keeping you company." A look of confusion distorted Carl's face.

Diego shook his head. "No, idiot, I mean when we get back to Earth." He waited in anticipation for Carl's response. Ever since the ship spiraled out of control he couldn't get the thought of being stranded out of his mind. This could be a chance to see someone with a glimmer of hope that things would work themselves out.

Carl always claimed his God would keep him safe and get him home. Somehow that thought alone seemed to keep him dreaming of the future.

Carl sat up in his chair. "Honestly, the thought never crossed my mind. I kind of enjoyed my life as it was. Maybe I'll use the grants I get to start new experiments on atmospheric transformation. You know, so one day we can make Mars habitable. Oh, hey Trent."

"What are you talking about?" Diego looked up from his computer.

From behind him a gravelly voice spoke, "Hey beautiful."

Diego's entire body reacted as if he'd touched a power outlet. "Goddammit! Every time," he screamed.

His fist launched towards the source of the voice hitting Trent in the arm. Instead of a cry from pain, all he got in return was laughter reverberating off the walls adding to his embarrassment. "Anyway…" he struggled to regain his composure, "let's get this going."

Trent pointed towards the observation glass with his long finger. "Okay, see that bright light out there? That's Earth."

"Well then, just type in the coordinates, I'm ready to be done drifting." Diego finally felt better about their situation but not enough to completely relax. The next few months were going to require constant attention. Their speed was slower than anticipated. Diego had accounted for all of that in his program.

"It's not that easy. Joseph and I have to finish our calculations. I'm quite sure some of the ones from earlier are a bit off. And speak of the devil."

Joseph entered the bridge looking leagues better. "Am I too late?"

"Actually, just in time. Diego's finally ready for our numbers."

"He knows we're not done yet, right?"

"I do, and I'm willing to wait." Diego leaned back in his chair and closed his eyes. At this point the energy drink was kicking in, inhibiting actual sleep. Instead he kept his eyes closed and just remained that way until the two minions were done.

"We're ready for you Diego."

"Thanks Trent. Well here goes nothing." He entered the final commands. The ship began to spin into place within seconds of the program processing Trent and Joseph's numbers. The path home was clear.

Taking initiative this time, Diego reached down and pressed the intercom button. "Attention crew…" Hearing his own voice over the speakers made him wince. "…We are on our way home." He got up and left the room without saying another word, high on the idea of what he had accomplished over the preceding twenty-four hours.

The gym sat on the far side of the ship, allowing for plenty of time to think about where things would go for him once they made it home, but no matter how hard he tried he remained unable to convince himself that they would make it back alright. It wasn't like NASA to just give up on bringing astronauts back home, yet the whole scenario just felt off. He walked past the other members of the crew on his way through the halls. A few sitting in the dining room could be heard laughing about some TV show they were watching. His desire to be social just wasn't there. He continued on until he finally made it to the gym. As luck would have it the room was empty. After a few minutes of running on the treadmill, he was overcome by a dizzy spell. That's when it dawned on him that in all of the craziness he had been too distracted to eat. He left the room to find himself face to face with Sophie. She handed him a meal bar.

"Figured you'd be hungry." She stood still, rambling on nonsensically. Diego's attention being fully consumed by the process of eating, all he heard was "play game," and "the Captain". Having no idea what was going on he decided to just follow Sophie and figure it out as they went.

Carl

Soft music embraced Carl's ears lulling him into a relaxed state. His ratty old bible sat open on his desk covered in highlights and penned in annotations. A combination of his handwriting and those of the men before him. Tradition called for the bible to be passed down from father to son upon turning thirty, making him the fourth owner of this family heirloom. The coffee stain in the middle of the page was the result of him and his brother fighting near their dad. His brother Zach had stolen his favorite Warneg Hero action figure and had been preparing to test the fire resistance of said toy. Carl chased him around the house accidentally slamming into the back of his dad's chair launching hot liquid from the cup into the air and all over his dad. The memories brought back such nostalgia for him. He caught his mind wandering and returned to the passage which his dad had been reading all those years ago. "I will never leave you nor forsake you," he read aloud. He knew that as long as he held on to his faith, he would make it back home to his loved ones. He turned to his journal to write down his thoughts.

Year: 2058, Day: unknown

Yesterday we were finally able to make out landmasses on Earth. Thank God. I knew you would help us get home. My faith in you was shaken but never failed. You always take care of your children. Please lend me the courage and calm to make it through the next few days as it will take everything we have to get back to the station without any connection to Earth.

Carl closed his books and returned them to the shelf. His left hand gripped the metal cross that hung around his neck. It was a piece he made himself which is why the proportions weren't exactly even. He didn't remember even grabbing it. It was just a habit he had developed to help him deal with feelings of being overwhelmed. He removed his hand from the cross so he could clean up his room. Tidiness helped the small room feel a little more bearable, especially after being in space for so long. Clothes from the day before sat in a mound along with a damp towel. With a swing of his foot, Carl kicked the clothes into the air and towards the laundry shoot. His eyes watched as they fell through the hole.

"Score," he said, pumping his fist. "Okay let's try this again."

The towel launched into the air this time, falling short. "Dang it." He walked over and placed the towel in the shoot.

Out of sheer boredom, he took to the halls with no particular destination in mind, more of an attempt to just keep moving. He heard the Captain expressing concern about something. Poking his head into the bridge he saw her and Rocco staring out the observation window.

Captain Somers pointed towards Earth. "I'm telling you, it doesn't look right. That's not the moon. And even with all those storms I don't recognize any of the continents."

Rocco's voice broke from the nervousness, "I don't know what to tell you. That's definitely Earth." His normal confidence seemed to be absent.

Through the glass of the bridge, Carl could see Earth covered in large grey and white clouds. Along its surface were the familiar blue ocean linings and reddish and brown land.

Frustration boiled up in the Captain's voice. "Yeah it should be. I'm just not thinking straight. If only we could get ahold of NASA. FUCK!" She slammed her fist against the desk.

Rocco gave her a hug. "We're gonna make it back, I promise. Within a week we will be close enough to get ahold of them via a short-range radio Joseph rigged up."

"Sorry to be so negative. It's just, you're the only one I can be candid with."

"Don't worry, this doesn't go anywhere."

That was odd, Carl thought to himself continuing on towards Zea's room to see if she was up to anything. He approached her door, lifting his fist to knock. Without warning the door ceased to block the way, opening to a naked Zea standing in the middle of the room hunched over her dresser. She turned her head sideways triggered by the sound.

Her face turned red as she yelled at him. "What the hell!" The nearest piece of clothing turned into a haphazard cover for her exposed body.

Carl stumbled backward, placing his hands over his eyes. His feet struggled to find their footing and within an instant he found himself sitting on the floor. His heart was pounding inside his chest, and his face grew warm. Sweat started gathering on his palms. His thoughts were a complete fog. "I'm so sorry," he kept repeating as he turned and headed away from the door.

"It's alright," Zea's voice came from the doorway.

Carl stopped without looking back. "I didn't mean to... I promise I didn't see much."

"No, really it's my fault. I forgot to lock the door. What did you want to talk about?" Her voice soothed his embarrassment.

He turned around to see Zea's upper half poking out of the door, draped in a peach-colored robe. It drew out the beauty of her pale skin and the blush of her cheeks. Her beautiful hair graced the top of the robe, like a tree branch barely touching the surface of the water. The gleaming of her brown eyes. Everything in him wanted to grab her and pull her close. *No stop it.* He thought to himself. *Those aren't pure thoughts.* He looked away attempting to collect himself, despite the fact he had grown feelings for this shy young girl.

"I just wanted to chat. I was bored." He mumbled as he continued to stare at the ceiling. No matter how hard he tried he couldn't get the thought of her standing there out of his head.

"Well could you give me five minutes to finish getting ready?"

"Yeah sure." Carl turned and wandered off, hoping to clear the event from his mind.

As he sat in his bedroom, Carl found himself replaying the events, worried that he'd upset Zea. Time passed and he decided to forget about going back. It would be easier to pretend nothing had happened. The music helped distract his mind. Hours passed in isolation before Zea showed up to his room.

She brushed her hair behind her ear. "Hey so you never came back. What did you want to talk about?"

His mouth felt dry. The image of her standing naked was back. "I...I... just... Well, I was hoping to just hang out." He felt so stupid. He didn't have anything worth saying.

"Okay." She sat down next to him on the bed. A new song came on. "Oh I love this song."

"Me too. I prefer their earlier work over the new stuff." With that, Carl felt the tension in the room dissipate.

The conversation came easy as if they were long lost friends. Once he felt talked out they parted ways, leaving Carl to his own devices. He couldn't get past how well things went with Zea. It was the closest he'd been to anyone since the mission began. He finally had developed a real friendship, but being so close to home it felt like it was too little too late. Things seemed normal aboard the ship. Everyone went about their business. Over the next few days Carl saw Zea open up to him. They would eat lunch together and make use of the media room. Things appeared to be going great. Finally the ship was preparing to enter orbit around Earth.

The crew had been in the middle of eating together as a final gesture before meeting up with the CAPS for docking when Captain Somers spoke up, "Everyone please meet on the bridge. It's time we prepare to enter orbit." The team packed up their dishes and migrated to the bridge. "Now we still have yet to see the Space station," Addison continued, "but our plan is to remain in orbit long enough to line up with it. Our assumption is it's just been too far away to see. As for Earth, there seem to be several large storms covering up the mainland."

"Captain, we have a large object approaching the ship," Joseph hollered.

"What are you talking about?" Rocco inquired, his voice full of confusion.

"Well, the radar picked up on a massive object that appears to be coming directly at us."

Captain Somers ran over to verify the information. "Everyone get to your stations."

Carl felt useless. He found his hand once again gripping onto the cross around his neck. *What could possibly be coming at them this close to Earth,* he wondered. Out of the corner of the window a massive asteroid came into view.

"Quickly, set boosters to full, we have to get out of the way," Captain Somers commanded. The green lights flooded the room. They had seen the Asteroid too late. The Phoenix VII was hurtling towards the oncoming projectile unable to get out of the way in time. "Everyone, brace for impact!"

Carl watched as the crew buckled themselves into their seats. He had been ahead of the game, making sure he was locked in upon reaching his work station, knowing in his heart that something was bound to go awry. Earth took center stage, the boosters playing their cacophonous song to usher it in.

"We're almost clear," Joseph's voice could barely be heard over the defining roar. "Come on, just a little …." the sound of twisting metal stopped him mid-speech. Grinding sounds hummed through the framework. The bridge lights faded from green and into red. The sound of the engines faded away. The ship began to lose its gravity as the momentum was interrupted.

Carl felt his limbs lift up, a puppet master controlling his every movement. "God, please don't let us die," he cried out. The only thing that came to his mind was the Lord's prayer.

"Our father who art in heaven. Hallowed be thy name," The crew was panicking around him. Over his prayers, the only voice he could distinguish was that of Captain Somers barking orders to the crew. "Seal the doors. Change our trajectory now!"

"Thy Kingdom come, thy will be done." Everyone but Carl worked furiously to alter the incoming fate, but no matter how much they tried, the outcome remained the same. The ship was hurtling towards Earth, completely unhindered. Carl was in disbelief. His skills were of no use. It was the exact same feeling he got during the emergency scenario training, the only difference being that this time there was no door he could walk out of after failing to prevent disaster. "On Earth, as it is in heaven." as the lines came out he stared at the planet growing ever closer.

"Zea I need a life support status." The Captain tried to control the panic-filled room.

Carl continued out loud, "Give us this day our daily bread."

"We lost a lot of air from the ship. We're running on backup. It's enough to last a few hours."

Carl watched Zea. "And forgive us our trespasses as we forgive those who trespass against us." He caught himself clinging to her visage to try and get through. The thought of being with her gave him the motivation to try anything he could to get them out of this. He sprung to life, pounding furiously at the computer, attempting to recall the training procedures. He checked engines, nothing. He ran the systems checks on his computer hoping something would catch his memory. It was in this moment of furor that the sound of muffled sobs and sniffling caught him off guard. It was coming from Sophie. He hadn't realized that in all the confusion she was even more terrified than he was. With all the focus he could muster he attempted to tune out her cries of desperation. The Earth was getting closer with each second. All concept of time went out of the window. The sobs grew less frequent, a sign Sophie was getting worn out.

As if to wrangle the entire crew into its open arms, the Earth's gravity swept over Carl's body. The odd sensation of weight, after being in zero gravity for so long was enough to temporarily confuse his mind. The effort it now took to lift an arm or shift in the chair required some thought.

Captain Somers screamed out, "Shit, we've hit the upper atmosphere." The ship was gaining velocity, its trajectory now headed directly towards the Surface.

Carl's body slammed into the seat. A red glow obstructed the observation window. Heat flowed into the ship. The warmth became unbearable, making it hard to breathe. Sweat began beading on his skin. His body remained immobile as the ship flew out of control. Every attempt to hold his eyes open was met with incredible resistance. He could only catch glimpses of the horror around him.

"Joseph, what the hell are you doing?" Rocco groaned over the crackling of the ship's hull.

The sound of bay doors opening hit Carl's ears. *Why would he open a door right now? Such a waste.* He just couldn't figure it out. *We're going to die and...* his thoughts got cut short, as the ship suddenly decelerated. His body slammed against the restraints testing their capacity to hold him in place. His arms and legs flew in front of him, and his head jerked forward. Then just as quickly, they snapped back. The muscles in his neck tensed up. Out of the window, parts of the ship could be seen flying past, independent of the bridge.

Rocco grinned from ear to ear. "Did you just deploy the solar sails?"

"Yeah I hoped it would slow us down. Seems to be working so far." Joseph's face was a mix of surprise and relief.

There was a twang of metal snapping, followed by the ship speeding up, though the pace was much slower than their initial descent.

"One of the wires snapped!" Trent bellowed.

Another one could be heard snapping, followed by another.

The ground was approaching quickly. The ship started turning, being pulled along by the remaining grasp of the solar sail.

Captain Somers's whole body tensed up. "Everyone, hold on, we're about to hit."

Carl closed his eyes and grabbed his cross. *God won't let anything happen to me that I can't survive.* He repeated this mantra to himself. The ship began crunching into the ground. A cloud of dust flew up from the far end of the ship blocking the window. The impact threw his body around inside the restraints. The cross ripped from his neck. In an instant, the roof of the bridge slammed into the ground and started to collapse. Carl watched the chaos around him. Glass, metal, and plastic flew everywhere. Computer parts collided with the framework around him. He closed his eyes trying not to watch the disaster unfolding. Something punched him in his stomach. A moan crept out of his lungs. Finally, the ship came to a complete stop. Carl opened his eyes. The stomach pain was gone. In fact, he couldn't feel much of anything. An itch hit his lungs and out of instinct he coughed to relieve himself.

A fine red mist sprayed from his mouth followed by a sharp pain. *I must have gotten hit harder than I thought.* He took a deep breath and wailed out in pain. Zea hobbled over to him. In his dizziness, her visage seemed to light up. The voice was muffled as if he were underwater. She climbed over bits of wreckage. Standing a few feet under him, her warm hands embraced Carl's face. His arms hung down past his head. He reached over with his right hand to touch her arm. She was all he had wanted. He couldn't figure out why she had tears in her eyes. It was at that moment that he felt a warm sensation moving down his body. It crept over his chin. A warm metallic taste filled his mouth. The liquid continued and ran into his eyes. He wiped away the liquid. *Why was it raining? He* thought. *Why was Zea upside down?* He struggled to speak through belated breaths, "I'm getting really tired."

Zea stood there with tears rolling down her face. In an unsteady voice, she spoke, "Don't move. I'm going to figure out how to get you down."

"What do you mean down?" He forced out. He looked towards the restraints that held him in. "Why is there a metal pole sticking out of my stomach. Where's my bed? I'm ready to lie down." The world began fading around him. "Is it night already? How far am I from my house?" Everything was a blur. His entire body shook uncontrollably. "I'm freezing. Is it snowing out?" Carl closed his eyes, letting the fatigue overtake him.

Zea

Smoke billowed out of the ship's smoldering core, carrying the scent of burning metal through the air. Chaos had broken out around the site of the crash. Strange whooping noises accompanied a chorus of shrieks and howls. The voices of the crew were faint. Despite all this, the only thing Zea cared about was Carl. His body was staked to the seat, a river of blood flowing from the wound. Training would have her leave the rod in until a way to stop the bleeding was available, but deep down she knew there was no way for Carl to survive. Zea unlatched the belt meant to keep him safe. With every ounce of strength she could muster, Zea began pulling at the rod. As she braced herself, searing pain shot through her leg. Instantly she lurched over in agony. Letting out a loud moan she pulled herself back up. Determination drove her towards her goal. Her hands wrapped around the metal. She struggled to pull with all her might, but any signs of progress eluded her.

Struggling to stay on her feet, she pulled again but still to no avail now sobbing at her inability to do anything to free her friend. Zea placed her head on the pole unable to focus past the crying. Suddenly a hand graced her own. There stood Nova, her suit torn to shreds, blood trickling down her arm. Without a word, she picked up where Zea had left off. Finding her strength, Zea joined in once again. This time the pole budged a little. A few attempts later and the long pole finally released its hold upon Carl. Zea threw her arms underneath the falling body in an attempt to slow its drop, but the lifeless body crumpled to the ground. Zea dropped to her knees and grabbed Carl's head, stroking his hair.

She screamed at the top of her lungs, "Come on Carl! I can't lose you like this!" She slapped his face, hoping to awaken him despite knowing full well he was gone. "Wake up, dammit." Her sobbing grew louder.

"Zea! Are you alright?" It was Nova, trying to yell over all the ruckus.

In her grief, Zea was unable to be swayed away from the tragedy which she cradled in her blood-soaked arms.

"Watch out Zea."

Her gaze never left Carl's body, as a sharp pain shot through her head. Her eyes slammed shut in an attempt to deal with the pain. With no control over its actions her hand jerked up and clutched the left side of her head.

"Shit," Nova rushed to Zea's side. "You're bleeding."

Zea's quivered as she showed her two bloody hands. "That's not my blood. I tried… but…but….I couldn't save him. I should have been able to do something."

The smoke burned her lungs making talking painful.

Nova's gentle hand graced the side of Zea's face. "No I mean your head. I'm sorry about Carl. I promise we'll give him a proper burial but right now we need to get your head taken care of."

"I can't leave him here."

You're not leaving him. Let's get you up." The hand moved from Zea's head to Carl's body, removing it from her lap. A gentle pull brought her to her feet.

Zea slumped in Nova's grip. "Just leave me here." A blow struck the side of Zea's face, tossing her head to the side. Without any warning Nova had slapped Zea full force. Her cheek throbbed.

"You need to get your shit together. You're the only hope the rest of the crew has to survive, but you're so caught up in your own fucking self-loathing that you're fucking useless." Nova turned and stormed off.

What am I doing? With pain shooting through her injured leg, Zea grabbed Carl's arm and slowly began dragging him out of the wreckage. Whether it was her animal instincts kicking in or maybe hope that Carl could still be saved, she found herself determined to ensure Carl's body didn't remain in the smoldering ashes. The deadweight dragged along the ground fighting every pull and tug exerted on it. Her lungs ached. Her leg was in complete agony. Still, she worked her way around the broken metal and broken computers. The adrenaline was wearing off, leaving her sapped of energy. She let go of Carl's arm and struggled to catch her breath. The light was streaming in through the haze, meaning escape from the fiery hell was near. With all she could muster, Zea gave it one more try. Two figures came into view on the edge of the smoke.

Trent had his arm wrapped around Captain Somers's neck, leaning on her for support. The Captain's mouth had a strip of cloth wrapped around it. Trent's free arm held a similar strip up to his mouth and nose. "Rocco I found another one," Captain Somers attempted to shout, her voice completely horse.

"Good." Rocco's gruff voice came through the ambient noise. His large figure broke into view. "Between the four we have outside, you finding Trent, and Nova finding two others that just leaves Diego unaccounted for." Rocco made eye contact with Zea. "You finally made it out."

"Of course I did" Captain Somers responded with confusion. "I've been com…"

"No, not you. I was talking to Zea," he gestured towards her with a nod of his head. "Why the hell are you trying to take stuff with you. You need to get out of here."

Unable to speak, Zea grabbed the body and pulled it towards them. Bits of glass jetted from the blood-caked skin and clothes.

"Oh God," Trent heaved, his face wracked with horror by the sight that lay before them. "Is that Carl?"

Captain Somers removed Trent's arm from around her shoulder. "Can you walk on your own?"

"Yeah but there's no way I'm touching that."

"You won't have to, I'll help Zea. Just get yourself out of here. Rocco, finish looking for Diego and make sure to keep your mouth covered."

The smoke thinned out as Zea and Captain Somers bore the load of her friend through the gaping maw of the ships, that was once a gargantuan observation window, with the assistance of the Captain. Her eyes were greeted by a strange land. Blueish dirt crumbled under her feet, soft but seemingly dry. What could only be described as a forest in its quantity of objects alone, surrounded them. Tall, stretched out, cone-like structures covered in orange ribbons that seemed to emerge randomly from the reddish shell. They twisted out to form several canopies like layers up the entire length. Bunches of squirming blue tentacles stretched skyward with translucent bowls that seemed to pulsate in the wind. Large, smooth, green, bubbly masses appeared to be erupting from the ground, a yellow liquid running down them. Tiny red branching growths sat in clumps amongst the plants.

Captain Somers stood steadfast before everyone. "Keep moving. We need to get away from the ship. Just get to where everyone else is." There, just ahead, huddled beneath the strange plants, sat the crew. Joseph was spread out on the ground, Taylor seemed to be in shock, curled up in front of a large plant, and Nova was talking to Sophie.

"Where the fuck are we?" Zea asked in complete shock.

"I don't know. Let's worry about that later."

They followed Trent as he slowly made his way towards the others. Drawing closer, Nova could be heard attempting to soothe Sophie's fragile nerves. "Breathe Sophie. Calm down."

"Don't fucking touch me," Sophie screeched, tearing Nova's hand away. "I'll calm down when I goddamn well feel like it. I'm not a fucking kid. Diego!....Diego!... Where are you?!" She stumbled on unsure feet towards the inferno. Trent stepped into her path, unflinching as she pounded on his chest screaming. Her war path seemed stalled until she kicked Trent's leg forcing him to the ground.

Zea watched Sophie run past a crumpled up mass of a man on the ground that was spewing profanities, and disappear into the thick smoke. As the scene stole Zea's attention she instantly felt the full weight of Carl's body. Before she could comprehend what was going on, Captain Somers ran after Sophie. Looking at the remaining crew, Zea knew precisely what the Captain would have her do. She released Carl's body and hobbled over to Trent. She ran her hand down the length of his right leg checking for any signs of injury.

In response, Trent screamed in agony, "She broke my fucking ankle."

Zea lifted his pant leg to see the injury, swollen, and contorted. "Does this hurt," she asked, touching just around the edge of the ankle.

"Goddammit, yes it hurts."

"Bear with me for a second," her right hand wrapped around his foot and her left hand around his calf. A loud pop emanated from his ankle.

Screams of agony leaped from Trent's mouth and his fist dug into the dirt.

"Stay here while I get a splint made up." A nearby scrap of metal and cloth torn from her jumper made quick work of the ankle. "You should be able to walk but try and stay off it."

She gave him a hand up and guided him towards those who remained outside the burning ship. With Trent situated against a boulder, Zea went about checking on the others. She found Joseph unconscious on the ground. His vitals were dim. Each shallow breath was barely perceptible. Lacking any equipment, all she could do was keep an eye on him and make him comfortable. Just as she finished her checkup, Rocco emerged carrying Diego.

Rocco spoke with a commanding voice through his face cover, "Zea, Diego needs your help."

He collapsed to his knees dropping Diego who moaned as he hit the ground. A bloody stump now replaced what was once Diego's left arm. Pale skin indicated severe blood loss. Not far behind them came Sophie yelling out orders, but it was clear she was in a state of panic.

"I'll be right back. Keep him distracted while I work on him." Zea grabbed a metal scrap and ran towards the ship. She reached the metal into the fire but its heat caused her to retract. The flames licked the air in front of her. She once again placed the metal into the fire, her hand burning from the heat as the metal began glowing red. She scurried back to Diego and touched the metal scrap to Diego's wound. The skin sizzled and the blood baked. Its heat was dissipating quickly. She ran back towards the fire and repeated the process. With the wound fully sealed, she realized the Captain still wasn't back. "Sophie where's the Captain?"

"I don't know. She was with you."

"No, she ran in after you." Before she could go any further Rocco was up and walking back into the wreckage. Zea followed closely behind. "Wait for me! Get Diego over by the others. I'll check on him when I get back."

She hadn't realized before but the heat was overwhelming. What was left of her undershirt got pulled up over her mouth to filter out some of the smoke. She held onto Rocco's shirt so as not to lose track of him. The two made their way slowly over bits and pieces of the ship. Leaning up against one of the shattered desk frames sat Captain Somers.

"Captain, we need to get you out of here." Rocco knelt in front of her.

Zea followed suit checking for a pulse. She placed her ear against the Captain's chest. "She's not breathing. We need to get her out of here."

As a team, they struggled with what little strength they had left and pulled her out into the fresh air. Zea immediately went to work. The Captain was placed on her back with her head tilted back. Both hands placed on the ribs produced a cracking sound as Zea began compressions. A few breaths into the mouth and right back to compressions, she went over and over hoping for some signs of life. She refused to lose another one of her companions. She placed two fingers on Captain Somers's neck searching for any signs of life. No such luck was afforded her. The pain in her leg grew as she remained kneeling over the body which only succeeded in driving her on.

Finally the body lurched to life in a coughing fit. Zea sat the Captain up rubbing her back with tear-filled eyes. She sobbed, "Welcome back. Don't talk. Just sit here and rest."

She took a seat next to the Captain. With everybody at least in stable condition, she could rest for a minute. Now that her focus was no longer divided, the full force of the pain in her leg came back. Until now she had just assumed something cut her, but upon closer inspection she noticed a large shard of glass stuck in her calf. She started to touch it but the pain increased tenfold. It had to come out before it caused any more damage than it already had. She pushed through the pain in her next attempt and managed to slightly move the shard but couldn't hold on long enough. "Rocco," she grunted, trying not to scream. "I need you…ugh…to help pull…ugh… this out."

Rocco made his way over to where Zea sat. He took a close look at her leg like he had seen this before. "Okay, but this is gonna hurt."

"Please just get it out."

"I want you to grab my shoulder and squeeze as hard as you can."

Zea placed her hand gently on Rocco's shoulder as if she were comforting him.

"On the count of three. One…….two…..three."

The pain cut through Zea and shot up through her back and into her head. She'd seen people in situations like this but never truly experienced what they were going through. She wailed in agony. Her nails dug into Rocco's fleshy shoulder. The glass broke free and blood gushed from the wound. Rocco quickly grabbed the piece of cloth previously protecting his mouth and tied up the wound. Zea closed her eyes and began taking deep breaths. She tried to focus on her favorite childhood memories to draw away from the pain. Gradually her composure returned and she was able to block out the pain enough to run rounds checking on the crew. With such limited supplies she could only do so much. Normally she would use things around her to take care of injuries in a pinch but nothing seemed even remotely familiar.

"Anybody know what's going on?" Trent asked as Zea checked his leg inside the makeshift splint. "I mean what kind of freaky sci-fi shit is this?"

Still short of breath, Captain Somers answered through wheezy breaths, "We were on course for Earth." She stopped to catch her breath, "But nothing here seems familiar."

"Well my numbers weren't off."

Sitting with his wrapped up stump clutched against his chest, Diego struggled to speak, "Maybe my program was off. I only had a short time to put it together."

"But that still doesn't explain where we are."

Taylor stood up and wandered over towards the nearest cone-shaped object. "These aren't like anything I've ever seen."

He picked up a rock and scratched at the surface. "It's definitely not a tree." The surface cracked under the pressure releasing a white smoke. "He jumped back. "Nothing we know of does that. And look at these big blue things. I have no idea if they are alive or not."

A large black misshapen rock with wings was flying circles around Sophie's head. She flailed wildly attempting to scare it away. "The hell is that thing? Someone kill it."

Holy shit what is that thing?" Nova hollered, following suit.

A rock flew past the creature causing it to fly off. "Nice arm, Rocco," Trent said.

"Are you kidding? That was a terrible shot. I should have hit it. Guess I'm getting rusty. We need to get back to the issue at hand. The first thing we need to do is find shelter." Rocco stood staring out into the wilderness around them.

Zea knew that wasn't a wise decision given the state of the crew. "We can't go anywhere right now."

"We don't know what's out here or what kind of weather is coming. I'll start looking around."

Zea wasn't going to let someone ignore her this time. "No. We're not going anywhere until everyone can at least move on their own. Joseph's still unconscious."

"Fine, but I'm still going to scout the area. We need water."

"I'll go too." Taylor offered up.

Zea stood up and made her way to Taylor. With a scowl on her face and determination in her eye, she locked on to Taylor's eyes.

"Don't you dare try and leave. I'm not kidding." She remained steadfast. Taylor finally gave in and sat back down.

"Rocco, just get out of here." She refused to even turn around to watch him walk off. With Rocco gone, Zea went back to check on the wounded. The scene reminded her of pictures from war: Captain Somers covered in Soot, her blonde hair turned black from ash, Taylor with his broken nose and bruised eyes, Trent in a splint, Nova's head bandaged up, Diego missing most of his arm and Sophie taking care of him, Joseph still unconscious, and as for herself she was caked in a mixture of everyone's blood. She worked tirelessly. After an hour of hopping back and forth between crew members, Zea finally managed to bring Joseph to. Aside from a minor concussion he seemed alright.

"Zea, give yourself a break." Nova invited her to take a seat with a small tap on the ground. "Everyone will be alright for ten minutes. Come on."

The adrenaline was wearing off and the thought of sitting down was tempting. Zea settled into the soft dirt beside Nova. She laid her head against Nova's shoulder and stared off into the strange surroundings. The sunset on the alien world, shining the last of its rays past the distant mountains, and streaking through the distant clouds, turning them lovely shades of pink and orange. The remaining flames from the ship fought off the incoming darkness. Strange sounds echoed through the wilderness yet somehow Zea felt a sense of peace.

The camp began to form around her. Captain Somers began harvesting plants near the ship that appeared to be flammable and constructed a small fire pit. Taylor and Trent were busy working on a rough lean too that could shelter the group near the fire pit, consisting of scraps thrown from the ship during the crash and broken pieces of the plants around them.

Out of the darkness stepped Rocco, his demeanor filled with disappointment. "There's no water anywhere nearby. As far as I can tell these woods go on for miles."

The news only added to the confusion of the group. Zea watched as they all struggled to come to grips with what had happened.

Captain Somers pointed up towards the sky. "Let's see, there's the big Dipper, and Cassiopeia. Taurus is over there, and that's Venus. Based on their positions, that would put us near the 47th parallel. Assuming its Fall."

"Then where's the moon?" Diego asked, choking back the pain from his arm.

Without looking up from one of the plant samples he'd taken, Taylor replied, "It's probably a new moon."

"Actually we didn't see the moon when we were coming in." Captain Somers corrected him. "In fact we were closer to the moon's orbit when we got hit."

"So what are you saying, are we on Earth or not?" Sophie asked hesitantly.

111

"I don't know."

At this stunning announcement from the Captain everyone fell silent and remained that way. One by one, they began wandering off to the shelter to get some sleep. Nova passed out against the rock with Zea laying against her. Zea watched everyone else sleeping but couldn't manage to get her own mind to shut off. *How can this be Earth? How long are we going to be stuck here?* She remained plagued with questions. *I refuse to die here*, she thought as she laid against Nova long into the sleepless night.

Rocco

The dining hall was in shambles. Broken plates were scattered everywhere. Narrow beams of sunlight gave an eerie presence to the room. In the corner sat the 3D printer twisted and split open, wires poking out. All hopes of repair were gone. With no power there was no hope of ever using it again even if it could be repaired. Rocco knew the situation was desperate. His trip through the woods had revealed a complete lack of any recognizable food sources. The wreckage was their last chance. In a pile across the way some silver packets covered the floor. A glimmer of hope. There were a few hundred packets of dehydrated snacks with everything from beef jerky to ice cream. "Joseph, Taylor, get in here." Rocco took his shirt off from under his tattered jumper and tied the arms together sealing off the neck. He crammed as many food packets as he could inside the makeshift bag, and busted one open for himself. The other two walked in to find him pouring the powder out of the bag and into his mouth. He wiped off the crumbs before speaking. "Guys, I need you to take the food out to the others. I'm going to keep looking for water."

Taylor got on his knees and started grabbing bags. "I think I can carry a few. It's gonna take four or five trips."

Joseph looked at Rocco trying to hide a smirk. "Should I tell him?"

"Nah this is more fun. I'll let you guys sort it out."

"Sounds good." Joseph grabbed the shirt bag from Rocco and followed suit but kept from filling it up until Taylor stood with his arms full.

Taylor stopped and stared at Joseph holding one full shirt and his own shirt which he had just tied up. "Really?" He threw down the bags in frustration.

Rocco walked off laughing, "Good luck."

He squeezed through the broken door and out into the remains of the hallway. At one time this hall led to the rooms, now it just opened to the world outside. He worked his way through the broken parts of the ship and into the rooms, scavenging as he went in hopes of finding something of worth. Half his room was gone but the space where the bed laid was still intact.

"Please still be there."

With a little work, he managed to pry open a panel he'd personally modified to house his survival pack. It was a true stroke of luck that it wasn't blown away. The pack was just one of several survival preparations he had put in place. NASA knew if anything went wrong Rocco would be prepared to keep the crew alive until help arrived.

Inside still neatly packed were a few MRE's, a knife, a flashlight, first aid kit, and a few other random supplies. He dug through to the bottom of the pack. His hand searched through and found a cold metal object. He pulled out a steel canteen full of water and took a small sip before placing it back in the bag.

The search continued. It took Rocco past several rooms before leading to Carl's.

"I wonder."

He walked through the doorway and rummaged through the rubble.

"Come on, there has to be something of his still in here."

He pushed aside the litter on the floor. A small plastic arm rose through the dirt. The dirt brushed away to reveal Carl's Warneg Hero.

"That'll work."

He placed it inside the bag and went back to his search. The next step was to locate the equipment room. He worked his way through the iron jungle, climbing over steel branches, and carbon fiber rocks. The screeching of metal moving around kept him on edge. A long section of the ship protruded from the ground. Rocco wandered into the tube and climbed up the steep slope. In large letters, a door reading Equipment Room sat still sealed. The railing along the hall provided grips allowing him to clamber up to the door. He gripped the emergency release handle giving it a hard twist, producing a loud click, and half the door slid open.

A burst of musty hot air flew from the room. Rocco clicked on his flashlight. The beam illuminated a room full of machinery, pipes, and electrical wires. Oil coated everything. He passed through the entryway, hovering over a long drop to the wall that was now the floor. It took some shimmying to reach the water storage unit without slipping on the oil. His flashlight showed a giant hole in the side of the water storage tank. All hope he had sunk. He turned the light towards the bottom of the room hoping to not see what he expected. The water had collected but shimmered a rainbow glow from the mixed-in oil.

"Shit."

The situation just got more desperate. He climbed back out of the room and made his way back to camp, all the while wondering how to break the news.

Everyone was huddled up, too busy filling their stomachs with food to notice him coming out of the wreckage.

He threw down the bag of supplies and began pulling things out. "I found a few items we might be able to use. Hey Zea I thought you might want this." The action figure landed in her lap.

"Oh my god, thank you." Her eyes welled up with tears.

"I also have a first aid kit so we can start cleaning some wounds." Rocco pulled the canteen out next. When the moment finally came, he couldn't bring himself to tell them about the water. He knew morale was more important than the truth in these situations.

"Everyone take a few sips." The group drank through the water in a matter of minutes. "Well I'm going back out to see what else I can find, I'll be back later."

He zipped up the bag and slung it over his shoulder. It was easier to go alone. With his goal of finding water in mind, he headed back into the wreckage. Once he was sure no one in the camp could see him, he turned and headed straight into the bizarre surroundings. The large ribbons above him produce beautiful shadows along the ground. Strange creatures scuttled through the strands and tentacle-like protrusions.

A tiny brown creature was stopped in front of him. It had no eyes yet it knew exactly where he stood. Whenever he moved its rounded face and long pointed slender snout followed him. Two feather-like objects seemed to be sensing him, trying to figure out if he was food or danger.

Unable to determine its motive, Rocco froze in place. As if determining he posed no threat, long teeth emerged from the end of the snout. Rocco tried not to seem terrified while he continued to hold his ground.

It's snout raised up, arched over a gelatinous green sphere that rested on its brown and white striped back and bit down on something. It pulled out what looked like a marbled leave with a rounded mass in the middle, and began consuming it. A purple juice burst forth when the bubble in the middle broke open. Once it finished, it pushed itself up onto six razor-like legs and ran off. Figuring it would lead him to water, Rocco began following. He made sure wherever he went, he placed a pebble on the ground.

The creature weaved through the plants stopping to pick things up off the ground to store in its bubble. It felt like the creature was going nowhere.

Rocco began seeing strange orange poles reaching into the sky covered with tumor-like masses all along its length. Some were split open with colorful fingers sticking out covered in a light green fuzz. The creature ran up into one of these and began clucking. Suddenly hundreds of the tiny creatures emerged from the orange tumors. It was completely surreal. He sat and watched them scurry around briefly before disappearing again. With enough of his time wasted. He continued towards the nearby mountain. At the very least he would get a good view of the land.

A gaping hole opened into the mountain. The entrance seemed sturdy, so Rocco whipped out his flashlight and wandered into the cave. Its roof sat high above him. The moist air hung heavy around him. He wandered through shallow puddles and mud. The mud soon turned to rock and the entrance fell further and further away. His flashlight shone through the dark revealing an enormous carved-out room. Water dripped from the ceiling and ran down the walls. Small clear creatures scurried around the sides of the room. They seemed completely oblivious to his light. One of them passed over a strange red mark. The more Rocco looked at the walls the more he realized the walls in here were covered in these markings. The highest ones reached fifteen feet off the ground. Everything about this place was surreal. At the back of the cave, laid a narrow passage just big enough for Rocco to walk through. A low rumbling sound emanated from deep within. It was the unmistakable sound of flowing water.

Wagering it would be worth the risk, Rocco ventured further into the cave. The smooth walls pressed close to his wide shoulders. The path veered down cutting off any light afforded from the entrance. The further he went, the louder the roar of rushing water became. Without warning, the walls disappeared around him. The beam from the flashlight barely reached the far wall. He swept the light around the room trying the find the source of the water. Not having any luck he moved his light up towards the ceiling. A peculiar thing happened at that moment, wherever his light hit a purple glow appeared. Pulling his light away the area continued to glow purple for a few seconds. Rocco decided to try scribbling his name with the light. It worked perfectly. Feeling like a little kid peeing in the snow, he reverted into a teenager. Completely amused with himself, he scribbled out a giant purple dick. The darkness slowly erased the drawing like an upset parent trying to remove their child's indiscretion. The drawings quickly lost their appeal with no one else around to get a good laugh.

The flashlight was no longer providing enough light. The pack contained just what he needed to create a makeshift torch. A metal shovel doubled as the stick. Some cloth wrapped around the handle formed the perfect head. A few flicks from his lighter and the entire room sprang into view. He found himself standing on a ledge six feet above a large lake and a flowing river. Its source was a waterfall running down a large rocky outcropping near the ledge he was on. The rocks appeared to be covered in a fluffy white substance looking like cotton ball clouds. Rocco walked over and threw his bag on the ground. He cupped his hands under the water and pulled it up to his face. Normally his instincts would keep him from drinking strange water, but if he didn't find water soon, he and everyone else would die from dehydration. The crisp clean water felt so good on his dry lips. The cracks welcomed the moisture. Chills ran along his body while the cool feeling worked its way down his throat. As light from his homemade torch died away he realized this cave was the only way to ensure everyone's survival. Time was limited. If they didn't get water soon it wouldn't matter how lucky they were to escape the wreckage. Rocco filled his canteen up and exited the cave. He journeyed back to the camp as quickly as he could.

Rocco arrived to find everyone huddled under the makeshift lean-to, trying to escape the heat. The stench from Carl's body was unbearable. He gagged from the sheer putridness of it. Zea was obviously not doing well as Carl's body sat covered in small flying blue creatures. The sunlight reflected off their pearlescent exterior, producing flashes of red and purple. Realizing he was the only one who could ensure the others didn't wind up like that, he took the canteen to them and helped them take sips. "I found a cave with fresh water. It's just a few klicks from here."

Captain Somers was the first to move. She struggled to stand but made every effort to look strong while she did. Her body wavered despite her best efforts. "Let's go everyone. We can relax once we get there." The horde of Zombies shambled behind Rocco on their way to the new shelter, their thirst soon to be satisfied.

During their journey, the crew ran into the little creatures Rocco had been following earlier. They appeared to be waiting for Rocco's arrival into the orange forest. This time they didn't scatter, rather they trekked along like little guides. Once the entrance to the cave drew closer the creatures scattered.

Rocco led the group through the throne room and down the dark passage using his flashlight to guide them. The ground was slick with moisture. Trent suddenly lost his balance and fell to the ground, sliding into Nova and Diego knocking them down inside the narrow passage. The flashlight was making it too difficult to take care of the fallen, so with his flashlight held between his teeth, Rocco cut a strip off Trent's shirt. Trent tried to argue but was too weak to have any effect. A new makeshift torch was in order. A flick from the lighter set the cloth aflame atop the shovel, filling the empty void around them with light. The waterfall room lay just ahead. The three fallen companions made their way to their feet and continued. The grand room opened before them with its purple roof and white sand beach lining the river. No one seemed to even notice the brilliance of what was around them. They ran straight to the waterfall, pushing each other aside trying to get water except for Zea, Rocco, and Addison who all stood back waiting for their turn.

Joseph climbed his way down the small ledge and tested the water. "Wow, that's cold." This didn't appear to slow him down as he waded in. He found himself suddenly waist-deep. "Oh God! Huuu. Okay it's getting better."

"Did you just pee in the water?" Sophie said absolutely disgusted.

"Come take a sip and find out."

"Fuck that. I'd rather die of dehydration."

He waded further upstream and into the lake and dove into the water. "Man that's refreshing," He said floating in the water shivering.

Rocco stood with the others, staring at his pal in the water acting like an idiot. "Zea I think he may have hit his head harder than we thought."

"Sssscrew...you," he stammered. Joseph slowly made his way back out and attempted to climb up the ledge out of the water. His hands struggled to grip the rock sending him back down into the water. "IIIIII...got this."

Feeling some pity for him Rocco walked over and offered him a lift. The sight of Joseph completely soaked through, hair dripping wet was enough to make Rocco erupt with laughter. "You know you're a dumbass right?"

"Wwwwwhat are...you tttalking about. IIII feel...Great."

"Tell me that when you're still stuck in those wet clothes tonight."

"Shit!"

"Let's get you warmed up." Rocco walked him back to the front of the cave. Addison built up a small fire in the middle of the room for Joseph to huddle by while attempting to dry off. A strange sweet scent drifted off the smoke. The shadows outside spread across the ground with the setting sun.

The rest of the group took their places around the fire. Nova began to hum a soft tune to herself. The others around her caught on and soon everyone was singing along. Their voices filled the cave stirring tiny brown creatures from the cracks in the walls. Their tiny bodies leaped into the air and large golden wings emerged from their sides. The group fell silent unsure of what to make of this new scene. The creatures circled the cave. Light from the fire reflecting off their wings looked like dancing flames above them. Its beauty was astounding. The floating flame flew out the cave on silent wings and into the coming dusk.

Addison

Days passed by slowly for the crew. The discovery of a dead battery inside the distress beacon was stirring unease. Their last hope of rescue was gone. Addison was trying everything she could to keep the crew from giving up hope, which was easier said than done. Now everything was calm.

Zea was attempting to clean Diego's festering arm wound. It's stench grew unbearable whenever it was left unattended for more than half the day. "This one's going to hurt. Just try and stay still." She pressed the edge of Rocco's knife against one of the rotting pustules. It sliced into the soft skin releasing a flow of rancid goo.

"Ahhhhhh!" the scream of pain from Diego echoed through the cave's chambers.

Sophie grabbed ahold of Zea's arm preventing progress. "Please, you have to stop. I can't handle seeing him hurt."

Wincing through the pain and holding back the screams, Diego pushed her away. "Back off." With tears in his eyes, he looked at Zea. "Keep going."

Zea handed a wet cloth to Sophie. "Put this on his head to help with the fever, otherwise fuck off."

Sophie jerked the towel away from Zea and pressed it against Diego's head. The water dripped down his face and into his ragged red beard.

The tension was palpable. Addison only wanted to keep the peace. She walked over to Sophie and placed her arm around her. "I'll take over, you just go get some fresh air."

Sophie didn't budge.

"Go on, I've got this."

Sophie slowly walked away looking back over her shoulder as she wandered off.

"Thank you," Zea said, returning to the wound. "I was never going to get this done with her around."

"You're good. Now let's get this finished." The heat from Diego's forehead was pouring through the wet cloth. The screams started up again even more agonizing than before. Diego's remaining hand gripped onto Addison's arm and his untrimmed nails dug in.

A chunk of rotting flesh fell to the ground. Zea poured a tiny bit of rubbing alcohol onto the wound. "Diego you rest for a bit. We'll do some more later."

Addison and Zea wandered off, leaving Diego to sit in silence.

Zea's face was worn from a week of caring for everyone's injuries. Her once beautiful brown hair was now a mud-caked knotted mess. The weight of her body seemed to have doubled judging by the way she dragged herself along.

Addison figured a couple of snacks would do Zea some good. The pile had dwindled down to the final few packets consisting of freeze-dried ice cream and cheese. She grabbed two packets of ice cream and followed Zea outside. "Here, get some food in you." She threw the packet.

Without a word, the packets got ripped open and Zea devoured their contents. Their empty shells got cast aside.

Seeing their shiny foil sitting on the ground, Addison realized she had not really seen any empty packets lying around the camp. Her mind wandered imagining where they could have been thrown away at. All of hers had just been scattered in the cave as she ate but now she couldn't recall seeing even those. It was almost like when she and Daniel went camping and she would just throw corn cobs and fish bones on the ground but come morning he had picked them all up and hung them from a tree inside a bag. Living outdoors was his forte but Addison preferred a nice hotel unless the two of them were together. If only he could see her now. Her eyes welled with tears. No matter what, she had to survive to get back to him and feel his embrace one more time. Seeing Zea sitting there with her mouth full of food, she knew that the first thing she would tell Daniel was that she was finally ready. Ready to move to Europe. Ready to put their lives ahead of her work. Ready to finally have kids.

"Feeling a bit better with all that sugar?" Addison inquired.

Zea swallowed her last mouthful. "Not really but at least it's something. Captain... Did you ever imagine something like this place?"

"Not in my wildest dreams. It's like something out of Doctor Seuss."

"How are you managing to stay so calm through all of this? I mean this place terrifies me."

"I just know that Daniel will find a way to get me out of here, and as long as I'm around nothing will ever happen to you." Despite her best effort even she wasn't fully convinced they would make it out of this. "Let's change the topic a bit. Tell me about your fondest memory."

"Oh, my. Well...I don't really have many."

"Come on you've got to have a few. What about that ring you always wear?"

"What, my mom's ring? When I was a kid, I would always sneak into my mom's room to play. Sometimes I would walk out covered in make-up. Other times I would try on her clothes and leave them lying all over the floor. My favorite though was when I would get her jewelry box open." Zea began fidgeting with the ring as if out of habit. "Anyway, this one time I was covered in jewelry and I found this ring with a large red gem on it. My mother's birthstone. So I put it on and started running around the house acting like I was a witch with a magic ring from the Warneg Heroes. I would summon my pet veglot and ride around the kingdom. As I waved my hand around, the ring flew off and landed in the sink. I tried to catch it but it went down the drain. No matter how hard I tried I couldn't get it out. I was so embarrassed that I left it in there. That night my mom ran the disposal with the ring in there. I thought I was going to be in so much trouble that I ran away. Being little I only made it into the tree at the neighbor's house where my mom found me crying. Rather than getting mad she climbed into the tree with me and just sat there. It was half an hour before I was finally ready to climb down. After that she got it fixed and would let me play with it as long as I asked her first."

"She sounds amazing."

"She was the best person I've ever known. Kind of like you."

The beautiful moment ended abruptly as Taylor came barreling out of the cave and tripped over Addison. "What the hell," she yelled grabbing her side. Suddenly a rock whizzed past her head.

"You cheated you bastard." Trent's voice carried out of the cave.

"What are you talking about? You can't cheat at Tic-tac-toe." Another rock hurtled through the air. "Are you kidding me? It was just a game."

"Get back in here you bastard."

Two more rocks came flying out of the cave. "That's it!" Addison got to her feet. "Trent, I swear if you throw one more rock I'm going to lay you out. Taylor you're coming with me."

His voice filled with hesitancy, Taylor asked, "Where are we going?"

"Don't worry about it. Let's go. She grabbed his arm and dragged him away from Trent and Zea. Addison refused to let go of Taylor until the cave was out of sight. "Now that we're out here you're going to help me look for food. We're running low."

"You know I don't recognize anything out here, right?"

"I figured, but we've only got a short time before we're all too weak to do anything about it."

"Our best bet would be to follow one of the creatures around here and try a small sample of what they eat."

"That'll work. You head that way and I'll go this way but don't wander off too far. If you find a creature let me know." She went off making sure to keep Taylor within eyesight. A tall beautiful specimen appeared in front of her. It had three beautiful jade eyes on each side of a horseshoe-shaped head with a long snout squarely in the middle. The skin was cracked like tree bark all along the body. Four legs branched off the flattened core and split into two pairs that stood upon four kidney-shaped masses.

"Taylor, get over here," Addison spoke softly, trying to get Taylor's attention without startling the beast before her. He didn't seem to react. She slowly reached down and picked up a rock, never taking her eyes off the beast. She lobbed it towards Taylor, realizing the irony as it flew from her hand. He immediately turned. Silently, Addison gestured for him to join her.

Taylor crept towards Addison, staring at the ground to ensure each step fell silently. Once he reached her, they waited for the beast to move. It wandered gently through the forest, lowering its snout, and sifting through the soft dirt. Small jerks pulsated through the creature's body.

Addison was entirely fascinated by the scene. "What's the bark beast doing?"

Taylor attempted to whisper back, "bark beast? I kind of like that. I was going with horseshoe head but yours is definitely better. Anyway, I have no idea."

The dirt seemed to be breathing around the creature's snout, moving in sync with the beast's movements. The dirt mound opened its gaping mouth releasing the hidden treasure inside. The snout bore a large white root-like mass in its grip. A pouch opened on the bark beast's neck and in went the mass.

Taylor was lost to the world, taken aback by what he was witnessing. Addison couldn't blame him. For him this must have been like a dream come true. They sat and watched the beast repeat this cycle two more times.

Once seemingly satisfied that there were no more roots worth pulling up, the bark beast continued its journey through the forest and into a field covered in tiny red branching growths. Up to this point they had only appeared in tiny patches. In the middle of the field sat strange structures made of what looked like boulders jammed into the dirt by a giant. One large boulder stood tall with five rows of boulders radiating from it. Each successive boulder appeared to be smaller than the one before it. Their gray surface was covered in pockmarks and holes. Overhead, strange winged creatures flew as if guarding the boulders. The bark beast made its way towards the formation and struck the surface with one of its feet, knocking a chunk free from the boulder. A slice of shiny black meat lay inside the hole created by the bark beast. The snout reached inside and consumed part of the boulder.

Addison and Taylor had assumed they were far enough back to remain unseen, but a loud shriek from one of the creatures above caused the bark beast to leave its snacking and stare directly at the two stalkers. Addison's heart leaped into her throat. She had no experience with situations like this. If it were a bear she would know what to do but here the rules were different. All she could do was hope the bark beast was docile. Her hopes came true as it sprinted off.

Addison and Taylor emerged from the forest and into the field. Addison walked over to the hole that the beast had knocked open and reached inside. The meat was moist and warm in her grip.

The next thing Addison knew, she was sitting in a rocking chair surrounded by Christmas decorations. Daniel was playing his guitar and singing to her. Snow was falling outside coating the world in white. The red ribbon trees and tentacle plants were beautiful this time of year. Wrapping paper was strewn about the floor, and boxes were piled haphazardly in the corner of the room. Suddenly a warm coffee mug sat in her hand and three children were eating breakfast in front of the TV watching the Parade. It felt like her time in space had been so long ago. As if it almost hadn't happened. She checked her body but all the scars from the crash were gone. Why couldn't she remember anything else? "Cory would you like to help me with Breakfast?" she asked her oldest daughter.

"Of course mom. Can I make the biscuits? They're my favorite."

"I think I can let you do that."

"I want to help too," the youngest of the three said, running up to Addison. Her hair was a mess. It appeared to have been cut by one of the other kids with a pair of scissors, missing random chunks.

"Okay but you need to change out of those pajamas first."

"But mom I love my princess pajamas. Please can I wear them? I promise I won't get them dirty."

"Okay, fine but you have to try your hardest to stay clean." Addison patted her on the head.

"Yeah!" She disappeared into the kitchen.

"How about you Jake? Would you like to help too?"

"No thanks I want to play my new video game with dad."

"I like that idea." Daniel got up from his chair.

"Have fun boys."

"Yeah have fun boys," the girls' voices rang out in unison.

The kids started growing before her eyes. The room morphed around her. A chandelier was hanging from the ceiling above a dining room table. The family was sitting around the table discussing their days at school.

"What did you learn today Cindy?" Daniel asked the youngest daughter.

"We studied multiplication. I learned that twelve times twelve is one hundred twenty-one." Her face filled with pride.

"Don't you mean one hundred forty-four?"

"Yeah that's it."

"And how about you Cory?"

Cory struggled to speak with her mouth full of food. She gestured for Daniel to give her a second to swallow. "We're studying the Aeneid today. The teacher had us discussing the entrance to the underworld called Avernus. Apparently, it's a real place. "It's a volcano with a lake inside it. They say that any bird that flies over it dies."

On cue, loud shrieks filled the air, and the ceiling fell away, but the conversation continued around Addison as if nothing had changed.

"Well what about the Phoenix." Jake jumped in "I bet it could survive."

No, it couldn't. The phoenix is a bird. That means it would die too."

"Come on guys stop fighting," Addison told them. "And what did you learn Jake?"

"I learned about World War Two. Mom, were the wars you fought in like World War Two? Did you get to drive a tank or drop bombs?"

"Not quite. I…" The room changed again. She now found herself sitting in a chair outside in a field covered in red branching growths surrounded by her extended family. Her husband was sitting next to her, his hair now mostly gray. In front of them Cory was draped in the most beautiful white dress Addison had ever seen. A strange man dressed in a tux stood facing Cory.

"Cory do you take Ryan to be your lawfully wedded husband?" The man behind them asked.

"I do."

"And Ryan do you take Cory to be your lawfully wedded wife?"

"I do."

"By the powers vested in me...I now pronounce you husband and wife. You may now kiss the bride." The crowd roared with approval. "I now present to you Mr. and Mrs. Feldhaver." As the couple faced the audience, Cory and Ryan's faces melted away and Zea and Taylor stood in their place.

Addison gave the two a big hug. "Congratulations Sweetie. What a beautiful ceremony."

"Is she okay?" Taylor asked, trying to break from the embrace.

"She seems to be tripping." Zea grabbed Addison's face swiping the flashlight back and forth.

The cave now replaced the field and crowd of family members. "Ugh. what happened?" Addison grabbed her head.

"Well we found that crazy plant and both started eating it to see if it was safe to eat. It tasted amazing so we took more. That's when the weird creatures circling above us attacked. One of them scratched your arm. Within seconds you were a blubbering mess. I managed to scare off the creatures and get you back here. You've been mumbling about some people named Cory, Daniel, Jake, and Cindy. Oh and then you started calling me Ryan and Zea Cory."

Addison tried to sit up but her entire body ached. "I don't remember any of that. I could've sworn I was back home. I and Daniel were with our kids." Grief overwhelmed her.

Zea handed her the canteen full of water. "But you don't have any kids. Here, drink this and don't move. We need to keep you hydrated."

She attempted to stand but found her legs were shaky beneath her. "What about the food? I have to go get food. Plus my family is out there and you took them away from me. Bring them back."

"Addison listen to me. Your family was never here. All of this is real. Whatever you saw out there wasn't." A deep gravelly voice spoke from behind her.

"No, Rocco you don't understand, I have to find them."

Zea ran off. "Come back Cory....I mean Zea. I promise I'm alright."

Zea came back with some of the blankets they had scavenged from the ship and covered Addison in multiple layers. "You need to stay here and warm up. Rocco, keep an eye on her." Zea searched the cave. "Anyone seen Nova?"

"Yeah I believe she went to wash off in the river."

"Thanks Rocco. I'll go get her. Maybe she can snap Addison out of this."

Everyone was huddling around her but all Addison wanted to do was get away from them. The feelings she had been experiencing were unbelievable. Now all she felt was an unshakable sense of dread and despair. Her skin felt like tiny bugs were crawling around on it and they wouldn't come off.

"Okay I'm here Addison." Nova stood there, hair still dripping. The soft water brought relief to Addison wherever it touched. "I need you to tell me where you are right now."

Addison burst into tears. "I don't know. I was just at my daughter's wedding and then suddenly she was gone. Where are they?"

"How many kids do you have?"

"Three." She licked her lips. "I need water."

Nova handed the canteen back to Addison. "Here. Hold on to this. We'll refill it as much as you need. Just nod your head if you understand."

Addison nodded her head.

"Now tell me what you mean by a wedding."

"I was so happy. I had made it back home. God get these blankets off me! All of you just back off. Quit crowding me."

"Okay, okay. No more blankets. Do you know my name?"

"Of course. You're Nova, That's Zea. Taylor, Trent, and Joseph are over there. And that's Rocco standing behind you. But why am I back here? I was safe. I was gone for several years."

"I need you to listen to me. The Phoenix crashed. We are still waiting to be rescued. You're our Captain."

Addison couldn't stay focused. Her mind kept wandering back to that wonderful place. *This must be a dream. They'll all disappear soon. Just wake up.* She slapped her face. It was the only way to snap herself out of it.

"Addison Stop! Hurting yourself isn't the answer."

"Oh god what's happening to her?" Sophie's voice came from far away.

"She's detoxing from whatever got in the wound." Zea sounded terrified.

Addison closed her eyes trying to escape. When she opened her eyes the world was dark. Panic set in. "Help! Help!" The words wouldn't come out no matter how hard she tried though she felt like she was screaming at the top of her lungs.

"She's awake," a voice broke through. "Bring over some light."

A bright light drifted towards Addison. It hurt to look at. She closed her eyes. A cold wet rag graced her forehead.

"Here drink."

The metallic canteen pressed against her lips. She forced her mouth open to let the water in. she was so thirsty it was all she could think about.

"That's enough. You need to take it easy. Here have some cheese."

Addison opened her eyes. The light was less harsh this time around. "Ugh what happened to me?"

Nova stood by Addison's side. "You were detoxing. Something on the creatures you encountered got you high when they scratched you. You've been in and out for three days. Come on, sit by the fire. It'll warm you up. We're going to let you rest and we'll explain everything again once you're feeling better."

The warmth of the fire felt great on her skin, though the light still hurt her head. She was willing to work through it.

"We're glad you're back, Captain," Trent said.

"Agreed." The other voices rang out.

"I'm not your Captain anymore. Just call me Addison from now on."

Everyone remained silent.

Addison stayed there by the fire all night. Her strength slowly returning. The next day she managed to get up and walk around. She was still weak but she survived. Now would be the hardest challenge of her life. She longed to go back. That feeling was undeniable. She knew she would be stuck in a struggle to fight off the need to get high again. With the food stocks taken care of, she had no reason to go out for now, but it would soon run out and there was no way for it to just replace itself.

Sophie

A chilly morning greeted Sophie as she awoke. The sunbeams lit up the far wall of the cave. She laid there with her head on Diego's chest, unwilling to leave his side. He was so warm and safe. The need to pee was outweighing the need to sleep. She fought it until she could no longer hold it in. If she went inside the cave they would yell at her so she decided to spare herself the fight this time and headed outside. The forest was alive with the scurrying of little critters everywhere and sounds that were becoming more and more familiar. The croak of the paddle flyer was her favorite. It reminded her of when she would catch frogs with her cousins down by the creek.

A new sound struck Sophie's ears. It was unlike anything she had heard since they arrived on the planet, a strange series of grunts mixed with the rustling of foil. She couldn't stop herself mid-stream so she remained squatted hoping to go unnoticed. Her eyes caught sight of a strange new creature.

Its body was covered in hard scales whose color seemed to resemble the blue and brown dirt. Curved spikes grew out from the back and pointed in all directions. Two spiked tails waved through the air. The head was flattened like that of a snake with four compound eyes, two looking forward and one to look at each side. It was using a long almost beak-like toothed snout to rustle through the food wrappers. A large gray appendage came out and wrapped around the foil pulling it into the snout. The appendage then reached out towards the next foil package but just couldn't reach it. It tried again, stretching its head forward but still fell short. As if pissed off, the creature suddenly rose into the air on four thick legs made up of multiple joints. The back legs ended in three large claws. The front two appeared to have one claw each that resembled clamshells. It finished picking up the wrappers and wandered off.

Terrified and unsure if the creature would come back, Sophie quickly pulled up her pants and ran into the cave. Diego was still asleep, so she decided to see what everyone else was up to.

Trent was holding onto the knife. "We're all set to head out. If everyone goes together we should be fine. Addison, you'll stay here with Diego and Sophie."

"That's probably for the best."

Sophie couldn't believe their audacity to even think of leaving her behind. "Really, you were just going to leave me here? Seriously? Just because I'm worried about Diego doesn't mean I can't be useful."

Nova handed her the backpack. "Actually, we just thought you were sleeping and didn't want to drag you away from Diego."

"Yeah, sure. I'm coming along. I'll show you I'm not useless." She grabbed the backpack away from Nova.

"We never…" Trent was stopped mid-sentence by Nova.

"She needs this," Nova whispered. "It'll be good for her to get her mind off of Diego for a bit."

Trent just turned and walked away. Everyone followed behind. Sophie positioned herself directly behind Trent in an attempt to distinguish herself as the group's leader. "Let's go everyone," she shouted. This was the only way to show them she was still as sharp as ever.

"Ugh," Trent sighed, "You don't even know where we're going."

"I'm pretty sure we're going to look for the animals that hurt Addison."

"She got the animals that hurt Addison part right at least," Joseph joked.

It was Rocco's turn to speak. "We're going to get the food Taylor and Addison found a few days ago. But we're prepared in case the Trippers show up again."

"Well then what are we waiting for?"

Sophie led the charge until she realized she was heading in the wrong direction. Without a word, she turned and caught up to the group. The trip out was silent except for her opining about Diego and wanting constant reassurance from Zea that he would be alright. She just couldn't help herself. This was the first time she had ever really felt connected to someone, and it was hard watching him suffer. The field came into view ahead. Sophie walked on ahead but realized that no one else was with her.

"Guys aren't you coming. Or do I need to do this alone?"

"If you had been at the planning meeting you'd know we were going to start by grabbing some roots, that way if the trippers do show up again we don't go home empty-handed. But then you already knew that, right?" Trent turned away from her and started digging into the dirt with his hands.

"Whatever." Sophie couldn't believe they would just dismiss her like that.

If the boulder fruit was as good as they said it was, shouldn't it be the priority? All their belittling was really getting to her. She sat down on the ground in defiance while the others toiled away digging up the white roots. The group worked hard to procure two large root clusters. "Okay guys let's go get the boulder fruit." Sophie stood up and started walking to the field. Behind her, she could hear the others talking.

"Should we let her go alone?"

"Shut up, Trent."

"No, Rocco, I think I'm with Trent on this one."

"Joseph, Trent, we're all doing this together." Rocco held everyone back while he checked the field first. "Sky's clear. Move in."

They were easily able to cut down two of the smaller fruits and haul them away. Nova and Zea had both root clusters. Each fruit took two people to carry back to camp meaning Sophie didn't have to do any of the heavy lifting. All along the way back to the cave, she kept shouting encouraging things at the others trying to keep their spirits up. Despite her efforts the encouragements were just met with moaning.

The cave entrance was in sight now. Sophie ran ahead of everyone else and headed for Diego who remained as she'd left him. "Has he been asleep this whole time?"

"Yeah, I've not seen him move," Addison said. "That infection seems to be getting the best of him."

"Diego come on get up." Sophie touched Diego's shoulder, jostling him onto his back. His skin was cold to the touch. "Zea get in here. Something's wrong with Diego."

Zea dropped her roots and ran inside. Her hands felt around Diego's neck and arms.

"What's going on? Is he alright?"

"Bring me the canteen."

Sophie searched frantically. "I can't find it."

She threw everything in the cave around. It wasn't turning up. About to give up, she remembered she was carrying the backpack. Her hand shook violently as she unzipped it. There sat the canteen. She threw it over to Zea who placed it under Diego's nose.

"He's gone."

"What are you talking about? You were supposed to take care of him. It was your job."

Sophie ran over and laid her head on Diego's cold lifeless body.

"You can't take him. He's still alive. I love you, Diego. You can't go."

Her crying was overwhelming. Tears and snot ran down her face. Loud labored breaths were the only thing capable of interrupting her wailing.

Addison pulled Sophie away from the body but Sophie pushed her back and resumed her position on top of Diego. Rocco's arm gripped around Sophie this time and pulled her off. All Sophie could do was stand there helpless. She turned around and faced Rocco unable to stand the sight of her dead lover. What she saw next was incomprehensible. Rocco was silently sobbing to himself. She laid her head into his shoulder and wept uncontrollably, his grip remaining steadfast. By this time everyone else had returned and were just getting the news. Addison remained strong as she told the others, whispering to keep Sophie from hearing, but Sophie overheard every word only making the grief more poignant.

Sophie cried until she could cry no more. She refused to let the others handle the body so they came to an agreement. They would carry the body from the cave with her help. Sophie cradled the head to keep it from dragging on the ground. They reached a rock in the ground beneath one of the orange bubble trees, Carl's name etched into it, marking an undisturbed mound. Under the same tree, a shallow hole.

Joseph grabbed a large rock and handed it to Sophie. "You do the honors."

She picked up a tiny stone and etched Diego's name into the rock's surface. She couldn't believe he was gone. They were just cuddling that morning. Why hadn't they done more to save him?

The men lowered Diego into the ground and began burying him.

Feelings overwhelmed Sophie. She couldn't trust these people she thought were her friends. All they ever did was criticize her and let her down. Now that Diego was gone she had nothing. The rock rolled from her hand. At that moment, Sophie fled away as fast as she could. The setting sun barely left any light, producing dark shadowy figures all around. The purple sky taunted her every step. A rock found her foot, sending Sophie flying headfirst into the ground. The dirt stuck to her wet face. A howl pierced the air. Cracking sounds came from all around her. Sophie got up and wandered aimlessly, until she could no longer see anything but the stars above. She curled up beneath the nearest ribbon tree and stared up at the Milky Way streaking across the sky. The only thing she felt was loneliness. The universe itself had abandoned her. She wanted to leave but the darkness was so overwhelming, her only available option was to stay where she was. Sleep escaped her weary eyes.

The longest night of Sophie's life finally came to an end with the rising sun. The favorite sounds of the morning creatures had lost their charm. All joy seemed to have melted away with Diego's passing. Sophie no longer felt anything was worth doing. Songs had no meaning. Her whole body felt numb. She picked up a rock hoping to distract from the pain in her heart. The jagged edge produced a sharp pain into her arm as she pressed hard against the skin. She dragged it up her arm letting out a scream of pain. Her sole focus was on the pain in her arm and for a time she felt less sad. This would let her be with Diego. The rock cut into her other arm, less successfully this time. Blood poured down her limbs. She laid down praying for the sweet release of death. The pain lost its veracity after a while.

Sophie opened her eyes to find the blood dry on her arms and small creatures lapping at the puddle around her. Any other day, this would terrify her, but realizing her plan had failed and being unwilling to feel that pain again, she resigned herself to sit under the ribbon tree all day. The lack of blood had left her woozy and unable to move.

Sitting there for a while brought along pangs of hunger. Sophie forced herself to stand on uneasy feet and venture on, unsure where she would end up. Through the mess of trees the hint of red caught Sophie's eye. It was the field. She ran towards it. Somehow this field looked different than the one before. It had the same familiar clusters of boulder fruit, and red branching broths sitting waist-high. All that mattered was getting food into her.

The fruit tasted so magical. It was the nectar of the gods. Sophie took a seat in the shade and filled her belly. As she digested her meal, dark clouds rolled in from the horizon. No shelter was available in the field. she crossed the open plain and entered the other side of the woods where a gigantic ribbon tree towered above the rest. Its shell was a hazy dull red, mixed with what appeared to be white ash. A large hole was bored out of the base. Sophie climbed in just as the lightning storm hit. Its thunderous clacks rang out. At times the air around her seemed to sizzle. Then the rain began. Light at first but in the distance a wall of water formed. It drew closer and closer, enveloping the world as it went. Its roar was comparable to the sound of Niagara Falls. Water seeped into the hole, soaking the ground on which Sophie huddled. It was unpleasant, to say the least, but at least she wasn't completely exposed. The rain went on for hours. The sound changed from a cacophonous roar to a melodic hum. Her tired body gave into its enticing song and she drifted off to sleep.

The smell of fresh rain clung to the air. Water dripped from the plants around Sophie. The sun was just rising. It seemed like only hours ago that she had tried to kill herself. She was losing track of time. Sophie emerged from the damp hole and into the cleansed world. The field should have been just ahead. When she initially reached the tree the field was easy to view. But what she looked at now made no sense.

Large grey tree-like plants had emerged. Their roots jutting in and out of the broken ground. Their size was on par with the other plants of the ribbon forest yet these looked more Earth-like. They had a few branches growing off the main truck. Large round fans adorned the ends of the branches and trunk running from red at the base to yellow at the tips, with consecutive smaller rings above them. They waved about in the gentle breeze. Their surface was rough to the touch. A thick blue moss-like substance grew in patches around the base. Cup-like growths were spread out along the trunk. From the branches dangled strange blue silk spheres.

Strange magic seemed to be at work. "Did I fall into wonderland? Where the hell did these come from? How did a rainstorm make all of this grow so fast?" Perhaps she was in such a daze from blood loss that she had missed them completely. But there had been a large empty field that was thick with red branches. "Did those small red branches really grow into these giant things? None of this makes any sense."

Sophie was at a loss. She found a puddle in the ground and splashed the cold water on her face. She was awake, that much was certain. The only thing she could do was head back to the cave and apologize to everyone. She passed through the field of newly birthed trees looking for the boulder fruit she had partaken of the day before. Sophie wandered aimlessly for hours until, finally, encased in a set of roots, she found the boulder fruit with fresh holes in its surface. If she remembered correctly the path home was straight ahead, though given her circumstance even that might be wrong.

Deciding it was worth the risk and trusting her instincts, Sophie headed into the ribbon forest. It never seemed to end. No matter where she turned there were only more tentacle plants, orange bubble trees, and ribbon trees. Nothing looked familiar, even the spot where she bled out was not to be found. The sun was no longer overhead but she was no closer to escaping the labyrinth. Even the way back to the hole she had survived in was now obscured in her mind. All she could do was continue and hope for the best.

The path's scenery gradually changed around her. Bizarre yellow and pink ribbed funnels replaced the bubbly green masses. Tall plants rose into the sky with green comb-like branches on both sides. Small volcano-shaped mounds opened with purple umbrellas growing out of their tops. The ground under Sophie's feet turned from solid to mush, and then into shallow water. She was no longer in a forest but what appeared to be a large bog. *All kinds of strange things could be hiding in this water. It's not worth the risk.*

Sophie turned and headed away, but her feet found no ground. Instead the soft sand sank under her feet, slowly swallowing Sophie. Her body started shaking with terror. The cold wet sand oozed into her clothes. She struggled to free her legs causing her body to sink faster. *This can't be the end. I don't want to drown in sand.* Now up to her waist in quicksand, the only way to survive was to pull herself out. She tried to keep herself from panicking further. Every movement of her body was amplified in her mind. Her hands were unable to find any solid ground and their attempts to grasp earth only caused her to sink deeper. "Ahh," she screamed out, desperately hoping someone would hear and come running, but she was afforded no such luck. If she was going to get free she had to do it herself. The cold sand was now pressing up against her chest, making each breath difficult. The sounds of the creatures around her seemed to be taunting her. In her moment of despair, her eye managed to catch sight of a funnel plant nearby. Sophie grasped its silky surface, pulling herself free. The sand was in every crevice. Every inch of her body was trembling. Her breathing had become heavy from all the exertion of freeing herself. She stripped down and shook the sand loose. The cold air nipped against her wet body, but having just saved herself, she was grateful for the feeling. *I made it. Holy shit.* She threw the wet clothes back on and sat down to regain her composure. She had faced so many life-threatening scenarios in the last few days.

Thinking she was safe and feeling more composed, Sophie ventured on in search of her lost comrades, unsure where to begin. It seemed no matter where she went nothing around her resembled the area she knew. With no food, water, or shelter her only option was to carry on and hope that she would find the others soon.

Trent

"Sophie!" Trent hollered. At this point he was certain that she was lost to them. Even if they did find her, she would probably just be a mangled corpse. It was the fifth day with no sign of her whatsoever. Adding to the losses of Diego and Carl, Sophie's absence weighed heavily on everyone. Trent had definitely had his spats with Sophie but even she didn't deserve whatever terrible fate would befall her out there. Blame consumed his conscience, causing him restless nights. The only cure for the burden upon his soul was to keep looking. The rain had washed away all traces of Sophie's being. The odds of finding her now were dwindling to nothing. "Any luck, Taylor?"

Taylor walked back towards Trent. "Nope. We need to save our energy."

"Fine, you go back. I'll stay out here a while longer."

"At least take the flashlight and knife." Taylor unclipped the knife from its sheath. With the blade in hand he offered the handle to Trent. "Here."

Trent grabbed the knife and slipped it into his boot. "Thanks. I shouldn't be out here too much longer in case anyone else asks."

"Remember if you see the trippers get away as fast as you can."

"Got it." Trent took the flashlight and continued in his search. *If I were lost where would I go?* Trent mulled over the different possibilities. *Well I personally like food. But Sophie seems like the type who doesn't mind starving herself. I could check Diego's grave again. She could be anywhere by now. That's assuming she isn't nearby and just hiding. What if she went back to the ship?* All of them seemed like viable options.

There was no better place to start than Diego's grave. As he approached, a terrible smell caught his nose. It was the unmistakable smell of death. The graves were just ahead. Something was wrong. Piles of dirt sat around where the mounds had been. "What the hell?" The graves were opened and the bodies had been removed. A pile of bones and hair sat not too far away. *Whatever did this must be close. These were undisturbed yesterday.* Yellow slime coated the remains and the graves. Trent pulled the knife from his boot and readied himself.

Heavy steps shook the ground. Loud snorting sounds accompanied the incoming threat. Trent ran as fast as he could, but the quicker he traveled the more the steps sped up. Behind him a hideous beast loomed. The body seemed to ripple with excitement. The three eyes were locked onto Trent, following his every movement. Its blank face split down the middle. Both sides of the face parted revealing a mouth with four rows of teeth on either side. Yellow slime dripped from the mouth.

Trent leaped away and burst into a full-on sprint. The beast followed suit and pushed off the ground with its massive legs, coming to a stop in front of Trent. It turned its ugly head around followed by its massive cancerous looking torso. Without giving Trent any time to react, the beast raised its massive claw and slammed him into the ground. The claws formed a cage around Trent's body locking him in place. The mouth hovered over his face. Two strange feather-like projections popped up from the sides of the head and skimmed along Trent's body.

This was absolute terror. Unable to move, he was faced with imminent death with no one around to help him. The knife was on the ground out of reach. Trent bit the beast to no avail. All the kicking and screaming were useless. Without warning, the paw raised up, releasing Trent from his earthly prison. He pulled himself up just in time to feel the paw slam into his back. He hurtled through the air and slammed into a ribbon tree. Pain shot through his back and his lungs seemed incapable of working. He fell to the ground, hands out, slamming his face into the dirt. The paw came at him again striking his leg and sending him flying into the air. He crashed down landing on his leg with a loud crack. With one leg cut from the claw, and the other dislocated or worse, all he could do was crawl away. The beast reached out its paw and flicked Trent back towards itself. The mouth closed around him. The teeth punctured his skin. The beast swung its head back and forth and then dropped him onto the ground.

Trent begged for a quick death. Every attempt to escape was met with another swipe from the beast. If he could just reach the knife maybe he could put up some kind of fight. Gravity disappeared as the paw threw Trent against another tree, sending him whirling into unbearable pain. He could no longer focus. He had to hope he could get away. The second he stopped trying to escape the beast, he would be resigning himself to death. He tried once more to crawl away. It was working. He managed to put some space between him and the beasts reach.

The beast laid down watching Trent crawl away. It appeared to have grown bored of the game it had been playing. Trent dragged himself to his feet and limped off. From behind him, a large mass flew up and over his head. It crashed down in front of him. The mouth spread wider than before. The smell of sulfur surrounded Trent. This was it. He had nowhere to run. He closed his eyes and waited.

Instead of the usual roar, there came a strange kind of pain. Trent opened his eyes to the sight of a scaled creature with two tails, covered in spikes, latched onto the beast's side by its beak-like snout. The three black claws attached to each of its three back feet, disappeared inside the flesh drawing green blood. It's front claws, which had a much flatter and wider appearance than those on the back, alternated digging into the beast's soft naked flesh. The beast writhed in agony trying unsuccessfully to shake the creature loose. Its jaws turned from Trent towards the assailant, closing around the scaled flesh. In retaliation, the spiked creature bit down harder before being torn off, taking a chunk of flesh with it.

Green blood gushed from the wound. The spiked creature dropped the mangled hunk of flesh as if taunting the great beast. It raised its head and howled into the sky. The sound of crunching branches could be heard coming from every direction. While the first creature had been selflessly attacking the beast, the rest of its pack had surrounded the opening, waiting for the signal to strike. They moved in, snapping their mouth with a loud clacking sound. All at once they launched themselves towards the beast, jaws open. One managed to attach to the face, digging away at one of the eyes. The beast gave up on Trent and fled off into the wilderness, trying to rip off the few creatures that managed to remain attached.

The creatures turned and faced Trent. The one responsible for the attack broke from the others and approached him.

Trent stuck out his hand towards the creature's head. "Please don't hurt me. I just want to go home." The creature lowered its head and pushed into Trent's hand, nuzzling its body against his. "That's a good boy, good spiker," he said hesitantly.

At this point all he could do was go along with whatever was happening. The spiker pulled back and walked away, but stopped and looked back at Trent as if it were beckoning him to follow. Not wanting to upset it Trent followed along.

They led him to a large hole in the ground surrounded by foil wrappers. "Have you guys been taking all our trash?"

Seeming to respond to the question the leader let out a howl.

"I wish I had more for you."

The lead spiker climbed into the hole leaving Trent with the others. Little spiked balls crawled from the hole into which the big one had just entered. They bounced around growling at each other, biting and flicking their tails.

The leader carried out a contorted pink ring with white spots and laid it down in front of Trent. He wasn't sure what to make of it. The spiker pushed it closer. "I'm sorry do you want me to throw it?" Trent picked it up and tossed it into the ribbon forest. A look of confusion graced the spiker's face. It disappeared back into the hole and pulled out a second ring. This one got dropped directly in front of Trent's hand. "I don't know what you want."

The spiker cocked its head to the side. This time it brought out the third ring and ate it in front of Trent, consuming the entire thing.

"I gotcha." The cold ring squished in Trent's hand. One bite was all it took for the purpose to become clear. All the pain he had sustained during the attack was gone. "What the hell is this?" He took another bite. It chilled his tongue until all feeling was lost. The true test would come with resetting the ankle. He braced himself and pulled his ankle into place. There was a loud pop but no pain. It was time he returned to camp. The lead spiker rubbed up against Trent's leg. "Iph guuda guo," his words were obscured by the numbing effects of the ring. "Muph pwesh." They circled around his legs the entire stretch back to the cave.

There at the entrance, the party split up in all directions except Trent who was left standing alone. Talking was useless still. He made his way towards the crew, getting almost directly behind them before they had any clue he was there. "Guth I'm hewe."

Everyone let out a horrified gasp when they saw his bloodied body. Zea ran over with what remained of the medical supplies. "Tell me if this hurts."

"I'm mum. Mo phewing."

"You mean you can't feel anything?"

"Mo."

"Fine. I'll patch up the external wounds and we'll take care of the others later. These are superficial. Whatever happened, you got lucky it wasn't worse."

You can say that again. He thought about saying it out loud but he knew the only thing they would hear would be random grunts. He tried to remain silent until he felt the pain return.

All the pain flooded back at once. "Ahhhh. God it hurts. Damn it."

"I'm sorry Trent, but I need to check you for internal injuries now. Please don't hate me for this."

"Ugh. Hate you for what?"

"This." She pushed down on Trent's back.

"Shit! What the fuck!"

"Sorry. But I did warn you, so…."

If he didn't know any better, he would think Zea was getting enjoyment from his pain.

"What did this to you?"

"Some massive creature. I lost the knife during the fight….ow. Would you stop touching them?"

"I need to make sure the bite didn't do any other damage."

"Yeah, right. Anyway, it dug up the bodies and chewed them up. Like nothing left but bones and hair." Zea's hands wrapped around his leg. "No… no. not the ankle…Shit! I already reset it."

"Well better safe than sorry."

"How did you get away from it?" Rocco seemed deeply concerned.

"So, you know those wrappers from our snacks. It turns out some creatures have been eating the scraps inside them. They love them in fact. And I think they ate the foil too but I'm not really sure. They have a whole family out there. Anyway, getting back to the point, I was checking out the graves to see if I could find Sophie or maybe some trace of her and bam! This giant monster pops out of the wood, yellow slime dripping from its mouth. It chases me down and starts throwing me around like a rag doll. Just when I think I'm done for, those spikers who stole the foil wrappers popped out and took on the monster till it ran away. And then they led me to their home."

"Okay but I still don't get why you couldn't feel anything," Addison inquired.

"It was this weird cold, I don't know, maybe a vegetable, that when I ate it, it made all the pain numb, along with my tongue."

"So, you just found a random vegetable and started eating and got lucky?"

"Of course not. The spiker gave it to me to eat."

Taylor stared at him. "And you just ate it?"

"Yeah. There were ten of them and one of me. Plus, they just took out the monster."

Zea interrupted the conversation, "Let's get back to the numbing food. Would you be able to identify it if you saw it again?"

"Yes?"

"Good. Once you're better we're going to go find some. And please don't ever go off on your own again. We've already lost too many people."

All Trent could do for the next four days was sit and wait out his healing process. His nights were miserable. Nightmares of the beast attacking him popped up any time he fell asleep. Sometimes it was tossing him around. Other times, the beast succeeds in eating him alive. The results were the same either way. He would wake up out of breath, in a cold sweat thinking for a moment he was still in the dream. One night he woke up and punched Taylor who was asleep next to him, thinking it was the beast's paw.

Zea took it upon herself to order her patient not to walk around until his wounds had healed. Any attempts to wander around were met with resistance from Rocco or Taylor. Joseph didn't seem to care one way or the other when it was his turn to watch Trent.

Boredom was going to be the death of Trent. He could feel his muscles aching to move. The energy build-up was frustrating. He had never been forced to stay still this long ever, outside of the Sleep pods of course. The only thing he'd been allowed to look at was the cave walls.

"Joseph, can I just walk around the cave a bit?"

"As long as the others are gone, I don't care. That's on you."

That was enough leeway for Trent to feel comfortable heading outside. It was a beautiful overcast day outside. He took in everything around him. After being here for a while the plants and animals were no longer a spectacle. Rather, it was as if he had grown up seeing the ribbon trees and tentacle plants every day of his life. An untraceable crunching sound caused Trent to panic. His body tensed up preparing for the worst. The cave was right behind him providing a safe escape. The monster wouldn't follow him in there.

The source of the sound turned out to be the group returning. What a relief until he realized he was walking around and Zea was with them. She was going to kill him for not listening. He hustled back to his spot near Joseph. It hurt so bad to breathe. "Shit my ribs hurt."

"Ha, dumbass." Joseph didn't even turn to make eye contact.

"Shut up." He had to play it cool to keep suspicions down. "Welcome back guys."

Zea took one look at Trent, "did you stay off your leg?"

"Yes ma'am. Just like you asked."

"Good. You're finally taking my advice."

"Yeah he stayed off it, if you don't count him going outside before you got here."

"What the hell Joseph!"

"Hey, I never said I wouldn't tell Zea. I just said I didn't care what you did. And I still don't. Now if you'll excuse me, my turn's done."

"Okay, let me have it." It was better to have Zea rip him a new one now rather than wait for her to prepare her insults.

Nova

The whole day had been spent looking for the other parts of the wreckage in hopes they could find more resources. The mountain provided an impressive view of the area around them but it was as if the ribbon forest had swallowed all the pieces thrown out from the crash site. It was disappointing to say the least. Nova just wanted to rest by the fire for the night. That was the plan at least until they got back to the cave.

Joseph sold Trent out and now Zea was laying into him. Her fury was insatiable. This strong side of her was an amazing sight to behold.

When Nova first met Zea she was a shy little girl. It was a difficult hour to get through. At even the mention of her mom, any conversation would immediately shut down. Despite that her medical record was impeccable. According to the records Zea was able to graduate med school at twenty-three. She was living in Seattle when a bomb went off downtown. In all of the chaos, Zea managed to save the lives of forty-five people. Nova knew that pushing this part of the file would make up for the shy personality.

Now things were different. A confident woman stood before her, unflinching in her resolve. During the wreck, Zea seemed to have found her voice. "Trent, I swear If you pop your stitches, I'm gonna break your ankle again just so I can reset it. I swear you're so stubborn."

"If it makes you feel better." Trent stopped to wince in pain. "I'm really regretting moving now."

"Everything looks like it's healing alright. Just don't try that again."

It was like watching a mom dealing with her child. For Nova this was the first time the roles had changed. Normally she had to be the one to scold and then comfort everyone.

"Zea mind if I talk to Trent for a minute?" Nova wanted to see how he was doing since the attack.

"Sure, he's all yours."

"See you at our next torture session." Trent repositioned himself. "So, what's up?"

"I just wanted to check in with you. You've been screaming a lot at night and I figured you might want to talk about it."

"It's nothing really." Trent's hand began scratching the top of his arm. One of his obvious tells when he lied.

"Does that explain why you freaked out when we were heading back to the cave?"

"I just didn't want Zea to see me." He kept scratching at his arm.

"So, you're not at all concerned that the beast that attacked you is going to come back? And what about the hallucinations from the pain? The one you had about the creatures that saved you and took you back to their home?" She watched his fidgeting cease upon hearing her question. *He's telling the truth. But that means that something out there has signs of complex behavior.*

"Those were real. I can tell you how to get to them if you don't believe me. You head out of the cave southeast until you get to a ribbon tree entangled with some strange green vine. Follow the blood trail from there. I'm quite sure I left a decent one."

"Okay I believe you about that part. We're getting ready to head back out so I'll make sure we check it out. But as for you not being affected by the attack, well, just let me know when you're ready."

"Will do Doc."

"Everyone be ready to head out in five."

"Gotcha Rocco." Nova tapped Trent's shoulder. "We've all been through a lot. It's okay to be scared." She grabbed a quick nibble of boulder fruit before heading out.

It took them some time to find the marker Trent had described. The vine seemed to have bored holes through the tree. A trail of blood weaved its way through the forest and towards a large ravine filled with discarded plant bits, obscuring the floor. Beautifully colored rocks jutted out from the side walls. The group continued moving forward but Zea stopped along the edge just staring down.

Nova walked over beside her to take in the sight. "We should probably keep moving. We'll check it out later."

"No, I'm good." Zea turned to walk away.

In an instant, Zea was falling. Nova's hand instinctively grabbed Zea's arm and threw herself backward away from the edge. Their two bodies collided on the ground. Where Zea had been standing was no longer a part of the ledge, but an empty void. The ground had fallen to join the debris scattered at the base of the ravine.

"Are you okay?" Nova's heart was pounding. She dreaded to imagine what would have happened had she not been there.

"Yeah." Zea's hazel eyes locked onto Nova. Her body still laying against Nova's, she brushed her hair out of her face and behind her ear. "Thanks, I didn't even realize what was happening. I thought I was done for."

"Don't mention it." The two just laid there intertwined, completely lost in the moment. Zea's warm body against Nova's made her stomach start to knot up. Rather than settling down, her heart sped up. The air around them was electric. It was as if time had frozen still leaving them to revel in the moment.

Rocco's appearance jostled Nova out of the all-consuming trance. "You two alright? That was a nasty fall."

"Um… yeah… yeah. We're fine." Zea stood up and brushed herself off.

Rocco offered his hand to Nova and pulled her back to her feet. "Thanks, Rocco."

Nova glimpsed over at Zea. She had never felt this way about another girl before. The only thing Nova wanted was to be close to Zea again. Her beautiful hair tucked behind those lovely little ears. Her cute gestures while she told Rocco about what happened. Nova was completely engrossed. As they walked, the only thing on Nova's mind was that magical moment.

Taylor held up a strange twisted ring. "I think I found the fruit things Trent was talking about. He said it was pink right?"

Nova had been so distracted she had no recollection of the last half hour. All around her were arching brown plants. The pink fruits dangled in chains below the curves. They ran thick through the forest.

"There's only one way to find out." Joseph grabbed a hold of the fruit and took a large bite. Within seconds his speech lost all clarity, and instead sounded like a series of misconstrued grunts. Somehow it became a game. Everyone took turns trying to translate what he said.

"Guth theth aw awthome."

"I've got this one. Gut thieves are a thumb."

"No Taylor. It is definitely gun things are our sum."

"Wow Rocco nice one." Nova gestured to Joseph for another.

"Wilwy?"

"No, sorry no one wants to see that," Zea laughed.

"Wets jetht gwab a bunth of des."

Nova decided to join in. "Wets jet grub a buns of D's. Nope, that one sucked. My bad, guys. I'm just gonna keep picking these pain killers." She ripped a few of the vines and slung them over her shoulder.

"Ayy wun know how lun dese lath?"

"Four hours. If it lasts any longer please seek medical help immediately." Taylor was cracking himself up so much he had to stop picking fruit entirely.

The harvest went quickly. Nova was done and just pacing back and forth until everyone was ready to head out. Nothing was really catching her attention. She turned to make another lap when the sunlight glinted off something a little way off. The others were busy still so she decided to go check it out. Getting closer, the light turned out to be a piece of foil, and next to it, a large hole had been burrowed into the ground. Footprints littered the area. Dried spots of blood led up to and away from the hole. "I think I found the place Trent was talking about. I'm not seeing any creatures though." No one was close enough to hear her. She ran back to the group and led them to her find.

"Well I'll be damned," Rocco said, analyzing the prints in the dirt. "Looks like I owe Trent an apology. Whatever they are, it seems they moved on. Ok everyone, grab the fruit, we're heading back."

Nova picked up her harvest and followed Rocco back to the cave.

A strange new smell was filling the forest near the cave. It was completely intoxicating. Inside, Addison was roasting a pair of the gel-backed creatures over the fire.

Nova's mouth was watering. "Those look delicious. Is it safe?"

"Seems so. Trent and I tried some earlier."

"Outside's a little tough but the inside's amazing." Trent's mouth was brimming with chewed up meat.

No one seemed to object. Their stomachs were doing all the talking. Nova grabbed the flesh and tore in. She always tried to maintain some air of decorum but this was her first time having real food since they crashed. It was so warm, and tender. Even the residue was good enough to lick off her fingers. The only sounds anyone was capable of uttering were moans of pure satisfaction. Being so full was bliss. The others drifted off to sleep one by one. Soon it was just Nova and Zea.

The two sat by the fire, watching the embers glow. The moment was one of pure beauty. Zea rested her head on Nova's shoulder. "You know, the last few days have been so hectic. It's nice to just be able to rest."

"Agreed." Nova ran her fingers through Zea's soft hair, causing Zea's body to instinctively press into hers. "I've really taken to these quiet moments." Her hand made its way through the hair and transitioned seamlessly to Zea's arm. The sleeves were in the way, but the effect was still the same. Nova pictured what soft skin must lay beneath it. This seemed as though it could last forever.

"Why'd you stop. That felt amazing." Zea's hazel eyes looked up at Nova's. The flames reflected in her gaze. "Just a little more." She shifted her head down into Nova's lap.

This was the most beautiful moment Nova had ever experienced. Her experiences with men never seemed this natural nor romantic. Her right hand remained on Zea's Arm while the other hand made its way into the lovely locks. In return, Zea's hand gently caressed Nova's thigh. Her emotions became a mixture of excitement and nervous energy. Her body wanted more.

Zea rolled over onto her back, eyes closed. Nova's hand naturally found its place, gracing the side of Zea's face. All her training said that this was wrong. A connection caused by the emotional vulnerability of the profession. That no longer was enough to even slow Nova down. She slid her hand from Zea's arm onto her stomach, where she traced the portions of skin exposed in the tears. Her body quivered under the light touch. The passion was undeniable. In a moment of pure passion, Nova leaned her head towards Zea's. Eyes closed, she felt their lips touch. The response was immediate. The kiss was filled with desire. Zea's hand pulled her head in tight.

Nova's hands began exploring Zea's small body, finding their way between her thighs and around her firm breasts. Their tongues intertwined. As quickly as the moment started Zea pulled away and sat up.

"I'm so sorry. That was inappropriate of me." Nova's face grew warm with embarrassment.

"Why? That was amazing. It's just… I… Well, I've never been with a girl before, and everyone can see us."

"This is a first for me too. I just find you irresistible for some reason."

Zea's head pressed into Nova's chest. "I'm glad you're here."

"Me too."

"Is it alright if we take this slow?"

"Definitely."

"Thanks." Zea gave Nova more solid kisses before laying her head back in Nova's lap. Nova savored the moment until she could no longer keep her eyes open. Zea had already passed out. She lifted Zea's head and scooted her legs out, trying to get comfortable without disturbing her sweetheart. Insomnia she had battled for ages gave way to the high brought on by Zea's presence. Finally, her body was able to fully relax. All the heartache, stress, and loneliness were replaced by a feeling of belonging. That night Nova slept better than she had in ages.

When she finally awoke, the thought of last night flooded back into her mind. She refused to open her eyes should the illusion disappear. A small noise from Zea reassured her that it was all real. Nova weaseled her numb arm out from beneath Zea's head. Without her body to support Zea, she rolled onto her back still asleep. Nova gave her sleeping goddess's forehead a kiss before getting up to have breakfast.

A shadow ran through the cave. Nova got up to chase after it. The soft light of dawn outlined a spiked creature. It's mouth overflowing with the scraps from last night's meal. It took off into the woods and out of sight. Any attempts to track it down at this point would be fruitless.

The fire had gone out overnight, leaving smoldering ashes popping in the pit. The embers glowed like an ancient city set ablaze. She threw some of the red branches onto the fire. Tiny little flames licked at the food handed to them. Nova breathed life into the fire igniting the kindling, rousing it back to life. The fire thanked her with a series of crackles and hisses. She returned the favor by adding in more fuel. She located one of the remaining pieces of boulder fruit and chomped down. Eggs had always been her least favorite meal, but after eating what they could scrape together, the thought of a simple plate of fried eggs and toast sounded delicious. The simple things in life she always took for granted, now were luxury items she couldn't afford.

The others woke up one by one and made their way over to the fire. Her eyes barely open, and hair a mess, Zea greeted the group. "Morning everyone." Her face blushed as she made eye contact with Nova. "Morning." She grabbed some food and returned to her spot. "Hey Nova, after breakfast I was thinking of going to go watch the sunrise."

"That sounds fun."

"Hey, I want to go too." Joseph got all excited.

Trent put his hand on Joseph's shoulder and whispered into his ear.

Joseph's face fell. "On second thought I'm just gonna go for a walk." He wandered out of the cave.

"You know what, it was a silly idea."

"No, you two go," Addison reassured Zea. "We'll hang back here. The clouds are going to make for a beautiful sight."

The reassurance lit up Zea's face once again. "Come on Nova, let's go!" She grabbed Nova's arm and pulled her up from the ground.

Nova followed Zea outside and they made their way up the side of the mountain. Partway up they found a rock ledge and took a seat. The sunlight streamed through the clouds. The sky was painted with beautiful pinks and oranges. The feelings from last night had intensified. Their hands met. The situation might not be optimal but sitting here watching the sunrise with Zea beside her, Nova couldn't help but feel like she found a true connection. Life made perfect sense at that moment.

Sophie

Soft dirt streamed through Sophie's fingers. Nothing remained in her hands but some tiny pebbles which she promptly tossed aside. She dug back into the dirt with her broken nails. A moist patch signaled her prey was near. Her hands pushed through the dirt feeling for a soft lump. Something wriggled past her fingers. She clenched her fingers around it and ripped it from the dirt. The creature put up a fight, trying to save itself from the brutal end that awaited it. Not wanting to lose another one, she gave a swift tug. The creature released its grip.

In her hands, Sophie held a long, clawed creature with tiny toothed mouths along its underside and little hand like projections running down the sides. It bit at the air and swung its arm in futility. She crushed the life out of it to end its struggle for freedom and shoved the broken body into her mouth making quick work of it. It was so warm. Liquid poured down her throat. She savored the taste of sweet victory, though the actual taste was more akin to bile. The hunger was nowhere near satisfied with the tiny amount of food.

She dug right back in, hoping for another morsel before she had to move on. This time a blue diamond-shaped creature sifted out of the gravel. It's one eye stared up at her. She grabbed a rock and broke open the shell. The green insides were still writhing around. She placed the hole against her lips and sucked out the meat. It was dry but better than nothing. The shell got returned to the dirt hole from which it came. She brushed her hands off on what remained of her tattered pants.

"Sophie!" A voice called out through the forest. It sounded like Rocco.

"Hello?" Sophie got on her feet and looked for the source of the voice. "Where are you guys?"

"Sophie come back."

"Trent is that you?"

"It's getting dark."

"What are you guys talking about? Addison it's only noon." She was so confused. Why were they acting like they couldn't hear her?

"Let's head back."

"No, don't leave. I'm here." She ran towards the voices.

"God that hurt Zea."

What the hell is going on? There was no one around. The voices seemed to stay just ahead of her. "Please just stay where you are. I'm coming."

"Any more food?"

"Seriously guys, this isn't funny." She stopped moving. "I'm done playing around."

The voice matched her movements and held their place. "Stop throwing rocks."

"Screw you guys." She was getting frustrated now.

Footsteps crunched along the forest floor behind her. "Diego, come on get up."

Was that my voice? None of this made any sense. *Did one of those bugs make me high?* This time she was pissed. She ran after her own voice.

It stayed ahead of her despite her speed. She managed to walk it down, the source of the voice tiring out and remaining in place. "I can't find the canteen." Her voice was now replaced with Trent's.

If this was a joke, it was the cruelest one anyone had ever played on her. All she wanted was to get back to the cave, but it seemed the others were enjoying tormenting her, even going so far as to impersonate her. The footsteps were close now. It was just behind the tree.

Sophie crept up to the ribbon tree watching her every step. Each footfall was nerve-wracking. If whoever was behind the tree knew she was closing in they might run. She poked her head around. On the other side sat something inexplicable.

A dog-sized creature with powerful legs and a tiny body was sitting on the ground. A long neck extended towards a bulbous head. A series of flaps stood where the mouth should be. The body swelled before her eyes, enveloping the neck completely. As the body pressed back in the flaps waved around releasing an exact imitation of Trent's voice.

"I'm gonna pass on that."

It stopped immediately and turned its four eyes towards Sophie. They all blinked individually. It spoke again, this time as Zea.

"Did you stay off your leg?"

With the body deflated it ran off. Three others appeared out of nowhere and followed it into the distance.

All of the frustration and fear from the last few days hit Sophie like a truck. She dropped to the ground in tears. She had no idea where she was now and even the impossible forest was nowhere to be found. *Why did I have to run away? Fuck! This is all my fault.* She wiped the tears from her eyes. "No. I have to keep looking." Just ahead of her was a large mountain. If she could just get to the top maybe she could find the cave or at the very least the ship. She made her way up the face of the mountain. It took an hour before she couldn't climb anymore. The top was still another hour away at least. She sat down to rest and take a look to see if anything caught her eye. Standing up above the trees, the shiny metallic sides of the ship glinted in the sun.

She could barely contain her excitement. She jumped up into the air screaming. It was the wreck. All she had to do was get to it and she could find her way back to the others. The way down the mountain was strenuous. It seemed to be harder to find a way back down than to actually ascend. She tried to keep the direction of the ship in focus. As the treetops blocked out the line of sight, all she could do was follow the path of landmarks she had identified from atop the mountain.

"Okay if I follow this tree to the large boulder I should be heading in the right direction."

Once she reached the floor it was a straight line to the boulder. The first part was done. Now all she had to do was line up the next landmark. A dead tentacle plant sat a hundred yards ahead. She made it her goal. This pattern continued for what seemed like miles. By now she should have reached the ship. What she needed was a high point to search for the ship. Just out of her way was one of the orange pole trees. The masses seemed to be spread out just enough that she could climb up. It was a daunting challenge but if she didn't do this she could wander aimlessly forever.

Sophie grabbed onto the main stalk. It seemed solid. Her left foot pressed into the lowest mass. It pressed down forming a cushion beneath her feet. She pulled herself up putting her full weight onto the mass. It held up surprisingly well. Onto the next one. She pressed her hand against it making sure it was solid. Certain it would hold up, she continued climbing. Soon she was high enough to see the top of the ship. She was close.

Back on the ground she meandered towards the ship. There it sat in all its glory. The chunk of the ship was split in two. Half rested flat on the ground and the other half rose from the ground, propped up by the lower section. The plants around it were broken, some bearing char marks from the flames. Parts of the insides of the ship littered the ground. She made her way over to the horizontal portion. It had three rooms attached to it. She made her way into the darkness. Her eyes slowly began to adjust revealing a tangle of metal. The first door was shut tight. She gave the manual release a twist hoping the damage from the crash wasn't too severe. A loud click indicated the lock had disengaged. She pulled at the door, managing to barely open it. Just enough for the light to stream through. She pulled harder, separating the metal halves enough to get her head in. The entire side was ripped open. If she went around, she could squeeze in. the room was full of broken lab equipment. The chances of finding something useful in there were high.

The next door was broken in half. A tangle of wires hung from the ceiling. Broken gym equipment made it impossible to get inside. The final room was completely crushed by the other portion of the ship.

She headed outside to try the hole in the lab. The fracture in the lab wall bore its jagged teeth. They tried their hardest to grab ahold of Sophie as she squeezed inside. It appeared as though every piece of glass was shattered. Nothing remained undamaged. Red Martian dirt covered everything. A fibrous yellow material melded with one of the dirt piles. In the corner of the room the emergency shower was still standing. She pulled the handle more out of curiosity than anything. She didn't expect to actually get anything from it. A pleasant surprise greeted her. Water trickled from the showerhead. She opened her mouth and caught what little water she could. As quickly as the water started, it had dried up.

Upon searching the rubble, she discovered a bent-up strike. A few squeezes of the handle threw sparks into the air. It was still good. With the striker in her pocket she continued searching for useful supplies. Lab coats laid on the bottom of the closet. She threw a bunch of them out of the tear in the wall. The cabinets were a mess of broken glass and crushed plastic. Somehow one bottle managed to survive intact. Its label was hard to read in the dark. She pulled the bottle from off the shelf trying to keep the remaining liquid inside. One whiff and she knew it was pure alcohol. There was enough to start a fire. Finally, a little bit of good was coming her way.

Sophie left the lab and grabbed the coats. She tossed them into the ship's broken corridor. They would suffice as a makeshift blanket and pillows. For now, though her focus was on ensuring she could stay warm. The alcohol was a good accelerant but she needed kindling. She ventured out once again, trying to stay ahead of the setting sun. the broken ribbon branches scattered around the floor would maintain a sufficient burn. They were surprisingly solid. Now all she needed was a hand full of the red branching plants for kindling. She took her load and headed back to the safety of her new shelter.

Darkness crept in. A few clicks from the striker set the alcohol-drenched branches ablaze. A yellow flame engulfed the entire pile of scraps. White smoke billowed into the air. She gazed into the dancing flames. Not having anything to do felt amazing. The last few days had been so grueling. Her legs ached all over. Since they arrived on this godforsaken planet, every day was a challenge both mentally and physically. She took a seat on the metal floor and refused to move. If any creatures tried to disturb her, they would be in for a hell of a fight. Her stomach rumbled. The snacks from earlier had been just enough to satiate her at the time. Now the hunger pains were back, and they brought along cravings of food she felt she had only ever dreamed of. Her father's fresh hot pancakes drenched in pure maple syrup. Just the thought made her mouth salivate. He often got up early to ensure she had a homemade breakfast every morning. She longed to be that age again, sitting around carefree while her parents took care of everything. Now everything was dependent upon her staying driven to survive.

Inside her pocket were mushed up boulder fruit remnants, the last resort she had been carefully rationing. She scooped a bit out with her fingers. Just the thought of eating this fruit one more time made her gag. All she could do was close her eyes and swallow as fast as possible. It had to be done. The rumbling stopped momentarily. Hopefully, it would last her through the night if she rationed it. Boredom kicked in with her brain no longer distracted by the need to feed. She wanted so badly to just sit and relax but her body refused to participate. The lack of stimulus got her thinking of the time she ran through the house coating the walls in paint. Feeling that familiar itch, the only thing around that she could find were the ribbons in the fire. Sophie pulled one out and buried the flaming end in the dirt. All that was left was a chard piece of ribbon. The char left perfect markings along the inside of the metal hull. Drawings of flowers and stick figures adorned her new home. The drawing of her pet dog was her favorite. She even managed to draw a bone in his mouth. *This must have been why cavemen drew on the walls. They weren't trying to write stories. They were just bored.* She sat by the fire admiring her artwork until the light dimmed to a faint glow.

Her moment of bliss was ruined by the sound of metal creaking. Her first thought was that the chunk of the ship sitting on top of the one she was in was falling. Then footsteps on the metal changed her mind. A strange creature loomed in front of her. It's back narrowly missing the top of her shelter. Three tan-colored rings circled the head. Its body was coated in patches of green fuzz. The creature approached the fire searching the ground. The pile of lab coats Sophie was planning to use for bedding was within the creature's reach. It picked up the pile, A beaked mouth held the lab coats, pulling them away. Sophie's exhaustion turned to pure anger. There was no way she was going to let this thing mess with her. She grabbed the pile of lab coats and pulled back. The creature refused to give up.

The fire had all but gone out, leaving smoldering embers and tiny leaping flames. A quick grab produced a glowing branch. Sophie waved the stick at the beast. It dropped the coats and let out a deep roar that shook the ship. She continued to stand her ground, waving the stick through the air. Small flames leaped off the stick. The creature leaned its head in, attempting to steal the coats again. The stick made contact with the creature's head. The flesh sizzled beneath the burnt end. Sophie let out a primal scream. It was as if she connected with her animal instincts. She felt so powerful fending off this massive creature. Her foe retreated in pain, whimpering in defeat.

"I dare you to come back!" With the stick still in hand, Sophie took to the entrance planting the stick into the ground as a warning sign to any other creature that would dare to challenge her. Above her the stars burned bright across the sky. This was exactly how her ancestors must have felt. The last few days were filled with her running scared from everything around her, just struggling to find her way out of the maze. Now she felt connected to nature.

Joseph

Two hours had passed with no sign of activity. The ribbon forest was eerily quiet. Joseph was under the impression that the hunting expedition was a quick process. He could not have been more wrong. The trap had been laid between a pair of tentacle plants that straddled a heavily worn track. It had taken them all morning to collect enough branches to form a nest for a well-placed pod the gel backs were prone to eating. Beneath it was a large hole they dug for when some unsuspecting creature decided the pod was worth making a meal out of.

Addison swore up and down that the gel backs wandered through here about this time every day.

"Seriously, are you sure this is gonna work," he asked, breaking the silence.

"It would if you could shut up for more than a minute." Addison seemed aggravated. She had coated her skin in mud to prevent the creatures from seeing her.

"You know you look a bit ridiculous."

"Shh."

"Fine I'll just sit here on the cold ground." The wind chilled him to the bone. He was being forced to face it head-on because of something to do with the creatures smelling them. This was beyond boring. He picked up a rock to dig a little trench in the dirt. The edges of the trench got lined with tiny pebbles. In his head, this was an impenetrable castle that could only be reached by boat. His game got interrupted by the cracking of branches. He looked up to see a strange creature with a crescent-shaped head approaching the bait. "Addison," he whispered hoping not to spook the creature. "Something's coming from over here." She didn't respond. He raised his voice just a bit. "Addison. Addison." She was still looking the wrong way. *How did she not hear it walking?*

The creature emerged into full view. Its body seemed to be covered in a strange bark. It sniffed the ground, following the scent directly to the fruit pod. *Come on. Just a few more steps.* It passed between the two large tentacle plants. One step was all it took for the branches to give way, sending the creature tumbling into the shallow hole. Its front legs snapped back. A strange bugle called out for help.

That finally got Addison's attention. "Holy shit. Did we get a bark beast? Why didn't you tell me one of these was heading for the trap?" She left her cover for the captured prey.

"Well I did. You just didn't hear me… and since you told me to stay quiet." He raised his hands to rub it in. "So, what are we going to do with it?"

"We have to put it out of its misery."

The bugles continued as the creature struggled to stand. Its front half was stuck in the hole while the back legs were trying to pull the body free. Addison took the metal pole in her hand and unleashed her full force into the creature's head, sending it crumbling to the ground. "Joseph, I need your help twisting the head around."

Joseph hesitantly jumped to the other side of the bark beast.

"Okay, now grab that side of the head and we'll both twist clockwise."

This was the first time Joseph had ever killed anything bigger than a fish. He forced the head around until it let out a loud pop and fell limp. The legs spasmed in the dirt. "Crap it's still alive!"

"No that's just…."

It didn't matter, Joseph was already smashing the body with the bat. After a few minutes, and a pole covered in green goo, the creature's limbs ceased to struggle.

Addison was already attempting to pull the creature's front half from the hole. "Well that was excessive. Anyway, this definitely beats what I was hoping to catch. That's a good week's worth of food. Help me get this back to camp." She gave a few hard tugs, but the body wouldn't budge.

Joseph decided he would help her out. He grabbed one leg while Addison grabbed the other. They dragged the heaping mass through the forest. Branches and dirt piled up along the sides as the body formed a new trail through the ribbon forest. Getting the prey back to camp was an exhausting challenge. He had to stop every ten minutes or so just to catch his breath. The cave finally came into sight. His arms and legs were fatigued from pulling the corpse. All he had to do was get to the entrance, then he could relax.

"Everyone, get out here and help us." Addison still had the ability to order everyone around despite claiming she no longer wanted to be their captain.

On command, the others rushed out to meet them, shocked by the scene that greeted them. Addison was still covered in mud now mixed with sweat. Joseph was splattered in dried green slime. Between them, the mangled bark beast's body had flopped carelessly on the ground. Rocco had each person grab a leg. They carried the body to a clearing a little way off from the cave.

Feeling drained from the hunt, Joseph found a nice rock to lean against. He watched as Rocco tore open the beast causing the black entrails to pour from the opening. A rancid odor tore at Joseph's nostrils, coated his tongue, and churned his stomach. Yet, something about the sight of Rocco covered in blood elbow deep in the bark beast was fascinating. Watching him work to clean out the insides and chop up the meat was like watching a work of art. Normally being limited to a sharpened metal chunk from the ship would be a hindrance but it became an extension of Rocco's arm. He tossed the inedible parts away into a green goo coated pile.

Spiked creatures crept from the woods and ran off with the discarded pieces of skin and organs.

"See guys, those are the ones that helped me." Trent limped over to the putrid pile and knelt down with his hand extended out. It was greeted by a spiker twice the size of the others. A wave spread across the spikes in what appeared to be pure bliss. "Hey buddy. You came back."

It was beyond comprehension. Here on a strange planet, or at the very least in a strange environment, Trent had managed to form a bond with some of the creatures.

Joseph decided to give it a try himself. "I officially believe your story now," he said petting the large creature in front of him. There was no way anyone back home would believe him even if he had pictures.

"Really? I come back wrecked from being attacked and only now do you believe me?"

"Would you believe what you said? I mean it was like something out of a movie."

"I'll give you that one." Trent offered a hand full of flesh to the creature's open jaws. "Go on. It's all yours." The creature grabbed the scraps and disappeared with the others. "Damn. I was hoping they'd stick around this time. On the plus side, you guys have finally seen them and it's not just me saying they're real."

"I didn't see anything." Taylor mocked Trent. "How about you Zea?"

"I'm not playing this stupid game."

"There you have it. Zea saw it Taylor."

"Nah I don't believe it."

He laughed. "I tell you what. You can go out there and see them for yourself."

Joseph wasn't sure if they were messing with each other or being serious, though knowing them it was probably just the prior.

Rocco gestured to the others. "We'll leave the rest out here for 'em. Time to start roasting this sucker." Trent, Taylor, and Zea each grabbed a leg and helped haul their future dinner inside.

Nova and Addison had been hard at work making a large fire. "Hey Joseph, can you make something to hold the meat over the fire? Maybe some kind of spit."

"Fine, but I'm going to need to get supplies from the wreck first." It was going to be a long day for Joseph. "Who's going with me? Taylor, Trent how about you guys?"

"If it gets me outside for a bit, I'm in." Trent was up and on his feet before Joseph realized what was going on.

"Come on Taylor. You can suck Trent off, or whatever you two do when no one's around."

"Seems like you're projecting a bit. Something we need to know about you?"

Taylor high-fived Trent. "Nice. We doing this or what." He was already headed out of the cave before he finished his sentence.

There had not been much of a reason for Joseph to go back to the ship after they made the food run. When he got there, he found that the plants were merging with the metal frame, forming a strange ancient hidden city. This was his own Indiana Jones adventure minus the deadly traps preventing him from reaching the treasure.

"Hm, hm, hm, hmm, hm, hm, hmm." It was as if Taylor was reading his mind.

"Are you? Is that the Indiana Jones theme song?" Joseph had no other choice but to join in. Soon all three of them were loudly singing as they stood in front of the wreckage.

"Nice. Okay now we need to get to work. If you see anything that looks like this…" Joseph drew out a large Y shaped image. "Or like this…" He drew a handle and gears. "Make sure to grab 'em. I'll sort through everything before we go back." The first stop on their journey was the place where everything started. Broken glass still covered the ground. Some shards jutted straight into the air. The once splendid observation window was now reduced to a few jagged edges. Seeing the structure still holding up despite plummeting into the ground, was a testament to its engineering. Plenty of metal scraps were tossed around. He remembered seeing a suitable handle when he was on the initial food run. Now he just had to figure out which portion of the ship he had been in. If he was going to start anywhere the cafeteria was as good a place as any. "Guys, this way."

An obstacle course had been set up by the broken beams, made more dangerous by the onset of rust. The three of them clambered over the scraps and towards the open tunnel. The broken door still held its half-closed position, unaware that the contents it tried to protect were completely exposed by the missing roof. Puddles of water hid in the corners. If anything had the potential to hold the gears to make the spit turn properly it would be the three-D printer. Its metal frame was bent and contorted.

Joseph managed to slip his hand inside a gap on the front of the machine and pulled with all he had. The sheet refused to budge. "Taylor, toss me that table leg."

"This one?" he held up a metal leg bent in half.

"No let's go for the other one." The leg flew towards Joseph and past his hand, hitting him square in the chest. "Ughhh." a crushing blow left him unable to speak. A few coughs cleared up his lungs but the pain continued. "Thanks, I didn't want to breathe today."

"Any time."

"I thought it was a nice throw. Just like this." Trent threw a chunk of the plate right at Joseph.

He managed to dip past it. "Dude what the hell?"

I don't know. I thought it would be funny." The laughter from Trent was met by pure silence from the other two.

"Yeah no. Far from it. I need you guys to come and hold the printer while I try to pry it open." With Taylor and Trent bracing the machine, Joseph slipped the leg into the seam and yanked with both his hands gripped tightly around the pole. It refused to move. He needed more force. He placed his foot onto the metal frame and leaned his body back. A few more good tugs broke the panel free, sending Joseph spinning backward.

The insides exposed themselves to the world. The goop sourced for food assembly had begun rotting inside, turning everything a strange shade of gray, accompanied by a foul odor. Any useful components were now rotting away. Something inside caught Joseph's attention. It was a series of plastic cups used to hold the base materials. He got to his feet and began pulling the containers loose, ignoring the cut to his hands caused by the machinery inside. He didn't care, those containers were a game-changer. In total there were fourteen. "That'll work!" His excitement was uncontainable when the first set gave way. "Yes! This is perfect! I can't believe it!"

"What are you rambling about?" Trent came around to see the sight for himself. "I don't get it."

"I can use these to make a…. ughhh…" Another two cups broke loose. "To make a battery."

Taylor let go of the machine. "Wait you mean we can get electricity? We can have lights and music?"

"No, but I can do one better. I can use it to power the distress beacon. I didn't see any point in fixing it once we crashed." He pulled another two cups loose. "But now we can actually use it."

"So, you just, what, hook those things up and it turns on the beacon?"

"No…ugh…You just need…ah… a few metal screws and some copper. Oh, and if we can get some salt that would be even better." He finally removed the last of the containers. "We should be able to find everything we need in here. Just collect some screws and I'll take care of the copper." Christmas had come early and Santa had granted his wish. The wires would have to come from the printer. It would supply more than enough copper to build his battery twelve times over.

Taylor approached Joseph with some white packets in his hands. "Is this enough salt?"

"Yeah it is. How are we coming on those screws?"

"I've got twelve right now. Make that thirteen. Never mind, twelve." Trent disappointedly threw a metal sliver aside.

"That should work. I have three that popped off the machine over here somewhere." He scoured the ground. "Ah, here they are. Who's ready to make some magic?"

The difficult task of getting the Beacon in working order now lay before them. It happened to be attached to the generator room. Reaching it was a much easier task than getting to the cafe. To Joseph's amazement, the antenna was still connected to the signal box. He didn't have tools so it was going to take all three of them, along with some ingenuity, to repair any damage. The dish portion was smashed up. They worked together to expand it back to its original shape. The process took less effort than anticipated. The metal gave way easily, becoming a rough image of its former glory. A large hole in the side needed to be filled. The others were small enough to be of little to no consequence. A piece of metal scrap fixed the issue right up. The dish was stuck facing the ground. Joseph took a screwdriver and loosened up the connecting bolts. Its hinge opened, the dish was ready to be repositioned. There was little room to rotate the dish but some movement was better than none. After a few more adjustments and improvised repairs the antenna was fully operational.

"Now to make the battery."

Joseph grabbed the copper wires and used a rock to remove the insulation. He wrapped each screw up with a piece of hook-shaped wire. The screws were then placed into each of the cups. The copper hooks allowed him to connect the cups together.

"Now we put some salt in each well like this."

Joseph tore open the packets and evenly distributed the little salt available.

"And now we just need to fill these with some water. One of you needs to go get the canteen and bring it back. Taylor how bout you."

"Fine I can do that." He started to head away but stopped. "What should I tell them about cooking the food?"

"Tell em to just eat it raw for all I care."

"I think I'll try being a little more tactful."

"Hey if that's what you want."

With that, Taylor was gone leaving Joseph and Trent alone. Joseph tore the connecting end of the power line from the signal box. He attached the wires to his homemade battery. Now he just had to wait for the water. With everything he could do at a standstill he decided to sit back and relax. The wilderness was strangely beautiful today. He stared at the main hub of the ship before him. A loud metal creak rang out. The large chunk of ship shifted, and then without notice, collapsed into the ground letting out a loud explosion and shrieking of metal. Dust flew high into the air. The ground shook beneath Joseph and Trent.

"Fuck. I'm glad we weren't in there."

"You and me both."

It was a subtle reminder that their lives we're constantly at risk out here, no matter how safe they felt. Joseph and Trent distanced themselves from the ship while they awaited Taylor's return.

What seemed like hours went by before Taylor's voice could be heard.

"Guys, I got the canteen. Heads up, the others weren't as mad as I thought they would be."

"Hey Joe, I'm gonna scare Taylor. You want in?"

"Nah I'm good."

"Okay but you're missing out." Trent crept over to the new pile of rubble created from the collapse and wiggled under one of the beams. "Help Taylor. I can't get my legs out."

Somehow Taylor didn't see Joseph leaning against the hull fragment. It was quite the show. Taylor was freaking out about Trent trying to get the beam off him. "Where's Joe at?"

"He was inside when it collapsed." Trent let out a surprisingly real cough. He was fully committing himself to the prank.

"Are you serious?" Taylor was in full panic mode. He ran over and tried digging at the rubble.

While his back was turned Trent pulled himself out from under the beam. A few silent steps placed him directly behind Taylor. "Gotcha!"

Taylor leaped into the air. Joseph and Trent both let out a loud guffaw. Despite wanting nothing to do with it, Joseph found the sequence of events hilarious enough he couldn't stop the laughter. Talking was nowhere near possible like this. Instead he just walked over, tears of joy streaming down his face, and took the canteen from Taylor. He had to settle himself down before pouring the water. Every drop would count. A few deep breaths got him calm enough to complete the battery. Each cup now held enough water to almost submerse the screws entirely. The light from the signal box turned on. The sound of life came from the box.

Beep....

Beep....

Beep...

Beep....

The signal was active. Now they had to hope someone was listening.

Frank

The melodic sizzle of bacon played the chorus for Frank's breakfast symphony, joined by the bubbling oatmeal baseline, and whisking to keep tempo. Every step was an intricate part of the song creating a masterpiece. He was lost in the beauty of the whole thing.

The twins could be heard running down the stairs. They then passed the kitchen, Mia wrapped in a towel, running after her brother who was reading texts from her phone.

"Oh, I can't wait to kiss you tonight." Ben held the phone tightly, trying to stay ahead of her. He used the couch to help maintain his lead. "I miss holding you."

"Stop it you jackass. Give me back my phone."

"Are you going to wear that cologne I love so much?"

"Dad, tell Ben to stop reading my texts."

"Cut it out now." Frank had to stay focused to keep the food from burning. "If either of you wakes your mom up, I'm going to take both of your phones, and then no one will have to worry about reading any texts."

Ben fled around the dining room table for cover. "I love you so much. Oh, and you sent a picture of you making a kissy face. Man, this is pure gold."

"Ben I'm gonna kill you."

They had hit Frank's last nerve. He left the kitchen to run itself while he dealt with the little monsters running around his house. Just the sight of him walking into the room brought Ben to a screeching halt.

Mia ripped the phone away from his hands. "Fucker. God why are you so annoying."

"Ben go get your backpack and come get your breakfast. Mia, you finish getting ready. I don't want any more fighting this morning." The twins headed back upstairs. "Did you guys hear me. I said no more fighting."

"Yes dad." They both spoke in unison.

"I hate you so much," Mia muttered.

"You're no angel yourself."

"Shut up."

"I heard that." Frank watched them wander back to their rooms before he felt comfortable enough to return to the kitchen. The eggs were starting to burn. Smoke rose from the pan. "Shit, Shit, Shit, Shit, Shit." He pulled the pan from the stove. The batch was ruined. Black residue remained stuck to the pan as he scraped the eggs into the trash can.

"Hey babe." Kelsey was awake and standing in the kitchen. Her beautiful red hair was a mess, and she was wrapped in a light blue robe.

"Morning Sweety." Pan still in hand, Frank leaned over to Kelsey and gave her a gentle kiss. "Sorry the kids woke you up."

"Oh, no I was already up."

"Stealing my robe today huh?"

"Yep" Kelsey snuggled in the robe. "I like it better than mine."

"You know they're the exact same robe, right?"

He opened the fridge and grabbed the eggs out to start his second attempt. "I literally bought them at the same time. The only difference is yours is pink."

"Yeah but this one smells like you."

"So that's where your daughter gets it."

"You know it. Now what's for breakfast?"

"Oatmeal, toast, fresh-squeezed orange juice, and bacon."

He started cracking eggs into a bowl. "And if I don't burn these ones, some eggs."

She took a seat at the counter. "Sounds delicious. I love it when you cook. Mmmm. look at my big man whisking those eggs. Once the kids leave, I'm taking you upstairs."

That was all the motivation Frank needed to get the kids off to school as quickly as possible. He loved having time at home with his family in the mornings now that he no longer had to worry about going into work early. Having the family all gathered around the table for breakfast was great, even when the twins were in one of their moods. The moment got interrupted by the vibration of a phone. The whole table rattled.

"Who's calling you this early?" Kelsey said, mouth full of food.

"No Idea." The screen lit up with the words NASA. "I need to take this. I'll be right back." He took the call outside. "Hello?"

"Hey Frank, it's Daniel."

"Why are you calling me from work? You know I quit right?"

"Yeah, but we need you to get down here now."

"Why what's going on?"

"I can't tell you over the phone but it's big news. Just get down here now."

"Okay. I'll be down in a bit."

"No. you need to get down here as soon as possible. Trust me."

"Gotcha. I'm on my way." He opened the door and leaned his head inside. "Sweety, I need to get down to NASA. Something urgent came up and they need me. Can you clean up and get the kids to school?"

"Yeah sure. I love you."

"I love you too." Frank grabbed the keys from the wall and jumped in the car. The entire ride was spent trying to figure out what could be so important to bring him back in. He figured Daniel was exaggerating about the urgency of the situation until he pulled up to the gate.

"Morning Sir. Please head straight to the control room. Pull up in front of the building and we'll have someone park it for you."

Things were growing more bizarre by the minute. All Frank could do at this point was go along with the strange charade. He pulled up at the front of the building as instructed. Daniel was standing at the curb along with a security guard awaiting his arrival.

The security guard opened his door. "I'll take it from here."

It felt odd having to let someone else park for him but why not. Frank stepped out of the car and joined Daniel.

"Let's get moving. I'll explain everything on the way in." He held out Frank's security clearance badge. "You'll need this."

It felt good to have the badge back. "Okay tell me what's going on."

"The SETI Program picked up something interesting yesterday morning. It was a beeping sound being relayed by one of their satellites."

"But what does this have to do with me."

"I'm getting to that part. We analyzed the signal and we're sure it's the distress beacon from the Phoenix VII."

Frank couldn't believe his ears. "Wait what? You mean you found them? And if the beacon's going off then they must still be alive." This was unbelievable. He thought they were gone forever. Having lost the entire crew, including his childhood friend was the reason he had quit in the first place.

"That's exactly why we needed you to come back. We need your expertise and knowledge of the mission. We'd love it if you come back permanently but this will have to do for now."

They headed inside. Though he'd been gone over a month, Frank slipped right back into the routine. His office was still empty as if they anticipated his return. "Well this will take some time to make homey again."

"You'll have plenty of time for that later. For now, we need you in the control room." Everyone was busy running around the room analyzing data and passing along their work. The screens showed complex routes through the solar system and schematics of the ship.

"It seems the signal is originating from the far side of the sun. Our estimates place it coming from roughly 2 AU's away."

"Wait so you're saying they're in our path of orbit?"

"Precisely. We figure when the solar flare hit, it left them floating without the ability to correct their course on the way to Earth. We've been trying to account for every variable to see where their heading."

All of this seemed like some dream his mind concocted to deal with the mission's failure.

"Right. The first thing we need to do is try to get sight of them. I want all telescopes to turn towards the signal. Hopefully, we can catch a glimpse of it." He turned on one of the computers and attempted to log in. "Crap. they already blocked my user info. Daniel, I need you to get in. I want to get full control of the DSRS. We should be able to get it within range to communicate within a few weeks. Once it's in place we can get pictures to assess damages as well."

For the next few hours, Frank sat down with Daniel scribbling formulas all over a whiteboard. They calculated exactly how much thrust and how fast they would go. The plan was looking more and more like a slingshot maneuver around Venus to add more speed. They even figured out how far away they would be before the short-range radio communication would work. This was truly his niche. The numbers flowed out of him.

"Frank, your wife's on line one," Randy said standing in the doorway.

"Man, I forgot to call her. What time is it? Eight? I wasn't home in time for dinner. Kelsey's gonna kill me."

"You go home. I'll finish working. I don't have anywhere else I need to be."

"You sure?"

"Yeah. Go on."

"Thanks Daniel. I'll be back early to double-check the numbers before we start the maneuver. Randy let her know I'll give her a call on my phone."

"Got it."

Once Kelsey heard the news, he knew she would forgive him. That didn't help to clear his conscience though. He felt terrible for letting them all down. Tonight, was supposed to be his tutoring session with the twins to help them get ready for their math test. His wife's ringtone went off as he waited for his car to come around.

"Hey Darling. Sorry I didn't make it home."

"No worries. We got dinner figured out. Everything alright?"

"Yeah. More than alright. I can't say anything right now but once I get home, I'll fill you in. I'm just leaving now. Can you put the twins on?" The car pulled up to the curb and the security guard stepped out. "Thanks." He climbed in to start the journey home. Luckily, traffic was almost nonexistent this late.

"Hey dad."

"Hey pop"

"Hey, guys. Sorry I couldn't help you study tonight. Something really important came up. I promise I'll make it up to you this weekend."

"Yeah, yeah. We've heard that one before."

"Ben. I mean it. I will bring you guys to the office if I need to. I really am sorry. When I get home, I'll tell you what happened."

"Can you put your mom back on the phone?"

"Hey Frank."

"I can't believe I let them down."

"You didn't. They're upset but they'll get over it. You just hurry home. I love you."

"Love you too. See you in a bit." He needed something to ease the tension at home. A quick stop for ice cream made him feel a bit better. He managed to make it home before it had time to melt. Everyone was sitting around the TV in pajamas. "I'm home. And I brought a little I'm sorry treat".

Kelsey got up and came to greet him with a kiss. "Aww, how sweet of you."

The kids refused to even look away from the screen. He went to their spots on the couch kissed their foreheads and handed them their ice cream. "Listen, I'm really sorry, but they needed me. They found the signal from the Phoenix VII. I needed to do some work to get a rescue plan in place."

The frown on the twins' faces softened upon hearing the news. "Sorry we were mad at you." Mia got up and gave her dad a hug. "Ben, don't be a dick."

Ben followed suit. "I guess I forgive you, but this weekend you're all ours."

"You bet."

"Honey, listen we're glad you came home but don't they need you back tonight."

"Probably, but you guys are more important to me."

"Listen, we're fine. You go do what you need to do. I'll take care of the kids tomorrow."

"Yeah dad go ahead." Mia nudged her brother on the side.

"Yeah go on."

"Thanks guys. I promise I'll make it up to you."

Frank said goodbye and headed back to work. This time there was no one around to take his car. The parking garage was nearly empty except for the few overnight crew. Inside he found Daniel eating pizza while he worked.

"What are you doing back?"

"Well my family figured you guys needed me more than them right now."

"Well, have some food. I'm guessing you haven't had a chance to eat yet."

"Yes please." Frank grabbed a slice and started looking over the work Daniel had managed to cover in the last two hours. He set in continuing the calculations. Security checked in on them throughout the night, bringing around food and coffee in abundance.

With the arrival of the main workforce, Frank and Daniel were just putting the final touches on their strategy to reach the Phoenix VII. With notes in hand Frank took his familiar place at the front of the control room.

"Good morning everyone. Now as you have all heard, the distress beacon from Phoenix VII was detected by a satellite. There is an incredibly good chance everyone is still alive. We need to get the contact established as soon as possible. I've had Daniel send all of the data to your computers. We need to begin work immediately to get the Deep Space Relay Satellite up and running." He took control of the main computer and adjusted the front display. A predictive route showed up on one side, and the layout of the Satellite on the other. The keyboards clacked aloud. It was the sound of hope. The curvature on the predictive map slowly changed. The figure of the jet systems turned on the display. It was off to a rendezvous with Venus then on to the ship. This was the moment of truth.

Sophie

"Now which way was I going again?" Sophie needed to get back on track after spotting a puddle of water. Yesterday a loud explosion echoed through the forest, followed by a billowing cloud of smoke stretching into the sky. The only thing it could be was the ship. In order to keep herself heading in the right direction she used a little trick she discovered while working out the surroundings of the lab. Purple leafy projections, which sporadically grew up out of the dirt, always pointed north.

At this point she was outside the area she had memorized around the lab. The entire landscape was foreign. "Okay I was heading for the base of the five ribbon trees all growing together." She scanned the area. "Well I guess I'm just going to trust my instincts."

She checked the sky to see how much daylight she had left. The sun was still riding high atop its apex. The bright light that occasionally flew through the sky was there again. It had to be the asteroid that knocked them out of the sky. It was the only thing she could imagine it to be.

"Fuck you! You fucking piece of shit! This is all your fault!"

It helped to think that something tangible landed them here rather than just a string of bad luck. Once she got off this planet it was going to be her mission to destroy that asteroid.

The ground grew rockier underfoot. Soon all signs of dirt were gone. A large path of rocks weaved through the forest, devoid of any signs of plant life. It seemed to be some form of a river bed. Unfortunately, the water had dried up long before she got there. She ventured on. At this point the only thing distracting her from the pain of walking, was knowing she had a chance to get back to the others.

Little creatures darted ahead of her. Scampering could be heard in the branches high above. For a second, she thought she saw a familiar gray color. "No way. It can't be." The grey soon became more pronounced. She pressed on knowing what lay just ahead. Another grey shape appeared, followed by another. The definition of fanned out branches confirmed her suspicions. This was the magic forest from before. This time she refused to let it trap her inside the twisting maze. Instead of venturing into the middle she remained along the edge. They seemed to stretch on for miles. At one point she checked the ground just to make sure she was actually moving forward.

With the sun beating down on her it seemed like a perfect time to rest. The shade from one of the magic trees beckoned her with its enticing comfort and the promise of rest against the trunk. It could only be a short stop. Or at least that's what she told herself. Sitting down was a mistake. Standing back up hurt too much.

"Guess I'm just gonna stay here a bit longer."

Her weary body sunk in. Her heavy eyes drooped.

A new surprise greeted the exhausted Sophie. The ground beneath her shook violently. It heaved around, every which way. Sitting upright was virtually impossible. *Was this what caused the explosion? If so, were the others all right?* Without warning, Sophie found herself rapidly rising into the air. *The trees are growing again.* She had to get off now. By the time the thought entered her mind any hope of escape was gone. All around her, the trees shot skyward on the tops of large mounds. The large root system twisted around. A strange yellow gem appeared to be embedded inside the dirt mound. Trying to hold on for dear life she noticed that all the other tree mounds had the same gem.

Looking down, the roots attached to the base looked almost leg like. In fact, they were legs. The trees were attached to the backs of gargantuan beasts and Sophie found herself atop one of them. Fully emerged and standing fifteen feet in the air, the beast lurched forward. The idea of being thrown off terrified her. Her only recourse was to jump. A few deep breaths settled her mind. She focused on one solid point on the ground and launched herself into the air, narrowly missing one of the tentacle plants. A heard of the tree beasts carried the magical forest on their backs. The forest bowed to the sides making way for the bodies of the mighty beasts. Underneath their bellies, large, circular mouths lined with icicle sized teeth, closed up and retracted inside. The ground they left behind was crumbled and dusty. Heavy prints marked where the legs passed over. The weight so pressing, water rose from the prints.

Sophie was unsure whether to flee in terror or sit in wonder at the remarkable events unfolding. Tiny creatures whose backs were not much higher than Sophie's head weaved between the legs of the large ones. They continued playing around oblivious to Sophie's presence.

"Which would be more believable at this point? A magical forest appearing as if from nowhere or that the forest was truly a group of creatures buried in the ground." She laughed at the notion of trying to explain this to anyone back home.

With the forests gone now, the end of the field was exposed. An overturned boulder fruit brought back the memories of the night she had run away. The scar from her hands digging into the flesh was still apparent. All the feelings of hurt and loss came flooding back. A few tears ran down her dust-coated cheek. She was certain to make it back now. This stretch was the final push.

She headed into the woods, leaving behind the empty field. There was the ribbon tree she had clamored under. Her dried blood was still visible on the surface. Seeing the sharp rock laying there on the ground sent a twinge of pain through her scarred arms. Instinctively she rubbed the raised surfaces. A part of her longed to pick that stone back up and dig in once again. The pain would be the only thing that mattered. She drew closer to it and cupped it in her hand. It was soft and cool with a sharp edge. She stared at it, fighting the urge inside her. Summoning her newfound strength, she hurled the rock away. It clattered through the branches in the distance. The urge still remained but she had won the battle. Sophie needed to get as far away from this spot as she could least the desire to chase down the rock should appear.

A small clearing up ahead was littered in old footprints of both one of the crew and several creatures. The path was covered in broken branches. As she stepped down on one of the piles, a metal clang came from underfoot. She stepped down again and again came the metal clang. Her boot pushed aside the branches in search of the source. On the ground, slightly rusty but still good, was Rocco's survival knife.

"How did this get out here?" Her words fell on the silent trees. "Well Rocco will probably want it back."

She picked up the blade. There was nowhere for her to store it. The only option left was to carry it all the way back in her hand. The temptation to carve into her flesh returned. She ran her finger over the sharpened edge. This time she couldn't afford the luxury of throwing away the source of her agony.

A foul odor hung in the air, growing stronger the further Sophie got from the sight of the knife. The source was right up ahead. She followed it slowly. Caution was key out here. The two graves were dug up. She knew exactly what the source was without actually seeing it. She pivoted to her left. Bits of sinew clung to the bleached bones of Diego and Carl.

Her stomach became incapable of holding back its contents. With her mouth agape, Sophie unleashed all the food and water she had consumed in the last four hours. The stream flowed off and on like someone playing with a faucet. Her stomach emptied, but for the next few minutes it continued to try and expel what wasn't there.

Diego and Carl deserved better than this.

"What the hell happened here? Diego, why? I miss you so much. This isn't how it was supposed to go."

Convinced she could no longer even attempt to vomit, she grabbed one of the branches and pushed the bones through the soft dirt. The open holes awaited their former residents' return. The remains fell in with no regard for separating one set from the other. Fighting back the horror of seeing her love and Carl like this, she reburied their bones and put them to rest, hopefully for good this time. The soft dirt barely covered the bodies. Small portions of white poked through. There was not much she could do to remedy that situation.

"You would be so proud of me." Sophie sat down next to the stone etched with Diego's name. "I managed to make a fire by myself. I walked forever. Oh, and I caught my own food out there. I almost got crushed by some strange creatures with trees on their backs. And I fought off another who tried to take my stuff from me."

She sat in silence awaiting a response that would never come. All the memories were so fresh. His hands wrapped around her. That shy quiet personality of his. It was as if he had been with her all this time.

Sitting in misery was only making her feel worse. All those nights cold and alone, all those days trying to get back could not be impeded by this setback. Sophie got up, said one final goodbye to Diego, and made her way to the cave.

Knife in hand, she stood at the entrance. Everyone was busy hanging around by the fire unable to see her. "I'm back," Sophie called out.

The others stopped what they were doing, and once they were able to process what was happening, they rushed to meet her. Arms embraced Sophie from all sides. She couldn't move much less breathe.

"Oh, my God, you're alive!" one of the voices cried.

"We looked everywhere for you. Where were you hiding?" That one was definitely Addison. Her voice was unmistakable above all the others.

"I almost died trying to find you. You better have one hell of a story."

"Aww thanks, Trent. I missed you too."

"Seriously, I didn't think you could survive out there."

"Really Taylor?" Sophie weaseled her way out of the group hug. "If you don't mind, I'm really hungry. I may have lost my lunch outside." She stopped and turned around. "Oh hey, Rocco, I thought you might be missing this." The knife flew into the air and landed in the dirt. "Once I'm done eating, I'll tell you everything that happened, and then I want to know why the knife was out there."

The cooked meat was fabulous, juicy, and flavorful. It was better than any fruit or bug she had managed to scavenge up on her little journey. There were no little crunchy pieces to try and avoid. "This is amazing. Where did you find this?" She licked her fingers clean and then reached for a second round.

"Actually, Joseph and Addison caught it." Nova seemed to be worried about Sophie. It was written all over her face and in her voice.

"It was really more of a lucky accident. We were trying to catch something a lot smaller," Joseph added.

"Well whatever you did you should do it again." She filled her mouth. "I mean seriously, wow." Aside from answering her questions, no one seemed to have any intention of interrupting her feast. Halfway through the second chunk of meat, her pace was slowing to a crawl.

"Here, have some water, you look parched." It was so sweet of Rocco to be concerned for her.

"Thanks." The canteen drenched her face, leaving only half the water to actually enter her mouth. Finally feeling satiated, she was ready to recount her journey.

"Where should I start?" She was having a hard time thinking with her stomach so full. "I guess we'll go from when I ran away. So, I ran until it got dark and then sat under a tree crying all night." Sophie turned her wrists over making sure to keep the scars hidden. "Once the sun came up, I managed to find a boulder fruit, and I have to say it was so good. But this meat is definitely better. Though it probably tastes so good because I haven't eaten a lot. But anyway, I walked through this huge field and that's when the rainstorm hit. I got lucky and found a tree with a hole in it so I fell asleep there, and when I woke up, you'll never believe what I saw. I mean I hardly did myself. These large trees, yeah, they looked like trees, had popped up all over the field. I tried to find my way back but, well you know how well that must have worked out. I ended up getting lost and wandered around. At one point I found a swampy area. I don't recommend going back there. I ended up climbing up a mountain to try and find the ship, and I actually did. I found the lab and workout room. The lab was a mess. Broken glass everywhere. One of the samples had a yellow film growing on top of it. The only things worth taking were a striker, some alcohol, and the coats…"

"Wait did you say something was growing on one of the samples of dirt?" Taylor seemed solely focused on this one detail.

"Yeah." Sophie rubbed her eyes. The fatigue was catching up with her. "It seemed like maybe the bacteria had multiplied but I can only really guess."

"Did you smell anything?"

"A hint of sulfur." She couldn't hold herself upright to finish the conversation.

"If we all joined you could you get us back there?"

Why did he want to talk about this now? "I tell you what, I'm just going to lay here right now, but yeah I should be able to." It felt so nice to be back amongst friends. This time she was really hearing their voices and not seeing the mimics. She checked once more just to be sure they were really there. It was a truly calming sight.

Taylor

"Please tell me you've had enough time to rest." The last two days, all Taylor could think about was the bacteria they recovered from Mars. If what Sophie said was true, and he had no reason to doubt her, then the bacteria was adapting rapidly. It was going to be something to behold. Sampling it and running some rudimentary tests would at the very least give him something to do.

Sophie picked herself up. "Yeah I'm good. Now's as good a time as any."

"Yes!" His excitement boiled over. The pure adrenaline rush got him outside before he could say another word.

"Hey, you're not going to make it very far without me you know."

"Fine. But hurry up."

"Not like the bacteria's going anywhere. I mean what's it going to do run away from us?"

Trent spoke up, "I can't believe I'm saying this, but I'm with her."

Is Trent really siding with Sophie? "You know what Trent? I'm starting to think you missed her."

"Or I'm just a lazy motherfucker." A quick nod of Trent's head told Taylor exactly what he was planning to say next.

"Yeah it's definitely the second one." Taylor and Trent both said together.

"You sure we're not related?" Taylor asked.

"I wish man. I'd kill to have had you as a brother. Mine was a useless punk."

Taylor knew deep down that blood or not these people had all become his family. "Can't say I'd have been much better. Now get your lazy ass up and let's go."

"Come on everyone, it's probably best we all go in case the thing that attacked Trent shows back up."

"Yeah what Rocco said."

All Taylor wanted to do was get going. Finally, the rest of the group made their way out of the cave. They truly made a ragtag bunch. All their clothes were in tatters and barely hanging on. The guys all had beards, Taylor and Rocco's being nice and thick. Trent's was long and patchy, and Joseph's was almost non-existent aside from a few wispy hairs. The girls' hair was a mess. Addison was sporting a full unibrow. If someone saw a picture of everyone walking around, they might have confused them for a bunch of prehistoric cavemen.

"Okay Sophie, lead the way."

"Dude just chill. We've got a way to go."

The way into the woods took shape behind Sophie. They wandered between plants, with no real indication of their direction. Sophie would occasionally stop, stare at a purple plant on the ground, and then adjust her path. For whatever reason, these plants were her guide. This continued on and on until they reached a large dirt field.

"So, this is where the magic forest was." Sophie grabbed a chunk of flesh from the nearby boulder fruit. Rather than taking a bite Taylor watched her stuff her pocket full. "We have to cross all the way to the other side."

The excitement Taylor had felt was starting to wear off at the immensity of the field ahead. "You're right. The lab is pretty far out here."

"Oh, we're not close yet. Make sure you keep up." Sophie trekked ahead, leaving boot prints in the soft dirt.

The sun beat down on Taylor's unprotected skin. His boots filled with soft dirt. *There was no way Sophie made this trek.* He watched her lead the group without looking back or even stopping to rest. Occasionally one of the others would force her to stop just to catch their breath. In these moments, the canteen would go around. The water was limited to a few sips each. This continued on for what seemed like hours before they finally reached the far edge. The welcoming sight of shade was just ahead.

The group stopped once more upon entering the forest. This time, however, was at the behest of Sophie. "Things might get a little weird out here. If you hear anything, you know voices, beeping sounds, god forbid screams, don't go after them."

"What kind of screams?" Zea asked seeming nervous to get an actual reply.

Sophie let out a blood-curdling scream, "Wahhhhahgghgh. Something like that."

For a moment Taylor was concerned about Sophie. *Had she really gone crazy out here?* He leaned over to Trent. "I'm worried about her. She seems a bit...unhinged."

"I don't know man. With what I've seen I can't discount her."

The screeching of nearby trippers sent Taylor into panic mode. He looked around for a branch to defend himself.

"Taylor what are you doing?" It was as if Sophie couldn't hear the cries.

"The trippers are back."

No, they're not. Remember how I said not to trust anything you hear?"

"Guys I found food." It was Rocco's voice but it seemed to be coming from somewhere far away despite Rocco being right next to him.

"See? Strange things. Some kind of mimicking creature. Though they're pretty cool looking if you do see one." A gentle wave of her hand and Sophie was off again. "If we don't keep going, we'll never make it there by the end of tomorrow."

The strange sounds followed the group for the next several hours until the sun set. With the oncoming darkness, and no real source of light to speak of, the only option was to stop for the night. Everyone slept, with Rocco and Sophie agreed to take shifts keeping watch.

Taylor and the rest of the crew were awoken by Sophie before the sun's rays had reached the horizon. Groggy, they plodded along. All Taylor wanted to do was get sleep. Walking this much was more than he had been prepared for. This time he was the one dragging the group down. The woods went on endlessly, every plant looking just like the last.

The sun was setting when the sight of the ship came into view. Taylor couldn't believe they were finally there. "Are we actually at the lab or is this some other trick the planet is playing on us?"

Trent punched Taylor's arm.

"Ow! What the hell?"

"Good news," Trent smirked. "You're not dreaming."

"Thanks," Taylor said, rubbing his arm for emphasis.

He hoped the sarcasm was coming through enough. As they approached, the sulfur smell was everywhere. A yellow moss-like layer coated the ground around the ship. Tiny little yellow pods grew from the ground cover. This was even more impressive than he had imagined. "I thought you said the yellow was contained inside the ship?"

Sophie wandered to the edge of the growth. "I never said contained. But it was all still inside the lab when I left."

Taylor took a knee to get a closer look. "The growth rate is incredible. If this is really the stuff we dragged from mars, then that means it was capable of lying dormant on Mars for god knows how long. And as far as I can tell those small yellow bulbs are the means of distribution." He needed to find out as much about it as he could. He grabbed a nearby stick and tested it out. The moss squished under the pressure. The pods bounced around when struck only to resume their position when left alone. He pushed a small clump away from the main bunch. Heat radiated from the pile as if reacting to being separated.

In the dying light, Taylor noticed another peculiar feature. Some of the pods had begun splitting open. A fine white powder coated the insides. "Rocco, hand me the flashlight." He waited for a response refusing to divert his attention from the pods.

A beam of light illuminated the mossy growth. Taylor reached back searching for the flashlight. It made contact with his hand. He used it to scan the opened pods. The gentle breeze picked up the fine powder in a small cloud, particles dancing in the light, and then released them back to the ground. The powder landed on parts of Taylor's face, and clothes. He reached up and brushed himself off. A strong taste of rotten eggs coated the inside of his mouth. He got up and tore the canteen from Addison's hand.

"Ugh I think I'm going to vomit." The taste was overwhelming. A quick swish of water in his mouth cleared it right up. "I need something to eat. Anything that doesn't taste like vomit would be preferred. Hey, Sophie you still have that boulder fruit?"

"Yeah here you go." A lint covered mass emerged from Sophie's pocket.

"You know on second thought, I'm good."

"Whatever, more for me." Sophie bit into the fruit. "We should probably start a fire and hunker down for the night." Juice oozed down her chin as she talked.

Rocco was ten steps ahead of her. A pile of cloth strips sat in front of him waiting to be lit. The steel struck the flint, throwing sparks in all directions, igniting one of the scraps. A few breaths and the fire grew, into a blazing inferno.

Taylor took up next to the flames. Smoke drifted toward him, scratching at his lungs.

"Hugh."

He tried to resist the urge to cough a second time. The more he held back, the more it hurt. Moving spots became the only way to overcome the unbearable smoke. This made no difference, as the coughing fit continued. He put his arm over his mouth to keep from coughing on anyone else. Blood now speckled his skin.

"What the hell?" The coughing fit grew harder. His mouth tasted of metal.

"What's going on?" The surprise from Joseph's voice told Taylor it wasn't just his imagination.

The only response Taylor managed to muster was the word *blood* between coughing fits. His chest felt like it was being pressed down and burned from the inside at the same time. All he wanted was to shake lose the buildup settled deep down. A chunk of phlegm flew up to his throat but brought little relief.

"Zea, I think Taylor's in trouble."

His eyes were watering, making it almost impossible to see Zea walking over.

Her hand pressed against his forehead. "No fever."

Taylor felt his coughing fit grow worse. His reaction time was dropping. His head was dizzy.

"His heart's racing." Zea's cold hands held his left eye open and a brilliant light blinded him. The right eye was next.

Once his eyes readjusted, he saw Zea seated in front of him. His coughing continued. Suddenly Zea's face was covered in blood. It was hard to focus but he was certain she tried to wipe her face clean. Each breath was a struggle.

Nova rounded the fire to join them until Zea stuck her hand out.

"Stay back." Even in his distressed state Zea's worried face was unmistakable. Something was wrong. "I need you all to keep…, ach hugh… Sorry. Keep back. We need to … hughch…Get out of here."

The back and forth of Taylor and Zea's cough grew louder.

"What's going on?" Rocco brought a burning branch nearby.

"The yellow…." It was all Taylor could manage to muster. Talking was impossible at this point. He pointed to the yellow moss that infected him.

Rocco nodded his head. "Okay we need to get moving. Zea will you be able to walk with Taylor?"

"Should be able to."

"Good. Everyone else we need to treat this like a chemical attack. Keep your distance from both of them."

The ground was swelling beneath Taylor's feet. His legs struggled to hold his body up. A few steps and he succumbed to the coughing, falling to the ground pulling Zea down with him. Spots drifted across his field of vision. All he could think about was the pain inside his lungs. Every breath grew shorter and more labored. He had to muster the strength to keep going. A few deep coughs released a bunch of red mucus. He spit it out. His breathing improved enough to get back on his feet and keep walking.

Zea, however, didn't appear to be doing quite as well. She laid curled up on the ground, hitting the dirt with her fist. The coughing was violent and rattling.

"Zea!" Nova stopped and headed back towards them.

"Nova, please…. ughhhh….Zea wouldn't want you to get sick too." Taylor wiped the blood away from his mouth. "You need to stay back."

"Come on Nova. The only thing we can do is lead them back to the cave." Addison wrapped her arms around Nova.

On the ground, Zea's breathing became sparse. Her quiet spell was interrupted by a cough.

"Hack it up." Taylor pounded his fist against her back, hoping to loosen up the mucus building inside her. The pain grew again inside of his lungs. It felt as if he was drowning this time. The agony was immense. He forced himself to stay awake. Falling asleep could spell the end. He realized at that moment that Zea's breaths had stopped altogether.

Addison

Blood encrusted yellow clumps sprouted from the mouths of both bodies. The moss which previously had consumed the lab in a small circle, now formed a larger ring with arms spread up the nearby ribbon trees, and tentacle plants. Red dust was all that remained of the once vibrant life in the center. The metal of the ship's hull was now completely rusted out. It was as if the entire scene had rapidly aged.

Addison was in denial. She refused to accept that she had lost another two members of her crew. The promise she made to protect Zea was broken. There was no time to mourn the dead.

"Let's get back to the cave. We need to get away from this stuff, whatever it is."

"What about the bodies?" Nova was visibly shaken. Her eyes were bloodshot from crying all night.

Joseph placed his arm around her shoulder and pulled her close. "You heard them. We can't take the bodies."

"It's my code to never leave a man behind, but we can't risk catching whatever that is." Rocco grabbed his survival pack off the ground and backed away from the scene.

"She deserves at least half the respect she gave to Carl."

Addison grabbed Nova's arm. "I promise we will have a funeral as soon as we get back to the cave."

Sophie popped a red creature into her mouth. "Yeah we better go. There are some vicious creatures out here. I'd prefer not being caught again."

The group led Nova away from the nightmare. Addison positioned herself between Nova and the bodies to keep her eyes from wandering back.

The further they got; the safer Addison felt. She took full responsibility for everything that had happened up till now. If only she could find a way to change the past. The entire trip back was a solemn journey and talking was kept to a minimum. Every time they would stop to rest the notion that the yellow moss was not far behind got them moving again. That night little sleep was had by anyone. Addison's entire body was on edge. The darkness would make it harder to tell when the impending danger was getting too close.

Light from the breaking dawn afforded the team enough visibility to move out. Addison was completely exhausted both emotionally and physically. She trudged along in silence, as did the rest of the crew. Before long they found themselves at the mouth of the empty field. Knowing they had to cross this large seemingly endless field broke what was left of her spirit. She fell to the ground and refused to move.

Rocco placed his arm around her and whispered in her ear, "I'm sorry for everything. It's alright to feel upset. Hell, I'm furious. But everyone here is looking to you. Just hold on a little longer. I know you have the strength inside you." He picked her up and handed her the last of his boulder fruit. "Eat this and take my sip of water. Then we'll move on."

The food was satisfying, but Addison felt guilty taking Rocco's water rations. She knew it was useless to argue though. Rocco took the canteen back and then led the way into the barren landscape. Clouds rolled in overhead, blocking the sun's vicious rays. Once they reached the other side it wasn't long before familiarity had returned to the surroundings. A sense of safety should have been there but now even the memories of the cave chased after her sanity. Images of open graves and broken friends consumed her. She fought them back with as much strength as she could muster.

Drawing upon the cave brought yet another terrible sight. Signs of a raid upon the encampment were everywhere. Scraps of the bark beast's remains marked the far corners of the clearing. Parts of cloth once rescued from the ship were now torn to shreds. The dirt around the entrance was littered with pockmarks. The team was ill-prepared for a fight. Whatever was inside the cave released a gravelly grunt that seemed to come from all directions of the cave.

A shadowed figure ran through the dark. The lack of light made it hard to distinguish its true nature. With one hand, Rocco pulled his knife from its sheath. The other hand grabbed a rock. Without a word to the others, he lifted his hand to his mouth and gestured them to remain silent. He crept quietly towards the cave, calculating each step he took to minimize the noise. Joseph followed suit with nothing but a stick to defend himself.

The pair disappeared inside the darkness. Rocco shouted from the void, "Trent get in here. You're going to want to see this."

"For some reason I don't trust you guys. Call it intuition if you will."

"No seriously, come check this out." Joseph sounded desperate.

He checked in with each of the others to get their opinions.

Addison couldn't care less about their immature pranks. They had grown stale over the last month. "You're on your own."

"You guys are no help." Wearily, Trent made his way inside. His next words could only be described as a mixture of terror, joy, and confusion. "Oh shit!" his scrawny legs carried him swiftly out of the cave. "Oh shit, oh shit, oh shit." Behind him, a large spiker and three babies poked out of the dark in a full sprint. Trent's footing gave way and brought him to the ground. The small spikers jumped on top of him. Their spikes shaking on their backs. The beaked snouts rubbed at his clothes, and their tails alternated wagging up and down.

The sight was a welcome change, but soon life would be back to the same old routine. Inside the cave the few possessions they had were being played with. A select few beasts were jumping up the walls in a valiant effort to catch the clear bugs crawling around, leaving behind red marks along the stone. One was finishing off what little food had remained in their stores.

The need to get away from everyone was gnawing away at Addison. She felt she could no longer be of any real use. What good was a captain who couldn't protect the people she swore to lead? "I'm going to look for some more food since apparently, these things decided to eat it all."

"I'll come with you."

"No, I'm good Sophie. You stay here and rest with the others."

"Don't have to tell me twice."

Addison left the group behind, unsure where she was going. The goal was to get out of earshot, but not far enough to not be able to get back. These drafty woods held no appeal to her any longer. The long flowing ribbons and large tentacles seemed so ordinary. A small boulder made a nice resting point. She sat there letting the sun warm her skin. With no one around, it seemed the perfect time to enjoy some pleasures from when she was young. The heated rock felt so relaxing under her bare skin. With her eyes shut, and the feeling of warmth fully embracing her she took in the moment.

Raghaagah. A familiar noise lurked overhead. She rolled over to come face to face with a lone tripper. The wings were folded in, and the tripper dove towards Addison. She reached for a nearby object to defend herself but no such item was within her grasp. The bird struck her body.

Addison found herself lying on a strange blue beach. The plants of the ribbon forest jutted from the clear blue water and sand. The smell of ocean air wafted over her nostrils. Her torn clothes had transformed into a tight bikini.

Daniel came running up along the sand. He carried a sea star in his hand. "Look what I found for you." Its pink body still glistened from the water.

Addison took it in her hands and as she did it was no longer a sea star. Now in her hands was a dead tripper. She threw the carcass aside next to the boulder. "Take me to see the boardwalk."

"Of course. We can ride the Ferris wheel while we're there."

He took her hand and pulled her along. Something about him seemed off. His skin was dark yet translucent. His hair resembled grass instead of the lovely brown locks of his youth. As they walked his height fluctuated from being taller than Addison to shorter. His feet left no prints behind. They drew closer to the boardwalk. From afar, Zea approached.

"Zea you're okay. I was so worried you were dead."

"Sorry do I know you?"

"Yeah, it's me, Addison, your captain."

"Sorry, I think you have the wrong person. I'm not military. I haven't even graduated from medical school yet."

Addison didn't understand what was going on. "You don't remember the mission, Mars, the crash?"

"Nope but you seem like fun. Hey, do you guys want to get corn dogs?"

Daniel's eyes lit up at the mention of food. "Honey I could really go for one of those."

"Sure, okay."

They walked off but Addison remained in place. The image of the boardwalk was gone, now replaced by plants. Daniel and Zea walked off into the distance with no idea Addison had fallen behind. The ocean rolled away leaving a barren forest. Her beach morphed back into the forest floor. The boulder Addison had started on was only a few feet away. Beside it a dead tripper laid bleeding out. Her hands displaying signs of a fight.

The sun was now sinking into the distance. If she didn't make it back with food soon, Rocco would start to wonder what happened. Addison grabbed a rock and dug a small hole just big enough to hide the tripper's body next to the boulder. With that out of the way, she located a boulder fruit to bring back to camp and harvested a few chunks.

Upon her return, everyone was gathered around the fire.

"You're back." Trent was sitting in the dirt. "Please tell me you brought me some Chinese or Mexican food. Ahh I could so go for some tacos right now."

The headache and nausea were killing Addison. She was having a hard enough time focusing on what they said to know how to respond. Instead she tossed the fruit at the others without a word.

"Hey you okay?" Nova put her arm around Addison.

"Yeah, just dealing with a lot."

"We hear ya." Joseph tossed her the canteen. "Take a seat. We just got the fire going. Rocco here was just about to tell us how he got wrangled into riding a bull."

"Yeah it's not that great a story."

All Addison could do was nod in agreement. If she didn't things would just get harder.

"All right. I grew up with two sisters and a brother. We always used to mess with each other. You know pranks and fighting. Typical sibling stuff. So anyway, there was this girl I had a crush on but was too afraid to talk to."

"Real shocker there."

"Shut up Trent." Nova wasn't having any of his crap.

"As I was saying, there was a girl I liked, and my brother knew it. He convinced both of my sisters to pretend like they heard the girl talking about how much she loved bull riders. Well, I wanted to impress her so I signed up for the competition. I practiced every day for weeks. Finally, the day of the competition came around. I was shaking in my boots. The bull's name was Ripper because he was known for goring guys. I was bound and determined to do it but my body was fighting me. My brother helped me get on the bull. The alarm went off and the door opened. The bull started rampaging with me barely holding on for dear life. It seemed like an eternity, but when I fell the clock only read three seconds. Spread out on the ground the bull's front hoof came down on my left leg. Lucky for me it missed the bone. Well after all that I found out the girl I liked wasn't even in town that weekend."

All the talking was getting to Addison. She just wanted to sleep off the hangover. Not saying a word, she left the fire and went to sleep in the corner. No dreams disturbed her slumber.

By the time she awoke the group was already active, milling about the cave.

"Morning sleepy." It was Joseph who noticed her first. "Man, you were snoring like a wild hog last night."

Addison gestured for him to go away. He was disturbing her before she even had a chance to finish waking up. She got herself up and scrambled over to the fire. The boulder fruit was waiting in a juicy pile. She bit in, uncaring about appearances. The juice soaked her hands and chin. Bits of chewed flesh flew from her open mouth. The piece she held onto vanished quickly. Her clothes made quick cleanup work of the leftover juice.

The day, from that point on, just dragged along. The group played a game of charades, but Addison felt no interest. In fact, the only thing she wanted was to go back to that boulder and dig up the tripper. She needed a reason to get away. After a few rounds she finally came up with the perfect excuse. She headed out of the cave knowing they would question her motives.

"Where you going?" Rocco asked exactly as she expected.

"Oh, my period's starting, and I thought getting some of those numbing fruits might help."

"All you," Trent said with disgust.

"I'll join you." Nova was always so willing to help with anything Addison needed.

"I kind of want to go alone."

"You sure? I mean it's kind of dangerous out there."

"Yeah I'm good. I'll be right back." She took off before they could question her anymore. She headed towards the fruit vines until she was out of sight in case someone should get the bright idea to watch her. Now was her chance to veer off towards the boulder from yesterday. It took some doing but she made it.

The fresh dirt still covered the hole she buried the tripper in. Addison pushed it away revealing the body inside. She picked it up and scratched the claws along her stomach so as not to draw attention from the others when she got back.

This time Addison was transported to the passenger seat of a car.

Zea manned the helm. Rather than a steering wheel, she gripped what looked like the wheel from a ship as she drove them through the ribbon forest. "You know this is my favorite place in the world. The colors are so pretty here."

"I don't know, I think I like the coastal highway better." She stared out at the tentacle plants and ribbon trees. They seemed to be moving yet the scenery didn't change. Even the lumpy plants remained stuck in place. The radio played a strange melody. It almost seemed familiar yet every time Addison thought she recognized the tune, it changed. "How's Nova doing?"

"Nova? Who's that?"

You know, your girlfriend." *Why didn't she remember Nova?*

"Oh, you're so funny. Just because my boyfriend's a little girly sometimes doesn't mean he is one." Zea placed her hand in front of Addison. "Actually, we're engaged."

"Oh my god!" Addison couldn't help but scream. She was so excited for Zea. Suddenly a boulder appeared in front of the car.

"Zea, watch out." But it was too late. The car slammed into the boulder and disappeared from around Addison, and Zea along with it. The forest was back to normal. The realization that she needed to get the fruit to belay suspicion hit Addison. She felt less sick this time. Her body seemed to be adjusting to the after-effects, though the trip didn't last quite as long this time. It took all her strength to find her way through the forest and to the painkillers. One bite was all it took to lace her breath with the scent. A few in the pocket would help her story later.

Sophie was outside the cave collecting bits of dead branches from the ribbon trees and orange bubble trees. Each stick she picked up had been sharpened to a point. "Oh, you're back." she picked up one of the spears and stuck it into the ground, the dull end pointing into the woods beyond. "The others are inside if you wanna join 'em. Otherwise pick up a stick and get sharpening."

Not wanting to seem suspicious, Addison wandered inside. The moment she entered the cave, all their eyes were on her, judging her. They knew what she had been sneaking off to do. Hoping to throw them off she pulled the numbing fruit from her pocket. "I got the fruit. Sorry I was gone so long. I decided to stop and play with the spikers."

"Really, because they were just here." Trent knew.

All her efforts went into figuring out how to get herself out of this one. The wheels in her head turned frantically. "Umm. Actually, I was playing with the babies. They were just too cute to ignore."

"They are cute, aren't they?" Nova joined in agreement.

It was working. She tried to keep a straight face to help sell the lie.

"Damn, and here I've been working this whole time," Trent said before resuming his task. He had a large hole dug into the softer portion of the cave entrance. "How much bigger do you want the hole?" He turned to Joseph.

"Not much bigger. I'll go get the metal sheets tomorrow and see if we need to dig more."

They bought it. She couldn't believe how easy this was. The thought of the wounds on her stomach made Addison place her hand over them. *Oh god I hope they didn't see that.* She needed to come up with an excuse in case anyone saw the strange gesture. "Man, I'm hungry. Anyone got any food?"

"No, we finished off everything we collected yesterday and Joseph wants to finish building an underground storage place for whatever we bring back." Rocco was busy working on his own project. He had small chunks of ribbon from the trees. A few square-shaped chunks laid on the ground in front of him.

Wanting to seem normal, Addison picked up one of the chunks from the ground. Its center contained the letter A and a diamond. "Are you making playing cards?"

"Yeah I figured it would give me something to do. Plus it's something we can all use to keep busy."

"Good thinking. By the way what is Sophie working on?"

"Who knows? She said something about a defensive border. I figured it was best to let her do her own thing." Addison sat down and watched Rocco work. Her gaze locked onto his hands but her mind wandered. The image of that rock with the means of escape buried next to it was all she saw. The feeling of absolute peace in a world all her own. Maybe next time would bring her back to her childhood or let her talk to a long-dead family member. These thoughts kept her up well into the night long after the others had given up their tasks for the day and made their way to bed.

The snoring of the group was sporadic and asynchronous. Addison needed to get out and clear her head, but first she made her way around to each person ensuring they were asleep. Rocco was passed out on his back. As a former military man, he could sleep soundly anywhere. Nova was more restless. Small whimpers crept from her mouth as she tossed and turned. Lucky for Addison, her eyes remained shut. Trent and Joseph were heavy sleepers and could sleep through anything. She quietly crept to the world outside. One of the crew could be heard rustling behind her. *Shit, I forgot about Sophie.*

Sophie sat up. "What's happening?" She rubbed her eyes as if trying to clear them.

Addison froze, there was no good way for her to explain where she was going. She stammered, looking for the words to cover her true purpose in leaving. "I... just...well...the air outside."

"Give me back my bear jerk. Don't make me kick you."

"What bear?" Addison had no idea what she was talking about. "No one has your bear."

"Leave me alone."

Addison realized Sophie wasn't actually awake. She was talking in her sleep. "It's okay. Go back to sleep."

"You know I never said that about you." Sophie laid her head back down.

With that out of the way and the assurance that everyone else was fully asleep, Addison stepped into the cold night air. The darkness was all-consuming. In her haste, she had forgotten that there was no moon to light her path. If she was going to get back to the rock, she would need light. Carefully she passed through the sleeping bodies and to the fire. One long branch caught her eye. She plucked it from the flames and held the burning end in the air above her head. The light provided just enough illumination for her to reach the source of her craving.

The red light bathed the stone, dancing along its surface. The fresh dirt covering the means of Addison's freedom remained undisturbed. A quick jerk from her hand planted the torch into the ground. She dug into the dirt until the rancid smell of rotting flesh brought tears to her eyes. She needed to work quickly otherwise, the smell would become unbearable. The cold body was hard to miss. It was still intact and hopefully was still powerful enough for one more trip. All it took was the claw scratching her hand and she was off.

The world around her didn't change but a shadowy figure of her husband appeared, unaffected by the red glowing light. "I packed your bags in the car, we're all set to go."

"What are you talking about?"

"What do you mean? Are you trying to say you forgot you're in labor? Man, I figured that would have knocked out your sense of humor."

"What do you mean pregnant. I'm not…" Addison looked down at her huge belly. It was covered in stretch marks where the scars from the tripper's claws had been. A strange sensation came from inside, moving and kicking around. A contraction hit her entire body. "Ahhh!"

"It's okay just breathe. Close your eyes and breath."

Trying to make the contraction stop, Addison did as she was told. Once the pain stopped, she opened her eyes this time to find herself in a hospital gown. Daniel was a little more visible. His face had a vague outline of cheekbones, and a nose. Black shadows covered his lovely eyes.

"When I say, I need you to push." Zea's disembodied head sat between Addison's legs. The hospital only had one wall; the rest of the room was comprised of the forest. Yet for some reason she knew she was in the hospital.

"I can see the head. Give me one more big push."

Addison pushed with all her might.

"Congratulations, it's a baby boy."

The baby let out a strange crackling noise.

"Can I hold him?" Addison saw the baby float in mid-air towards her. She put out her arms to grab ahold. The far wall changed as the baby flew. It now displayed a mountain with strange yellow tendril-like paths reaching around it. The baby moved into her arms disappearing little by little the closer it got. The wall dissolved and the IV morphed into a ribbon tree. Zea and Daniel were gone. In the distance she could see the sun rising. The embers on the tip of the stick had grown cold.

The only thing that remained from the high was the mountain with yellow arms. For some reason, the yellow looked familiar.

The whole way back Addison wracked her brain about the yellow pattern. Once back she noticed the others were still asleep. *Maybe in the morning I can give them a reason to follow me to where they can see it for themselves and I'll act like I didn't realize it was there.* Sold on her new plan, Addison laid down where she started the night and closed her eyes. *Where do I remember that stuff from? It's like I just can't get it straight.* As sleep began to take hold she sat up. "The ship!"

Rocco and Sophie stirred in their sleep.

Crap I said that out loud. Addison checked to make sure no one had woken up. Satisfied, she laid her head back down. *If that's the stuff we saw near the ship we're in trouble.* She closed her eyes and waited for the others to awaken.

Joseph

The sun shone through the red ribbons overhead, casting strange dancing shadows across the ground while large blue tentacles waved in the breeze. It was a perfect day to be out and about, yet the reason behind the outing seemed vague at best. Joseph agreed to go along after some convincing from Nova that it was better for morale if everyone stuck together. The path Addison led them on was a twisted one. Often, they found themselves passing the same green blob plant or circling a long-dead ribbon tree.

"Sorry guys we're almost there." Addison kept her eyes locked on the ground only looking up to stare off into the distance from time to time.

Trent seemed annoyed from all the aimless wandering. "You sure about that? I mean, you've been saying that for the last hour."

"Just a little further I promise." The forest seemed to open around them.

Through the thinning trees Joseph thought he spotted a large creature bounding along. He picked up speed breaking from the group only temporarily. His foot fell out from beneath him. He fell to the ground beside a small hole that had stolen his footing.

Nova ran over and clutched his ankle. "You alright? Does it hurt?"

"Nothing I haven't dealt with before." All Joseph could do was stand up and try to keep his weight off it. He winced as pain shot through his sore ankle, attempting to stabilize on the stretched tendon. "I'm good to go." He winced.

"Sit down. I'll hang back here with you." Her soft hands grabbed ahold of the quickly swelling ankle. She gave it a gentle rub. "Is this helping at all?"

"Seems to be." The moment was serene, with a beautiful girl taking care of him. Leaving this situation was the last thing he wanted to do, but if he didn't start moving his ankle it would stiffen up, and then he would be even worse off. Reluctantly, he stood up and limped around.

The blood flowing through his veins helped to dull the pain ever so slightly.

Nova looked on like a mother bird watching her chick learn to fly, ready to jump in but not wanting to undermine its efforts.

Joseph stopped to gain his composure, fighting back the need to rest. Looking off into the distance he noticed the mountain seemed off somehow. He focused his attention on its towering peak. What should have been a red and blue speckled landscape was being covered by yellow veins embracing the face of the mountain. The yellow seemed to branch out in all directions, masking any other colors it encountered along the way. He glanced around to ensure he was seeing things correctly. If what he thought he saw was real it meant the Mars moss was advancing faster than they had anticipated. "Nova look at that mountain." He pointed his finger in an attempt to guide her focus towards what he was staring at.

"Why is it yellowing? Is that what I think it is?"

"Yeah, I'm sure it's the mars moss. We need to get the others back."

"I'd say we should just wait for them to get back, but Addison seemed to be just wandering aimlessly, and I feel like it could go on forever."

His best course of action was to find the others, but being unable to chase after them, he decided to hold his hands up to his mouth and shout towards their last known location. "Hey Guys, get your asses back here. There's something you need to see." No response. "I really need you guys to get back here. Addison, Rocco, Trent, Sophie. The fuck are you guys?" Realizing shouting was futile he headed back to Nova to rest his ankle.

Hurried footsteps, which were barely discernible, traveled through the forest. They must have heard his pleas.

Trent was the first to reach Joseph. As he broke from the forest, he stopped in his tracks. His eyes widened. Sophie, who was right behind him, hadn't been paying attention and slammed into him, sending them both hurtling forwards.

"What the hell, why'd you stop?" Sophie brushed the bluish dirt from her knees and hands.

"The mountain. It's covered in yellow."

"Yeah," Joseph limped over to Trent. "That's actually why we called you guys back."

"What's going on?" A tired sounding Rocco asked, arriving well behind the other two.

"Just look at the mountain." Joseph was already tired of telling people that, but it was the only way to get them to understand the direness of the situation. "The mars moss is heading this way."

"But how did it reach the front of the mountain already?" Rocco stared in disbelief.

"Not sure. Taylor would have known, but since he's not here all we can do is guess really."

Addison finally returned to the others.

Not wanting to repeat himself, Joseph gave a glance towards Trent, who seemed to read his mind. "The Mars moss is heading our way. It's halfway down that mountain over there."

Her face inexplicably lit up. It was as if she knew they were going to see it. "That explains why you were hollering for us. What are we gonna do about it?"

Rocco stepped in. "We need to figure out a way to stop it. I'm sorry, Addison, but whatever you were looking for isn't worth finding right now. That needs to be our focus."

"Hey, no I get it." It seemed strange that Addison was so ready to shrug off the search for whatever it was she dragged them all out to find.

The options looked bleak. Joseph wasn't sure that they could do much of anything. "What do you suggest we do? We can't touch it or breathe in the spores. Maybe burning it might make an impact?"

"We need to figure out how fast it's spreading too." Sophie dragged her foot through the dirt drawing a mountain and a hole for the cave. "If it's advancing towards us, we could easily move. But we all saw what it did to just that small chunk of the ship. If it hits the main hull, we could lose any possible resources left."

"Don't forget the beacon. I need to know how long I have to make it portable."

"K, let's get back to the cave. Joe you can rest your leg, and we can figure out our plan of attack for tomorrow." Rocco was the planning type. He never seemed to make any rash decisions without thinking them through first.

Joseph struggled all the way back, placing all his weight on the right foot then briefly shifting his weight to the left one just long enough to bring the right one forward. By the time he arrived back his ankle was throbbing and his hip was sore. He tried to make himself comfortable inside the cave, but no matter how he sat it brought no relief only more suffering. *Maybe a nice cold dip in the river will numb everything.*

A piece of ribbon tree burned bright enough to lite up the path through the narrow passage, flickering against the smooth walls. Each step was deliberate and well thought out so as not to slip. Beyond the reach of his torch lied impenetrable darkness. Inch by inch he made his way towards the growing sound of rushing water. Sweet relief was not far off now. Just ahead, a soft light that was not his own, reflected off the tunnel walls. Someone had already beaten him to the river. A small pile of shredded clothes greeted him at the entrance to the chamber. Humming intermingled with the roar of the waterfall. It was unmistakably a woman's voice. Joseph crept towards the ledge to see who laid below.

Standing in the water, Nova was busy washing her hair. The fire danced across her dark skin and glistened off the water. She almost looked angelic standing there with not a care in the world, clueless that anyone around was watching her. Old scars covered her back. Since the first day of training, Nova's back had remained hidden from all but Zea. He had no idea that this was the secret she had been hiding. Deciding he would be better off leaving, Joseph turned and headed out.

"Joseph, what are you doing?"

The unexpected response caused him to do an about-face. "I was just coming to ice my ankle in the water, but I didn't know anyone was here."

"Don't let me stop you." Nova pulled her hand from the water and waved him over.

Joseph couldn't believe his eyes. This gorgeous lady standing in front of him was completely naked. Not only that but she now encouraged him to join her. He stripped off his pants to expose the bruised, and swollen ankle. He clambered down the ledge, stepping into a shallower region of the stream. The chilled current bit at his legs. He waded over to the sandy bank and took a seat.

"Does it feel like it's getting any better?"

"I can put a little pressure on it now. I'm hoping that'll get me mobile again."

Nova left the lake and joined Joseph on the bank. "You know Zea would have known the best way to treat that." Her voice wavered as she spoke Zea's name. The water masked the tears, but Joseph knew they were there. He stepped from the river and over to Nova, his arms outstretched. Her chilled body nestled into his and she placed her head against his shoulder. She began shaking, not from the cold, but from her feelings of loss. Joseph pulled her in tight, his hands touching the scars on her back. Whatever had caused these had left a wound she would never forget, but it seemed the loss of Zea had an even larger impact on her.

He tried to talk over the muffled cries, "She loved you, you know. You managed to pull that shy little girl out of her shell, time and time again."

Nova took her head off his shoulder and leaned back, locking eyes with him.

"If it weren't for you, she never would have left the wreck. And if not for that, you would never have had the chance to share that brief but beautiful time with her." Joseph felt drawn to her. His thoughts were no longer concerned with his ankle and hip. The flames created a romantic atmosphere. He closed his eyes and pressed his lips against Nova's. His passion flowed through him, yet the actions went unreciprocated. A strong force pushed against his chest. Nova's lips left his.

"What are you doing?" Nova broke free from his embrace and covered her exposed body. "Are you crazy? What made you think I wanted that? Don't come near me." She waded through the water in a furious march.

Joseph trailed after her trying to explain. "I'm sorry, I just thought we connected."

"Shut up. I don't want to hear it."

He followed behind her continuing to apologize, but it fell on deaf ears.

"Shut up. Just stay here and don't follow me." She made her way up the ledge and tried to pull herself up from the water when a rock broke loose beneath her foot. Nova tumbled backward and into the river. A large plume of water leaped into the air, temporarily shielding her body from Joseph's gaze.

As the water rained back down, it landed on a still body. Red strings spread through the water. Joseph tried to reach Nova, but the river pulled her away. He slogged through the water trying to grab ahold, always just out of reach. The water carried her into the tunnel ahead. With all his effort Joseph pushed forward. The water grew deeper and deeper around him. The light from the fires was starting to dwindle away. Nova floated away into darkness. The only remains were dark spots in the water surrounding Joseph that quickly followed along with the current.

There was no hope of seeing her in the dark. Joseph turned back and grabbed a ribbon torch. He jumped back down into the river and waded into the dark but no glimpse of Nova could be found anywhere. He searched till the flame was all but gone. Devastated, he turned back.

Nova's clothes still sat strewn about the landing above the lake. Seeing these brought tears to Joseph's eyes. He collapsed on the ground.

"What did I do?" He looked down at his swollen ankle. "This stupid fucking ankle. If I had just watched where I was walking. Why didn't I resist kissing her? It's all my fault. She shouldn't have felt like she needed to run away. Goddammit. Maybe she's still alive. If I wait here maybe she'll come walking out of the tunnel and be ok."

He stared hopelessly at the tunnel.

"If only I could turn back time. Do something different. What do I do? I need to tell the others. But they'll blame me."

The light went out but Joseph refused to move. The glowing embers crackled in the silence. He didn't know what to do next.

A light broke from the entrance to the room, breaking Joseph's self-punishment. Rocco stepped out bearing a torch of his own, blinding Joseph.

Rocco seemed confused. "Why are you sitting in the dark? Wasn't Nova with you? I swear I saw her come in here ahead of you. Have you been crying?"

He wiped away the tears from his face. "She's gone. I upset her and when she tried to leave, she fell. I chased after her but the river took her away. I looked. Really. But I couldn't find her."

"Where did she go?" Rocco picked up the torch and ran towards the water leaving Joseph behind on the ledge.

"I checked. No matter how far I went I couldn't keep up. I had to go back for a light and then she was gone."

"Was she moving?"

I mean, the river was carrying her but no she wasn't. There was blood pouring out of her." The guilt was eating away at him. He knew Rocco knew. His mouth moved as if on its own, "It's all my fault."

"I thought you said she fell?" The voice echoed back.

"She did, but she wouldn't have fallen If I hadn't upset her," he shouted, the guilt weighing heavily on him.

"I'm not seeing her. I'm afraid she's gone." The light drifted back upstream. Rocco pulled himself out of the water and over to Joseph. "Now listen to me. It wasn't your fault. When we get back let me do the talking okay?"

"Why are you helping me? I'm a monster." Joseph felt like throwing up at the thought of what happened. Visions of him smiling and forcing Nova up the ledge and making the rock fall, filled his imagination. He knew deep down he could find no redemption. Her judging face when he had kissed her would haunt his dreams. It was stuck on a loop. A never-ending self-torture.

Rocco comforted him the whole way back to the main room, but his attempts seemed disingenuous and shallow. Joseph knew exactly how the others would react. He plotted a way to run as soon as he got back to the others before Rocco could tell them what had happened. He was all set. His plan felt flawless, but when the time came, he couldn't move. Seeing the others relaxing just made him feel even worse. They had no idea what news was about to strike them. He tried not to sob.

"Addison, Sophie, Trent, come here," Rocco beckoned. "I have something to tell you."

"What's going on?" Sophie said nonchalantly.

Trent refused to move. "Just tell us from there, or you can come over here."

Addison reached out and slapped his head. "Get up you lazy shit."

He rubbed the back of his head. "Dude, seriously? I'm going. I'm going. Man, this better be good. I just got comfortable."

"There was an accident by the waterfall. Nova fell into the river from the ledge and drowned. Joseph tried to save her but didn't make it in time."

"So, you just left her in there?" Trent asked.

"Actually, she floated down the river. We lost sight of her."

Silence fell. This time the devastation seemed worse than with the others. Nova was the glue that held the group together. Instead of accusations and disparaging remarks, the group fell into a depression. No one said anything. His guilt felt even heavier.

Addison was the first to move. She took off on her own out of the cave. No one chased after her.

Joseph needed to make this up to the group some way. He wasn't sure how. He figured some fresh air might help. Outside the cave he still felt the judging eyes of Nova locked onto him as she fell. He wandered back to the site of the original crash. All the memories of Nova and the others came back one by one. Upon seeing the metal beast, he knew what he had to do. With the Mars moss coming, he could make the distress beacon portable all by himself. That would get the others to forgive him.

He climbed over the collapsed remains of the observation deck, now a twisted mess of metal and wires. It was a dangerous game he played in this broken jungle gym. The transmitter remained just as he had left it. The dish was still pointed skywards. The battery had run dry. If this was going to work, he needed to shrink the dish. There was no way a large object like that would allow for movement through the ribbon trees. To make the entire antenna system portable, he needed to first create a smaller version of the dish to connect the feed horn to. The ground made a passable substitute for a whiteboard. He scribbled tirelessly for hours, etching mathematical formulas into the surface. At last he had the perfect specs for his makeshift dish onto which he would attach the feed horn.

Joseph grabbed scraps of metal and bent them around, checking his curvature as he went. The outside edges folded over to help hold its shape and secure the overlap. He banged at the bottom and sides with a rock to curve the edges into the desired shape. It wasn't pretty but it would do the job. He found a clamp lying in the heaps around him and attached it to the dish. Now came the hard part. The feed horn was attached to wires and a metal box. He had to open the horn to remove the wiring. Without tools it was a delicate process. His hands were shaking while he tried to loosen the connections and feed the wires through the metal hull. He had no concern for the old dish, ripping it up to free the important part.

The relay box was already exposed from when he hooked up the battery. It was still attached to the wall. A few hard hits with a metal pole broke it loose. Joseph picked it up and hooked up the horn to the wires once again. Everything seemed to come together perfectly. The battery would have to be carried separately, but it was small enough to not be a problem.

One look at his work and Joseph noticed bloody fingerprints all over it. He had been oblivious to the metal tearing up his hands. It was a small step in his ultimate penance. His conscience still ate away at him but he could at least do something to help the others. The components all sat nicely inside each other. He carried the creation back to the cave.

Maneuvering along the forest floor, he stumbled on his still sore ankle and sent the dish hurtling forward, his body rammed face-first into the ground. The emotions took over and he started to cry uncontrollably. He had failed everyone twice now, first with Nova and now with the dish. The parts were in a clump a few feet ahead. He had wrecked all his hard work. There was no way he could repair it this time. He hit himself out of frustration. Failure was all he ever knew in life, and this was just adding to that. He picked the broken pieces up to check for damage. Despite his worries everything seemed ok, but something had to be wrong. He checked everything again. No signs of damage anywhere. He still believed that some internal damage had broken the system, but until he filled the battery backup there was no way of knowing. He put all the pieces inside the dish and continued.

Once he was at the cave Addison, Trent, and Rocco seemed to not realize he had returned. Without a word he set up the satellite outside and wandered in to get Rocco's canteen. At this point the three others had finally grown interested in what he was doing and were watching silently. He dumped the water inside the battery's wells. The box sprang to life and the antenna started beeping. It was a miracle. The others joined him in a cheerful shout. Should the Mars moss hit the ship, they still had a way for NASA to find them.

Rocco

Under normal circumstances, Addison's disappearance would be of no consequence; however, with the recent events Rocco was worried about her. She'd stayed out all night with no sign that she would return. He took to the cold morning in search of her. The ground was damp from the morning dew. Her tracks were still visible in the blue dirt. Judging by their direction she seemed deliberate in her path, and the large gap between steps meant she was in a hurry. Focused on only the footsteps, Rocco had no idea where he was, or where the trail would lead him. He had to find her. If her strange behavior the last few days was any indication, she was in danger.

A loud squawking noise came from just ahead. It sounded like the noise they had heard when Trent freaked out and screamed that the trippers were back, only this time there were multiple creatures ahead. A large boulder jutted from the ground. Overhead a set of hideous creatures circled in the air. They fit the description of the trippers to a tee. Addison's footsteps led directly towards the boulder. He removed his knife from his belt ready for a fight should the trippers decide to attack. One dove at him, mouth wide open, claws ready to dig in. He swung his blade, lacerating the underbelly. The mass crumpled to the ground, crying out in agony.

The others alerted to their companions suffering, dove towards Rocco. He knew that the claws were what needed to be avoided. He readied himself. The first one swooped down. His blade missed, but his fist made contact, sending the tripper colliding into a ribbon tree. The next one the knife cut into its head and stuck. Rocco hurried to pull the body free with his other hand. Anticipating their next move, Rocco kicked his foot into the air and the tripper hit headfirst into his boot. The last one seeing the damage flew off. Before the ones he had dazed were able to get back up, Rocco sunk his knife into their heads.

The threat neutralized, he wiped his blade clean and went around the boulder where a ghastly sight awaited. A blood-soaked body was spread out on the ground. Addison lay smiling, why that was seemed unclear. Her torso had been ripped open. Entrails spilled out of her stomach and onto the ground. Spurts of blood still pushed up and flowed out. She mumbled incoherently.

"Avernus," she struggled to say through blood pooling in her mouth. Her eyes stared directly at the sky. She was oblivious to Rocco's presence and to the fatal wound she suffered. Her hand gripped a desiccated claw from one of the trippers. Without professional help she would bleed out. Not wanting to prolong her death, Rocco mustered up his courage. He closed his eyes and spoke to Addison. "Thank you for everything. You were an amazing captain and friend." Tears streamed down his face. He knew what he had to do. "Goodbye Addison." He sunk the knife into her heart and twisted. Not a scream or flinch came from Addison. Life left her eyes. Her smile however stuck. He closed her eyes and kissed her forehead. There was no way to get the mangled corpse back, given the state it was in.

It was urgent that Rocco got back to the others. There were only four of them left. He refused to lose any other crewmates. This was the first time he had ever left someone behind. It took all his will power not to turn back and drag her broken body along with him. The doomed footprints led Rocco back to the cave. Once again it was up to him to reveal to the others that they had lost another one of their companions.

"I don't see Addison. No luck?" Joseph asked.

Rocco hesitated to respond leaving a long silence. Finally, he mustered up enough courage. "Nope. I can't seem to find her anywhere. Her trail went cold. The only thing we can do is hope she comes back soon." The lies burned his lips. He hoped the false information would appease their curiosity.

"So, you're saying she just ran off and what, decided it was better out there than here?" It seemed Sophie wasn't going to be as easy to convince. "Just seems a bit odd. First Nova had an accident that only you and Joseph were around for, and her body disappeared. Now Addison just happens to be gone, and we are supposed to take your word for it?"

"Fine, I'll tell you the truth, but you're not going to like it." He considered just saying something ridiculous but then thought better of it. "You know what no. Come with me. I'll show you." He dreaded going back to that scene, but tensions were high and this was the only way to hopefully restore some peace. "Well what are you waiting for?" he was already heading down the trail.

"I think I'll stay here. My ankle's acting up." Joseph leaned against the cave entrance.

"Your choice. I'm going. Whoever wants to follow can." He looked back as he marched forward. Sophie and Trent were right behind him. "You guys need to prepare yourselves. It's not an easy sight to see." He pictured their faces twisting in shock even at his statement. He glimpsed behind him hoping for that satisfaction, yet when he did Sophie and Trent seemed more nonchalant than he expected. This just aggravated Rocco. His friend had just died and now he was being forced to show off her body like some piece at a museum.

The moment arrived. The body was just around the boulder. "Go ahead, take a look. But don't say I didn't warn you."

Trent stumbled back. "Holy hell. What happened to her?"

"The trippers got to her."

"Tripper huh." Sophie stared at the body. She took a knee and got up close. "Seems like something anyone could do with a knife."

Rocco pointed off to the side. "There's four that I killed lying over there under that tree. Those bastards ripped her open."

Sophie picked one up by the wing. "Man, you did a number on them."

They finally believed him. "Okay I'm heading back. You can stay here if you want. I couldn't care less." As he spoke a heavy wind blew through the ribbon branches and tentacles. He looked up into the sky and saw a strange white cloud in the distance, that seemed to cling to the ground. "We need to get back now!" He screamed at the others.

"Why what's going on now?" Sophie seemed to still be uneasy about him.

"You remember the Mars moss spores that killed Taylor and Zea? Well there's a cloud of them blowing in on the wind."

It didn't take long for Sophie and Trent to see what he was talking about. Once it blocked the light from the early morning sun, the three instinctively fled away from the scene.

"You guys are back quick," Joseph said as they entered the cave. "Why are you all out of breath?"

Gasping for air, Trent tried to explain. "The Mars moss spores are coming. They were right behind us. We need to get into the other chamber."

"Grab all our stuff and head out." Rocco knew every piece they took meant a better chance of survival. Anything the moss touched might not make it. He then lit four large branches on fire and handed one to each of his companions. We're going to need these. He piled the extra branches into his bag alongside the canteen and remaining survival equipment. "I'll grab the shovel. Sophie you take Joseph's torch and he can carry the distress beacon."

"Are you kidding me?" She picked up the dish. "If he drops this because his ankle gives out, we'll be in trouble. If he drops a torch it'll just keep burning."

Joseph grabbed two torches from Rocco's hands. "I agree with her. I can hold both in one hand and use the other to stabilize myself."

One look outside revealed how quickly the moss was advancing. The sky was a dark haze, the sunlight barely making it through. "We've got to go now." The wind was whistling through the cave. "Hurry." He made his way down the tunnel towards the waterfall. He didn't look back to see if the others were following his lead. His only concern right now was himself. The others appeared one by one, with Sophie pulling up the rear. They listened to the sound of the wind in the chamber above. They sat down there with nothing to do but wait till the wind died down.

No one had any idea how long they had waited but Rocco decided it was worth heading up to see if the spores had settled. It did not take much to see that the white powder now coated most of the inside of the main chamber. There was no going out that way any longer. Any attempt to enter the room would stir up the spores. He turned around and explained the situation to the others. "We need to find another way out of this place. Our current exit's no longer viable."

"Well if it were me, I'd follow the river. It has to come out somewhere." Sophie's logic was on point.

"Let's do it." Trent picked up his torch.

Rocco could see the hesitation in his eyes. He was still being affected by the events form the day before. "Joseph do you feel like you can make it through the river? If you don't think you can make it you don't have to go."

"No… I'll go along." He picked up his torches.

"Okay, let's do it. Same set up as last time. Sophie you take the dish and follow behind me this time."

"I'll follow Trent."

"If that's what you want." Rocco stepped down into the water with his flashlight between his teeth. He waded through the water, venturing deeper into the cave. His beam was incapable of showing how far back the water flowed into the tunnel. He pushed through by the light of his torch, unable to see where his feet were stepping. It was all instinct below the water. The river bent up ahead. He turned the corner and the ceiling sparkled with silver flecks. He pushed on down the tunnel. The water grew colder and the ground slick with growth. His footing was anything but stable. The river turned again leading further down the rabbit hole.

Up ahead, a dark object floated in the water. His heartbeat grew faster. He had experienced so much death, yet the sight of a dead body was something he never grew used too. His light hit Nova's floating corpse. The skin was logged with water. Its color was all but gone. It seemed to be caught on an outcropping, continuously bumping up against the wall repeatedly. A large wound sat at the base of her skull. He made his way towards it. The legs tapped against his beneath the water. He tried not to flinch for fear of falling in the water. He could hear the others behind him gasping as they saw the same sight he had.

He continued past the nightmare. The river continued to lead them deeper and deeper. He was beginning to give in to the cold. He could feel his extremities numbing. The beam from his light continued to point into unending darkness, but something was different. He no longer saw a ceiling in the distance. Hope returned when he reached a large chamber. The light from his torch was no longer the only light. A large hole opened in the ceiling, exposing the sky above, with water trickling into a pool on one end. A series of large steps, each with their own pools of water, carried the water gradually down to the river.

He pulled himself from the water into the first pool. The water was much warmer than the river below. Strange creatures moved through it. Green plants floated along the surface, with bubbles in their stems. Blue moss coated the ledges. He reached down to lift Trent. Next, Sophie handed him the dish and pulled herself up to the first landing. Joseph was the last. He passed his torches up to Trent, and Rocco pulled him up. They could taste freedom. Each level brought them closer to the top.

Rocco pushed himself into the outside world. He stood at the forefront of a large shallow hot spring. Steam floated off the water's surface. It sat alongside several other shallow springs, all connected by white ridges. Strange plants grew out of the dirt with long pink branches that ended in funnels bent over the ponds collecting the steam. Flat mushroom-like plants floated in the middle of the water. A short way from the ponds were tan pillar-like objects, all deformed and rough. Intermingled between them were flat purple disks with white bubbles that pulsated on the surface. This whole scene seamlessly merged with the ribbon forest in the distance.

Rocco leaned down and pulled the others up into the enchanting scene. It felt like they had ventured into a fairytale. The warm water was a huge relief on his numb extremities. He decided that it wouldn't hurt to warm up for a while. He sat back, taking in everything around him. Sophie fell asleep in the pool. The others were leaning back with their eyes closed soaking in the warmth.

A herd of creatures that appeared to have hard double spiral brown shells and six hooved legs wandered over to the farthest pool. A small projection emerged from the front of the creature and then a black organ pushed out from the mouth. They began sucking the water into their mouths and with another trunk-like appendage spat out the white substance around the edge of the pool. After performing this task for a while, they seemed to dance about the pillars and discs. Rocco was seeing the real beauty of this place for the first time.

"Any idea where we're at?" Trent was pouring warm water over his head as he spoke.

"No clue. In all my trips over the mountain I never saw anything like this." It all seemed so foreign to Rocco. "I don't even know what direction the cave's in anymore."

"I don't know where we are either, but damn if this doesn't feel amazing." The swollen ankle of Joseph's emerged from the water. "Look at this, the bruising is nearly gone, and you wouldn't even know it was swollen a few minutes ago. I think I could get used to this."

Sophie roused from her sleep. "As great as this is, we need to find ourselves somewhere to sleep soon. After we sit here a little longer of course." She slouched down in the water.

"These plants are amazing. I've never seen anything like this." Trent touched one of the funnels.

"What about those funny looking creatures," Joseph said.

There was hope in the air, Rocco could feel it, but his own worries couldn't be held back. "I don't think we're getting back home."

"Are you kidding? I built this dish just so they could find us here."

"Say we're on Earth, logically they would have found us by now, but judging by the weird shit around here I would say we're on an alien planet. Now, even if we're in our own solar system, which I don't see how we could be, they would still have to build a ship, and train a crew before they could get to us. That could take ten years easy."

Sophie stepped out of the pool and pulled her wet clothes off. "Thanks for killing the mood. I think I'm ready to head out now. I'm going to go see what's around here."

Joseph joined her along with Trent. Not wanting to be the only one stuck behind Rocco followed along. He wrung out his wet clothes and put them back on. The feeling of damp clothes was awkward and they were difficult to get back on. He let Sophie lead them into the forest. The trees here were a lot farther apart and the tan pillars and purple disks were still present. They had no real idea of where to go, but they searched for anything they could use.

A black object bounced off Rocco's foot. He thought nothing of it until he looked down and saw the ground littered in them. They were all different shapes and sizes. In a neat pile were bits of bark beast flesh and the tail of a spiker. They were in the middle of a feeding ground. He noticed large footprints and a ground-out patch of dirt. Fear gripped him. From everything Trent had described of the beast that attacked him, this seemed like it could be its nest or at the very least it's feeding grounds.

It became obvious Trent felt the same way, as he frantically searched around them. He seemed to be looking for any sign that the beast was close. "We need to get out of here."

That was all the convincing they needed to leave. They spent several hours walking to get them a comfortable distance away from the nest. Clouds were on the horizon and the sun was setting. They needed to get a shelter together before darkness set in.

Rocco and Sophie got to work collecting parts from the ribbon trees to form a lean-to big enough for four. They then took turns using the knife to cut the large cups off a tentacle plant for the room. By the time they got back, Trent and Joseph had the branches set up. They finished the shelter and all settled in.

Trent

The rain fell all around the lean-to. Its soft drops tapped on the tentacle cups. Small drops passed between the edges dripping onto Trent's face. He tried to move in the small space afforded him by the others, but the drops always seemed to find him. Since the storm hit, there was no getting back to sleep. The only other place to go was up against the entrance by the dwindling fire. Its heat filled the space around him. He watched the rain fall next to him. All the creatures seemed to be silenced by the storm. A lightning bolt spread across the sky lighting up the world around him. For a brief moment he could see everything. The darkness returned followed by a loud clap of thunder that shook the very earth beneath him. It awoke his sleeping companions who had no idea what had transpired. Rocco rolled over and began snoring almost immediately.

Joseph, without even opening his eyes just said, "Fuck this," and continued to lay motionless.

"What...What's going on?" A tired Sophie rubbed her barely open eyes.

"Nothing. Just some thunder," Trent whispered.

Sophie crawled over to Trent and placed her head on his lap. "This rain's beautiful."

"It is isn't it?"

Despite all the loss, this moment was peaceful. All the cares washed away in the rain. His legs fell asleep beneath Sophie's head, but not wanting to wake her, he just continued to lose feeling.

"Reminds me of camping with my wife back home. This one summer we set up camp for a nice weekend. Somehow, we both forgot to check the weather. It turned into a tent only trip. At one point you could feel the rain flowing under the tent. It sucked to be stuck inside, but on that third day when it cleared up the sky was such a bright shade of blue, and the air smelled fresh and crisp."

"Sounds perfect. I'm sorry you've missed so much."

"Me too, but I have to imagine I'm going to see them again. I'll have so much to make up for, especially with my little girl. She barely knew me."

"I wish I had someone waiting for me to come home. My parents cared more about work and money than me. Don't get me wrong I had everything I ever wanted, but it just wasn't enough, you know. All of you guys though, you have family waiting for you. And what about the ones who won't ever make it home to their families. They have no idea what happened to them."

"That's why we have to make it home. We have to tell them how heroic they were."

"Promise me if something happens to me, you'll tell Diego's family how much he meant to me."

"If anything happens to you I will. And that's a big if."

The conversation drifted late into the night until Sophie fell asleep only to wake a few minutes later as if nothing had happened. The two of them watched the grey storm clouds lighten up with the sun's rays. The rain died down leaving a fresh layer of moisture coating everything. The sounds of nature returned to the silent forest. Sophie's stomach rumbled from hunger. In all the confusion Trent realized they had neglected to grab any food rations. In fact, it had been two days since they last ate.

"Sophie do you wanna help me look for some food?"

"Sure, let me grab Rocco's knife. He won't even know I took it."

A slow movement of Sophie's hand saw the blade freed from its sheath.

The damp ground hid their footsteps as they tracked down a pack of strange creatures with gill-like flaps on their sides. Every time air was forced through them, they produced a strange harmonica like sound. The limbless creatures glided along the ground. They managed to stay just ahead of Sophie and Trent, leading them through the pillars and purple discs. They finally slowed down to nibble on the white balls atop the disks.

It made the perfect opening for Sophie to sneak up. Trent watched her brandish the knife and carefully approach one of the creatures. Just as Sophie prepared to stab the creature it let out a sudden whistle from the folds. The entire pack took off in different directions. The one in front of Sophie and Trent fled for a stray ribbon tree. They had it dead to rights. Sophie closed in while Trent circled around to block any possible escape.

The creature curled into a crescent shape and rolled over onto its back. It seemed like a strange way to react to a predator. Then, what they had thought were strange ridges on the back, broke free from the body turning into clawed legs. The creature raised up from the ground and scurried up the Ribbon tree out of reach. At roughly the size of a dog, it was a wonder how nimble it appeared in the branches.

Sophie flipped the knife in her hand placing the blade against her palm. She bobbed the piece of steel up and down a few times before holding it out in front of her. In one fluid motion, Sophie pulled her arm back and then forward releasing the knife. It spun end over end. The side of the knife hit the creature. It didn't manage to pierce the flesh but the momentum knocked it from the tree. A loud thump and the body laid still in the mud. Sophie picked up the knife from off the ground and drove it home. Black liquid oozed from the body.

"I caught it so you get to carry it back."

"Deal."

Trent grabbed the corpse and slung it over his shoulder. The two of them headed back to camp. Up ahead a strange new object blocked their way to camp. The closer they got the more it looked familiar to Trent. "Was that there before?"

"No, I think I would have remembered something that large."

"Yeah same here. But still, something about it seems familiar. I swear I've seen those markings before."

The object rose on wavering legs and turned around to face Trent. Its three eyes locked onto him.

Now Trent knew why the marks looked so familiar. They were the scars it received from the spikers that attacked it. This time there were no trees to hide behind and the spikers were nowhere in sight. White powder clung to the legs and mouth of the creature. Black goo dripped from the gaping mouth mixing with the yellow saliva.

The sight of the beast made Trent freeze up. Sophie readied the knife in case the beast attacked. Trent watched the eyes remain glued to him.

"I'm going to give it the thing we just killed," he whispered trying not to startle the beast. "Maybe it'll let us go and eat the meat." He pulled the body off his shoulder and set it on the ground.

A few steps forward and the beast fell. It tried to regain its footing but continued to fumble around. It seemed to be sick. Trent was unafraid as he watched the beast struggle. This was not the same ferocious creature that had attacked him. What stood in front of him was now a feeble, shadow of itself.

Trent took a few steps back from the black mess on the ground. The beast tried to make it to the prize but found itself strafing from side to side as if intoxicated. It let out a roar mixed with undertones of sloshing water. The head lowered and a large glob of black and yellow passed between the teeth. It drew closer to Trent. He could now make out all the details of the creature's face, along with the white powder covering it. It was the spores from the Mars moss. Somehow the monster had wandered into the moss and ingested some of the powder not knowing the consequences.

"How is this thing still alive? The spores killed Taylor and Zea within no time." Trent was amazed at the beast's durability.

"Yeah it's unbelievable."

The beast tried to approach but fell. This time it stayed where it was, letting out a soft moaning sound. Trent and Sophie watched the beast's labored breathing slow and eventually cease altogether. Life drained out of the body.

Trent felt some remorse for the beast despite its previous attempt on his life. Seeing it humbled by something so small made for a sad sight. Then he realized this was their chance to test out a way to stop the spreading on a small sample. Left alone the moss would grow and take over, but it had yet to form a cohesive shape. Quickly he picked up the creature they had killed.

"We need to get back to the others now. We have a chance to figure out if we can stop this stuff."

Sophie agreed, "Solid idea." The two turned and made way towards camp.

Rocco and Joseph were awake and clearly awaiting their return. Rocco's face had a disapproving glare on it. "Where's my knife?"

Sophie pulled it from her boot. "Oh sorry. We needed it to get food. See this is a good catch but if I didn't have the knife there was no way I would have caught it. So, you're welcome."

"Just don't do it again. Give it here and I'll start prepping the meat."

"All you." She tossed him the knife. The blade landed in the ground between Rocco's feet.

"You can cut up the meat in a bit." Trent grabbed a branch from the fire. "Right now, we have a chance to see if we can burn up the spores."

"I don't even know where we are much less the Mars moss."

"That's true, but remember that beast that attacked me? It found some and now it's dead not too far from here. So, I figure we can at least try and burn it."

"And that'll take four of us?"

"Fine if you don't want to go that's up to you. Joseph, wanna join us?"

"Sure, count me in."

Joseph and Sophie each grabbed a branch and they headed off leaving Rocco to his own game.

The body was already starting to decay by the time they reached it. The moss had worked fast, taking root in the body and breaking down the organs. A large hole had opened in the side. The rate of growth was proving to be unparalleled.

"Remember, whatever you do don't breathe in the spores." A piece of cloth shielded Trent's mouth and nose making the words muffled. He reached his branch out and touched the still loose spores. They ignited instantly. "Looks good so far." The stench of sulfur was overwhelming.

Joseph was busy burning up the growths with less appealing results but something they could work with. The bunches shriveled up beneath the heat, but no flame spread. The heat was the only thing that affected it. Moisture inhibited the ignition process. "At this rate we'll be dead long before we burn it all up."

"As long as we have the body here, we can get rid of this patch. That's a good start." Trent held his stick up to the beast's body but the flame didn't take. "We need some kindling and branches to lite this sucker up."

The group managed to scavenge a fair size pile of kindling. Each piece was laid with care to prevent any pods from opening. All three threw their torches into the pile and watched it take hold. The flames started small, but quickly grew larger consuming everything in their path. Flames flew high into the air. The heat was so unbearable Joseph, Trent, and Sophie had to back up around twenty feet just to cool their bodies off. They stuck around to ensure the flames ran out of fuel. All that was left behind was a burnt husk of a corpse and white ash where the moss had once been. It wasn't a perfect plan, but for now they could at least stave off any growth that might come near them.

The hunger was getting worse, and the smell of the cooked flesh only strengthened it. Trent could feel drool pooling in his mouth. "I need to eat. Think Rocco's ready for us yet?"

"I hope so." Sophie picked up a hand full of dirt to throw on a small flickering flame, extinguishing it. "I'm feeling a bit light-headed. A little food could do me some good."

With their heads held high from their minuscule victory, the three joined back up with Rocco. Scraps were piled up neatly, a ways off from the camp. Meat skewers roasted over the open flame.

"Perfect timing guys. I just finished the last of the meat. I was hoping for more but this will last us a few days. Maybe more if we ration it."

None of them felt like talking. Trent was the first to grab a skewer. His teeth sunk into the warm meat. The pleasant aroma pushed out any lingering scent of sulfur. The juices coated his tongue and flowed down his throat. The hunger pains subsided. Sophie joined him, making a mess of herself tearing into the meat. Joseph was slightly less barbaric, taking small bites and savoring them.

"Good right?" It seemed Rocco wanted a response

Trent figured a grunt would have to do. "Mmmhhh."

Nothing was going to stop him now. Once they had all had their fill they settled in and watched the evening go by. It was a rare occasion to have a full belly. Now he just had to try and fall asleep.

Joseph

"You're breaking the branches all wrong." Rocco placed his hands around one of the ribbon trees. "It needs to be done like this. See how the fibers break off in splinters at the edge?"

Trent reached up, eyes locked onto Rocco, and grabbed a branch. With a twist of his wrist the branch broke in two. "Oooh so hard."

"You're such a child."

"And proud of it." Trent snapped another branch. "I prefer the easy way."

"That's obvious. If you'd take the extra second to do it the right way, then the branches would burn better. But hey, getting a fire going out here is easy."

Joseph watched the two of them bickering back and forth. He was trying his hardest to keep his head down and just pick up branches that were already on the ground.

"Tell him he's being ridiculous." Trent seemed to be wanting Joseph to respond. If he pretended, he didn't hear anything maybe they would leave him alone. "Joseph, come on. You know I'm right. Just tell him."

"I don't know, I guess." Joseph picked up another branch. His hands were full enough to give him an excuse to leave. Neither of them seemed to notice that he had left. The branches dug into his arms. Their weight added up making the short journey a struggle. A few smaller branches fell here and there but the bulk of his haul remained. Any attempt to regain them would just cause the large branches to fall.

The camp was empty when Joseph arrived. No sign of Sophie anywhere. He searched for something to do as an excuse to not have to go back to branch collecting. The answer to his prayers laid just outside the lean-to. The emergency beacon was still inactive. The battery had been disconnected but the rainstorm had filled up the wells. The water level had stopped just before overflowing, meaning none of the salt had been lost. He drained the dish and planted it firmly in the ground. This was going to be the true test of his engineering. Joseph took a deep breath, anticipating the worst. After everything that had happened, no one would fault him for thinking that way. He removed the end screws and attached the wires. Using the hooks, he latched them back into place completing the circuit.

Beep.... Beep....Beep.

The box was still working. Now they just had to hope NASA would get the signal. There was no way to know for sure. All Joseph could do was assume that it was working. He sat back and stared into the sky, imagining a satellite receiving their signal and transferring their location to earth. Nasa upon receiving it would pool all their resources into getting the crew back. Everyone would be cheering him on. A true hero's welcome. But what about when they learned what happened to Nova? Would they really welcome him home with open arms as some amazing legend? His mind created thoughts of everyone ostracizing him for his mistake, unable to calm their fears. He felt like a monster inside. The large asteroid that had sent them here passed overhead. He wished that the impact had killed him.

Trent's voice came ahead of the sound of crashing branches, "Fuck this. I'm done. If he wants a fire, he can do all the work."

Joseph snapped out of his zone at the unwelcome interruption. "If you pretended to take his advice, he wouldn't be such a dick to you."

"Yeah thanks for the advice. I've never had to deal with anyone like him before." Sarcasm dripped from Trent's voice.

"I heard all of that," Rocco yelled in the distance.

"Good. I wasn't trying to hide it."

"Maybe if you weren't so useless and actually did what I said the ship wouldn't have crashed."

Trent's entire face was a brilliant red. His entire body showed signs of agitation. "I'm done. Joe come help me?"

"Help you with what?"

"I'm building my own sleeping quarters so I don't have to deal with this jackass anymore." He ran into the lean-to and stole the knife from Rocco's backpack.

"I don't see why you need me."

"So that you can help me carry the cups from the tentacles."

Joseph didn't want to but he was finding Rocco more unbearable than Trent at the moment. "Whatever." he tagged along, twisting through the forest looking for just the right tentacle plant. "How about this one?" He held up a large flat cup. It was comparable to the ones Rocco used for the first lean-to.

"Sure. It looks like there's another one over there." Joseph continued.

Not wanting to cause any more tension, Joseph left the one he had to go help Trent with the ones he chose. He hardly noticed the forest change around him. When he finally looked around the trees were still the same, other than a few larger looking Tentacle plants, but strange almost net-like blue lattices covered both them and the forest floor. Large rainbow-colored bodies grew sporadically from the intersecting branches. Generally, they appeared as three spheres merged together but occasionally, they had strange projections separating them.

"Let's start with this one."

Trent took the knife to the branch. He made it seem infinitely more difficult than when Rocco had done it. The knife only got halfway through when his frustration set in. He pulled at the branch hoping to break it loose. His hands slipped and gravity sent him flying backward. A nearby rainbow clump exploded throwing juice into the air and all over Trent's face.

"Uch!" His hand wiped the juice from his mouth. "It tastes like a doctor's office smells. Aggh." He scraped fervently at his tongue. "I need water. I have to wash this taste out."

"All the waters back with Rocco."

"Never mind then. I'll just bear with it." He acted like it wasn't bothering him but Joseph could tell by his contorted face that it was pure misery. Trent picked the knife up and returned to cutting until the branch eventually broke loose. "Two more should do it."

"I'll take this one back for you."

"By the time you get back I should have the others down."

The sound of footsteps caught Joseph's attention. "Rocco that you?"

"Better not be you, asshole."

"It's just me." It was Sophie's voice. "I've been trying to find you guys."

"Perfect. Sophie can finish helping you."

"Sure, I can do that. Toss me the knife." Sophie reached her hand out as if she expected Trent to throw it.

Trent walked over and handed the blade to her. "Here, all yours."

Joseph and Trent were at a loss for words as they watched Sophie grab ahold of one of the cups, and with a single swing, bury the blade halfway into the stem attached to it. She then pulled the cup tight and ripped the knife through the rest of the flesh.

Trent stared unblinking at what they had just witnessed. "That was pure luck."

Sophie gave him a look of nonchalance. She started pulling the next cup, and with one swift motion drove the blade in and dragged it home. The cup fell free spilling water on her.

"See that's why I was taking my time."

"Whatever you have to tell yourself. So, what are you making, another shelter?"

"Yeah I'm not sleeping next to that pile of shit Rocco. Help us drag these back."

Each with a cup in hand, they dragged them through the forest and to the camp. Trent set to work grabbing branches from the firewood pile to create his canopy.

"I know you took my knife." It was none other than Rocco standing behind them, his chest puffed out, breathing heavily through his nostrils. His fists were so tightly clenched, that his hands were shaking.

"Yeah, I did. See." The blade glistened in Trent's hand.

"You son of a bitch." Rocco's fist rose in a flash and connected with Trent's face. A stream of blood poured from his nostrils. Trent's body went limp.

Sophie went over to check on Trent. "The hell Rocco. Not saying he didn't deserve to get hit but did you have to hit him that hard."

Joseph grabbed the canteen from the lean-to and ran it over to Trent's unconscious body. "This should wake him up. Used to work whenever I or my brothers would blackout." He emptied the water onto Trent's face.

It was enough of a shock to get him to open his eyes. He blinked a few times before he was able to speak. "What just happened?"

"Dude, Rocco laid you out."

Trent sat up. "Not cool man."

"Listen, I'm sorry."

"No, screw you."

"Really I didn't mean…"

"I don't want to hear it." Trent rose to his feet and grabbed all the wood he needed for his makeshift canopy.

Joseph filled his arms and followed along.

Behind them Sophie could be heard arguing with Rocco. "No, seriously Rocco stay here."

"I feel bad. I need to help him."

"Don't you think you've done enough to hurt his pride? I mean seriously. You knock him out and now you want to tell him he needs your help to build a shelter?"

Tears ran down Trent's cheeks keeping the blood from completely drying, as he struggled to place the branches in the ground. All Joseph could do was sit and wait for Trent to ask him for help, yet the longer he waited the more the canopy seemed to come together. Seeing how stable it was, almost came as a surprise to Joseph. He never took him for the handyman type.

Sophie joined Trent and Rocco carrying a lit branch in her hand. She piled together the leftover ribbon branches and set them ablaze. The trio settled in, leaving Rocco to stew in his own misery.

Sophie

Sophie awoke to a dried-out mouth. Instinctively she reached for the canteen. The lack of weight made no impact on her attempt to get a drink. A few stray drops graced her lips. Her entire body felt parched. Trent and Joseph were still soundly asleep. They looked so peaceful, she decided not to disturb them. She gently tried to step past Joseph who woke up. Trying to keep from waking Trent, Sophie whispered to him, "Sorry. I didn't mean to wake you."

Joseph blinked his eyes. "No worries. Where you going?"

"Well I need to get a drink. Want to come help me look for some water?"

"Sure. I could use some myself."

"Bring the canteen and let's go."

Joseph inched his way out, stepping ever so carefully. "Okay, so what's the plan?"

"After yesterday's little shower, I'm thinking we should be able to fill the canteen from the tentacle plants." Sophie headed out before Joseph had a chance to reply. There were plenty of plants nearby for her to choose from. She eyed one with a small puddle of water inside. "Joseph hand me the canteen."

"Why are you still whispering?" he asked, handing it over. "I don't think Trent can hear us anymore."

"No idea really." She returned to full volume. "Anyway, this should be a good start." She submerged the canteen into the stagnating water. The air bubbles stirred up the dirt that had settled on the bottom of the cup. Once the canteen was full Sophie raised it to her lips. The water managed to quench her thirst but left a metallic taste in her mouth. "Here have some."

Joseph took the canteen from her and went to take a sip.

"Oh, by the way there's a bit of dirt in it." Sophie tried to warn him, but it was too late.

"Wait Whagagag?" The words became unintelligent as the water filled his mouth. He started to choke.

"Sorry. I didn't mean to do that."

"Not your fault. Huhhhh. I shouldn't have tried to talk."

She filled the canteen back up. "Here try again. This time remember to drink the water, not breathe it in."

"I can manage that."

Sophie watched Joseph raise the canteen to his lips. "Remember you're not a fish."

A burst of laughter left Joseph's lips. "Goddammit. Quit trying to make me choke."

"But that's no fun." It was great to get in a good laugh. it seemed like life had gotten so serious that all the joy had disappeared over the last few days. "Fine. I'll be nice and let you drink."

Joseph's eyes were locked onto Sophie while he lifted the canteen once again to get a drink. He stopped short. "Don't you dare."

"I promise."

The canteen tipped a bit more and stopped short. "Seriously. Don't mess with me."

"I cross my heart. If I do you and Trent can make me sleep in Rocco's lean-to listening to that god-awful snoring. I swear I've heard quieter chainsaws." She burst out laughing tickled by her own joke, which in turn caused Joseph to start laughing along.

"Okay, that was the last one." He regained his composure. And poured the water managing to get a proper drink this time around.

"See I told you I could be good."

"Yeah for some reason I still don't believe that."

"That's on you." Sophie was feeling energized from the laughter. Going back to the camp seemed too depressing. "Hey wanna go chill in the hot spring for a bit?"

"Why not." Joseph filled the canteen up.

The two of them walked side by side, until they reached the steam covered pools. The clear sky reflected off the agitated surface of the water. Their warmth was so inviting. The smell of the beasts charred remains occasionally wafted through the air but was not enough to deter them. Sophie wasted no time stripping down and climbing into the water. It was a small concession to be able to return to dry clothes once she was through relaxing. It wasn't like Joseph hadn't seen it all before. The warm water felt as good the second time as it had when they first climbed out of the pit.

Joseph followed suit and climbed in. "Never thought we'd be able to have a hot tub after we crashed."

Sophie closed her eyes and let the warm sunlight hit her face. "Same. And we don't have to deal with kids splashing in it or cleaning it."

"All the pleasure with none of the work. The perfect scenario." Joseph went silent.

Sophie opened her eyes to see him staring towards the pit.

"Well maybe one kid." She slapped her hand down in the water sending streams skyward. The water crashed down on Joseph's head. He seemed to register her actions yet didn't respond. She was bound and determined to distract him from whatever he was doing. She sent a wave of water his way. Yet again he seemed not to care.

"Hey what's going on?" Sophie inched closer to Joseph. "You all right?"

"I just can't help thinking about Nova. The images of her body stuck floating in that tunnel, unable to continue its journey has been haunting my dreams."

Not knowing the best way to help left Sophie feeling helpless. She placed her arm around Joseph's shoulder. He immediately laid his head down. His eyes remained fixated on the opening.

"You know we don't blame you."

"Yeah, but I still feel like I need to do something to honor her." He stood up in the water and climbed from the pool.

Where are you going?"

"Something I have to do. I need to help her move on." Joseph's feet moved swiftly. He was already halfway to the second pool before Sophie understood what his intentions were.

"Wait, are you serious?"

"Deadly serious."

"Well, wait up. I'll join you." She stepped out of the pool and ran to catch up. Before she could make it halfway to him, Joseph had disappeared into the pit. She reached the edge and lowered herself slowly onto the first ledge. The water in the terraces was cooler than on the surface. No matter how quickly she maneuvered he was still ahead of her. She managed to clear the second terrace when he made contact with the river. "I'm almost there. Give me a minute."

"Fine. Just hurry up. The water's freezing."

Sophie sped up her pace, making it down two more terraces. She was prepared to descend the next terrace when she noticed something float past Joseph. "Hey, what was that?"

"What was what?"

"That thing that floated past you."

"I didn't see anything."

"Look, there's another one." This time its yellow color was visible. "No way. That can't be."

"What are you ranting about?" Joseph turned around. He began flailing violently in an attempt to escape the river.

Sophie's suspicions were confirmed. "Don't come up here." Slowly she backed up. She had to get away.

"Just wait for me."

"No, you're infected. Don't come up here. You'll only manage to spread it."

"I feel fine." He pulled himself from the river.

Sophie managed to make it to the top ledge. "I don't care. Stay down there. The three of us still haven't been exposed."

"This is ridiculous. I'm coming back to camp." He let out a gut-wrenching cough. Blood stained the water terrace.

"See you're sick. Just stay there."

"No, fuck you. I'm fine." She watched him struggle to work his way up towards her. He stood on the second terrace now. "It's just a cough from the water earlier. I swear."

"No. Stay back." Sophie got onto dry land and ran towards her clothes. She no longer cared about keeping them dry. Her only thought was of survival. The further away from Joseph she was the safer. His violent coughing changed from echoing through the pit to ringing out unhindered. He was on the surface. She turned her head to see him struggling to stand. She needed to place as much distance between them as possible before running to tell the others. He continued to follow her rather than heading towards the camp.

Sophie bobbed and weaved through the pillars. Upon reaching the edge of the ribbon forest, she ran until the trees completely obscured the open field. *I need to head back to camp.* There was no sign of Joseph but resting now could mean him catching up. She breathed through the pain and forced herself on.

Rocco's camp came into view. "Wake up. Rocco, get out here." Sophie was exhausted from running. She collapsed outside his shelter.

"What are you yelling about?"

"Sorry, I didn't want to wake you, but we're in trouble. Joseph's infected and he was following me."

"Sophie what's going on?" Trent came wandering up to join them. "Oh, it's Rocco. What the hell did you do to Sophie? And why is she naked?"

"It wasn't me you jackass. She said Joseph's infected."

Sophie struggled to catch her breath. "Yeah, we went down to the hot tubs to relax. Joseph got the crazy idea to free Nova's body from the river. Once he got into the river, I noticed that chunks of moss were floating downstream." She stopped talking to take a few slow breaths. "Anyway, he said he was fine but started coughing up blood. Next thing I know he's chasing after me."

"Well why would you run back here?"

"I didn't know what else to do after I lost him in the forest. I don't think he's gonna make it back."

"Well put your clothes on and then we can all go see if we can find him."

A quick nod of her head and Sophie put her clothes back on. She was still shaking from the thought of Joseph willingly trying to infect her.

"Let us know when you're ready," Trent said.

"No, we need to head out now." Rocco seemed intent on being quick to neutralize the threat.

"Dude give her a break. At least let her catch her breath."

"It's okay. Rocco's right. We need to head out. The longer we wait the closer Joseph gets."

"If you say so."

Sophie took the lead. She headed back, following her original path as best she could. So far, no sign of Joseph anywhere. She kept her ears peeled for any sign of him coming up on them.

"There he is." Rocco was the first to spot him. Joseph's body was spread out on the ground. A pool of blood flowed from his mouth. He wasn't moving.

A wave of relief stuck Sophie. Even after everything that had happened to her, the sight of Joseph chasing after her wanting to give her his gift of death had been the most terrifying. Perhaps it was because he was someone she had grown to trust.

"We need to go." Rocco turned and headed out. "I'll come back with a torch and take care of the body."

"Sounds good to me." Trent agreed. "I'll stay back with Sophie at the camp."

"No need. I'm fine, really. I want to help you Rocco. What if I stay here and gather up branches while you get the torch?"

"You sure that's what you want?"

"Yeah."

"You heard her Rocco, get moving." Trent still seemed agitated with Rocco.

Sophie set to work plucking branches and piling them up. Trent helped. He broke the branches exactly as Rocco had told him too. It sparked some hope in Sophie that maybe now that there were only three of them Rocco and Trent might be able to at least tolerate each other again.

A small pile of branches surrounded the body by the time Rocco returned. They took turns saying their goodbyes before he set the body ablaze. The trio remained until the flames had died down. For whatever reason Sophie felt no remorse for the loss of their companion. She left his smoldering body behind and headed off.

Trent

The smell of searing flesh, and hair overwhelmed Trent's senses. It not only afflicted his sense of smell but managed to cling onto his tongue. As far as he was concerned, his mouth contained a piece of Joseph that he was unable to spit out. The time had long past for him to leave this horrid scene behind and join Sophie back at camp, leaving Rocco to his own ways. *How did we get to this point? We went from ten to three. Even the water's poisoned. What kind of cruel joke is this?* When he arrived at Rocco's camp, he realized he was the only one left that could use the satellite. Left in Rocco's incapable hands the whole thing would probably wind up broken in some fit of rage, or from his fat ass rolling over it in his sleep. He picked up the battery in one hand, and the dish in the other. Only a few drops of water spilled from the cells on his way back to the canopy.

Sophie was already laying down. "Why are you dragging that scrap metal around? If NASA hasn't found us by now, I don't see how that dinky little thing is going to make any difference."

"I don't know if it will, but it was Joseph's way of taking care of us and I won't let his efforts be pulverized because of Rocco. Besides it is not hard to move."

"I don't think Rocco would destroy it."

"Better not to take the risk."

"Whatever you say." Sophie rolled over and went silent.

Trent set the Beacon up and reconnected the wires. *Beep.... Beep.* He'd forgotten all about the sound. It was too late to turn back now. He was determined to keep it there with him. He closed his eyes to drift off to sleep.

Beep.... Beep...Beep.

His mind refused to tune out the sound. He tossed and turned trying to get comfortable. The night drew on and exhaustion was settling in but the beeping kept him on alert. Each successive beep ground away at his sanity. He fought until the anger boiled over and he could no longer resist his animal tendencies. Trent leaped up from the ground in a fit of rage. His sole focus was on the adrenaline-laced rampage. Without thinking he knocked the entire setup over. Water covered the ground and over his feet. The source of his madness was gone, but a new issue arose. His feet were damp. He sat next to the fire attempting to dry them before returning to his spot to sleep. The silence was so relaxing, within minutes he had drifted off to sleep.

"Daddy I missed you." Little Lucy ran up, dragging her doll along the ground. Trent picked her up and wrapped his arms around her and gave her a kiss on the head. "I missed you so much."

"Are you staying this time?" Lucy cinched her arms tightly around Trent's neck. "I don't want you to leave again."

"I promise I won't."

"Good." She leaned back in his arms and looked him in his eyes. Her lips parted. "Beep."

"What?"

"Beep."

"I can't understand you, baby girl. You're just making noise."

"Beep."

Trent roused from his sleep. It was still dark out. Even with the source silenced his damn subconscious refused to let it go. All he wanted was to sleep and escape the memories of the last several months. The first dream not involving the mission in any way and he managed to ruin even that. The frustration kept him from getting comfortable. Not wanting to wake Sophie, but needing to get out, he grabbed a branch from the fire and set out into the woods. He always made sure the light from the fire remained in sight. The light was barely a flicker, easily mistaken for a firefly if he were on earth. "Ahhhhhh," Trent screamed at the top of his lungs until no more air was left inside. A quick breath and he was right back at it. Something rubbed up against his leg. In his fit of rage, he forgot to pay attention to his surroundings. Whatever it was must have taken advantage of all the noise he made to sneak up on him. He looked down prepared to see something terrible. His tentative glance was met with a pleasant surprise. Rubbing up next to him was one of the spikers who had rescued him. He was relieved to see they had managed to escape the white cloud of death. There didn't appear to be any other spikers nearby. Not wanting to leave his friend alone, Trent urged it to follow him back to camp.

The spiker kept pace, running around sporadically but still following Trent's ultimate path. They continued like this until they reached the edge of the camp. Trent stepped forward under the canopy. He turned and faced the spiker who seemed apprehensive to join him. Trying to keep his voice down, he went to the spiker and urged it to come along. It refused. He didn't want to leave it alone in the forest. The only option left was to pick up the creature and carry it into the shelter's cover.

The spiker fought violently as if crossing some unseen threshold that caused it great agony. The spiker clawed at Trent's chest and arms. Its mouth bit down hard enough to break the skin. Trent tossed the creature. "Fine get the fuck outta here." The creature responded appropriately and fled. He looked over towards Sophie, making sure he hadn't woken her. He nursed his wounds until his eyes grew heavy. A dreamless sleep overtook him.

A beam of sunlight hit Trent's face. He roused unsure that he had slept at all. Sophie was already huddled by the fire.

"Morning. Glad to see you were finally able to fall asleep." Sophie handed him a chunk of roasted meat.

"Thanks. Wait, are you saying I kept you up?"

"Yeah but I figured eventually you'd settle down." She took a bite of meat. As she spoke small chunks of food flew from her mouth. "Once you wandered off, I was hopeful. But when you came back with that spiker, I almost lost it."

"Sorry, I was trying to be quiet."

"Not your fault. I find that I tend to just lay on the ground for a while listening to the night."

"You're sure?"

"I'm sure. Hey, I'll be right back." She picked up another slice of meat.

"Oh, now you're afraid to eat in front of me?"

"No, I just have something I need to do."

"Well that's vague."

"Trust me, if I told you, you wouldn't like it."

"You're taking some to Rocco aren't you?"

"I told you that you wouldn't like it."

"Talk about reading my mind." Trent stood up. "Regardless, I should probably come along just in case."

She stared at him. "It's not like he's going to do anything to me. Fine, come on."

Trent was pleased that he had won. They walked together, enjoying their feast. It was only a short walk between their shelter and Rocco's but the trees did a good job of hiding it. He came around the final tree and beheld a terrible sight. Mars moss encircled Rocco's lean-to. The ribbon trees were caught in mid-transformation to a brilliant yellow. Tendrils ran along the ground, stretching out to gain a foothold. Rocco laid unmoving.

"Rocco, wake up," Trent called out. He hoped his voice would stir Rocco, but there was no change. Normally they would be able to hear snoring from this distance but right now there was only pure silence.

"Yo, Rocco get your ass up." Sophie tossed a rock into the shelter. Still no movement.

A small unaffected portion remained directly around Rocco that the moss had yet to breach. It seemed as if the trip around the lean-to had deterred the moss enough. If none of the spores had reached Rocco, there was no reason he should not be alive. Trent refused to lose another crew member. Nothing seemed to work. He tried not to give up hope. With all his breath he let out a wretched scream that could wake the dead.

Rocco's arm moved. Finally, some signs of life. "What the hell do you want?"

"You need to get the fuck up. Right now."

"What are you talking about?"

"You're surrounded by the moss. Get up but make sure you don't roll over." Sophie was searching the ground, most likely trying to find a way around the moss.

Rocco sat up carefully watching his every move. One wrong hand placement could spell death. "Get me the hell outta here."

"Hold on. We need to figure something out." Trent could feel his brain spinning. He looked everywhere for some way in. there didn't seem to be a good option. "What if you try burning your way out?"

"Already on it."

Rocco spoke the truth. He was two steps ahead of Trent. In his hand was a fresh burning stick. He crawled on his knees towards the edge of the moss. The burning flames skimmed across the surface without leaving a mark.

"No, you have to hold it in place to get any effect."

"Got it." Rocco held the flame in place for over a minute. Upon pulling the torch back a small charred pile remained, hardly large enough for a single foot. "It's taking too long."

Without warning Sophie ran off.

"Where the hell's she going?"

"No idea."

Sophie's voice came to them soon after. "Trent get over here. I need your help."

Those words terrified him. What could have possibly gone wrong in such a short time? He left Rocco where he was and ran towards Sophie's voice. He found her pulling the large tentacle cups from off his canopy.

"Oh, you did hear me. Grab one of the cups." She picked up the first two off the ground. "Hurry up."

Before Trent could get a word in, Sophie was already headed back to Rocco, dragging the cups through the dirt. Trent pulled the last one from the shaky mass of branches and rushed back.

By the time he made it to the first campsite, Sophie was already standing on the first cup and placing the second one a short way in front of it. "Hand me that." She crossed back to Trent.

"This isn't safe." Trent refused to hand her the final cup.

"Well it's too late to stop me now."

"No, it's too risky." He pulled back the cup to try and deter her from proceeding any further. One wrong step and she would be a goner. He refused to let that happen.

"Fine don't give it to me." Sophie hopped to the second cup and bent down to pick up the first one.

"Wait. Fine, here." Trent made his way onto the first cup and walked as it would allow. He raised the cup over his head to keep it off the ground. It was like playing a more dangerous version of the floor is lava. He stretched out the cup for Sophie to grab.

"I knew you would come along." She took the cup and placed it in front of Rocco's shelter.

Rocco crawled forward and had his hand out to place it on the cup when a loud creaking sound turned into a thunderous crack. The ribbon tree that sat near fell onto the structure, its base eaten away by the mars moss. A scream of pain was followed by silence. Only Rocco's hand could be seen under the mess of branches and cups. Small whimpers could be heard coming from him.

Attempting to rescue him would only lead to them getting infected. It was only a matter of time before he either bled out or the moss took him.

Trent panicked. "Get out of there. There's nothing we can do for him."

Sophie's eyes were full of tears. "I'm sorry, Rocco. We can't help you." She scurried back across the pads.

The coughing was painful to hear. They needed to get away. Despite all the horrible things Rocco had done, he did not deserve to suffer like this. Trent felt awful leaving him to die alone. If they stayed where they were, there was no telling how long it would take the moss to close them in as well. The two ran for safety.

Trent was the first to reach the hot spring field. A yellow border surrounded a sea of red dirt. All signs of life inside the ring were gone. A large red mass was at the very center of the spreading. It appeared to be the remains of the beast. Somehow, they had missed some of the spores when they burned the body. This part of the woods was no longer safe either. "We need to run deeper." he grabbed Sophie's hand and dragged her along. They reached the portion of the forest that was covered in the strange blue nets. A short distance away the moss seemed to have reached even this portion of the forest. Trent stopped. Something about the mars moss seemed different here. It was as if something was preventing it from moving. There were no tendrils stretching out. It was as if an invisible line had been drawn that the moss couldn't cross.

"Hey, does that look strange to you?" Trent dropped Sophie's hand and went to investigate. Where the blue nets ended the moss seemed to stop dead in its tracks. He couldn't be sure but it was worth testing.

"What did you see?" Sophie finally caught up to him.

"The moss seems to be repelled by this blue stuff." Trent pulled up a handful from the ground and chucked the clump into the moss. It bounced across the surface but nothing happened. "Well never mind."

"Hey, it was worth a try. I would have done the…" Sophie's words got interrupted by a light cough.

"No!" Trent turned to Sophie.

"I'm fine really. Just a tickle in my throat. Too much running." She showed her hand to Trent. No signs of blood.

He breathed a sigh of relief. "Thank fuck." He gave her a huge hug. He thought he was going to lose her too.

"Aww you were worried about me."

"Of course, I was." He refused to let go. Sophie pushed herself free from him.

He caught a glimpse of something white on his hand when he pulled it away. His body froze but his hand shook uncontrollably.

"Let's go." Sophie turned to walk away, but Trent stood where he was.

His hands shook harder as he turned them over. His fears were confirmed. White powder covered his palms. He looked up at Sophie who's back now faced him. Two hand-shaped holes broke up the white coating on her shirt. "Shit! Shit, Shit, Shit!"

"Uh you got Tourettes or something?"

"He raised his hands up to show Sophie the fate that awaited them both.

"But I feel…." A series of coughs overtook Sophie. Blood shot from her mouth.

"It's too late. We're both dead." He stared up at the sky.

"I feel…achugh" Her body collapsed onto the ground.

Trent rushed to her side. He knelt beside her and placed her head in his lap.

Sophie opened her eyes and looked up at Trent. "I'm sorry." The coughing picked up again.

"Don't be. We were lucky we made it this long. The fact that we survived the crash at all was amazing."

Seeing Sophie, He knew where he was going to be in an hour. It was like watching his future on TV just before it happened. Her skin grew cold and pale.

"Stay with me?" Sophie asked before once again coughing. Blood splattered onto Trent's face. He wanted to say something, anything to comfort her, even if it was only an 'I'm sorry'. "Hold on please," was all he could muster. Any other response and he wouldn't be able to be strong for her. Her bloodshot eyes locked onto his, leaving him staring into their dark abyss. With a bloody hand, she reached towards his face. Halfway to its destination the shaking hand came to a stop. He grabbed ahold and placed her hand gently on his cheek. "I've got you Sophie."

He resigned himself to sit there and die with her in his lap no matter what. The blood was just a reminder of the life that was leaving her. Through watery eyes, he watched as her coughing grew more violent, and then her breathing slowed. Her face twisted in pain. Between coughs she tried to speak. What came out were only raspy breaths. The warm sun beat upon them, but her body only grew colder. Her legs kicked violently at the ground, searching for some foothold on life. The arm he had been holding fell away. Then, with one final breath, the moving ceased entirely. She had died right there in his arms. The color had faded from her eyes. All around him the world was oblivious to the horrific scene that had played out. He knew this was his future.

The only thing left for Trent to do was wait. He looked out at the blue clump he'd tossed carelessly into the moss. Now instead of a solid field of yellow, patches of brown led to the final resting position of the clump. Around it was a ring of brown. Trent couldn't help but laugh. The stuff all around him really did kill off the moss. It was too late for any of them now. He closed his eyes and sat awaiting his fate. Soon enough he would start coughing and it would all be over.

Trent sat running his fingers through Sophie's soft hair. Time seemed to be going by so slowly. He wished it would take him already. Deciding that the waiting wasn't worth it, Trent moved Sophie's limp body aside. Seeing it lying there motionless, staring at him, was devastating. It had all happened so fast. He closed her eyes and rested her on her back. With a final kiss on her cold forehead, He walked towards the yellow moss hoping to end things as quickly as possible. He stopped at the edge of what was left of the forest and stared at her body one last time. She looked so peaceful. In a matter of minutes there would be nothing left of her. "I'm coming everyone," he said, walking into the yellow moss barrier. There he laid down and breathed deeply. It was only a matter of time now.

The longer he waited the more he began to question why he felt so good. The sun rose higher yet no symptoms showed. It was at that moment he remembered his first trip into the forest. The rainbow masses on the blue net had broken when he fell. The nasty taste returned to his memory. It all became clear. The juice had gotten into his system and provided some kind of immunity. He began sobbing uncontrollably knowing that, despite everything, he was now the only one left. For whatever reason Trent had been spared from the destruction caused by the god of war's servant.

Frank

Mission control was like a ghost town. The crew was out preparing for the media circus that would ensue once the Phoenix VII was discovered. Frank stared up at a large screen filled with twinkling stars. The satellite had been equipped with a telescope capable of viewing the ship in detail. They had to position it as close to the sun as it could safely allow, for the communication antenna to function. Until it reached the optimal position, the view remained locked onto a random set of stars. Once they were ready to start collecting data, the boosters would kick in and turn the satellite towards the ship. A large countdown clock indicated that it was just under an hour till go time.

There were so many what-ifs to answer surrounding the ship's condition that it would take a full week to process all the information and come up with a clear plan. What if the crew died after they found the signal? What if the crew survived, but the ship was venting atmosphere slowly? What if the crew is running out of food and water? What if the radiation from the sun is making them sick? What if they are out of fuel? The list never seemed to end.

Frank pulled his glasses off and held them loosely in one hand by the arm. The earpiece fit comfortably between his front teeth. He was nervous to say the least. They had invested so much money into this operation, that if they didn't show positive results, he would be without a job for good this time.

The first one to break the silence was Daniel. He looked like a vagrant with his disheveled hair, and rugged beard with crumbs lodged inside. The bags under his eyes were so dark they could be mistaken for a bad makeup job. He seemed incapable of getting comfortable as he came into the room, first trying to sit in his chair, spinning back and forth while shuffling through his papers, then getting up and walking over to the vending machine not to buy anything but just to stare inside. Seemingly unsatisfied with the view, he transitioned to the front of the room and flipped through the different satellite information diagrams.

Frank felt bad for him. After the loss of Addison, he just wasn't the same. The higher-ups had discussed dismissal as a possibility, but Frank had convinced them he was still invaluable to the team. He needed to think of something to help distract his friend for the next forty or so minutes.

"Hey Daniel, can you do me a favor and go get my cell phone from my office."

"Uh, yeah, sure." Daniel shuffled out of the room. On the way out he stopped in the doorway, "Where did you leave it?"

"I'm thinking it's in one of my desk drawers."

"Ok, I'll be right back."

The silence was back. Despite the lack of people, the computers were working at max capacity to ensure every detail was taken care of. The clock reached thirty minutes. It was time to call back the others. Frank picked up the phone and dialed the intercom system.

"All staff of the Seeker mission please return to mission control immediately."

He placed his glasses back on, wiped the sweat from his forehead, and tucked his shirt back in. It was game time. He set to work prepping his computer.

The team slowly trickled in, some without saying a word headed immediately to their stations, others were chatting amongst themselves, and a few who were thanking Frank for rescuing them from the carnivorous reporters. By the time they finished settling in the countdown was at five minutes. Daniel still wasn't back.

"Caleb, can you take over for me? I'll be right back."

"Yes sir."

Feeling satisfied that he could leave the team in capable hands for a minute, he made his way down the brightly lit hall. The door to his office was wide open. Daniel sat inside pulling drawers in and out in an act of insanity.

"Oh hey, you're here...that good, because I can't find it. You sure it's in here?"

"Well, I mean it's not in my pockets." He pretended not to know where the phone was while he tapped his front pocket. "Never mind."

He reached in and pulled it out. "It's right here. Not sure how I missed it. Let's get back to the control room. It should be time."

They walked back just in time to see the last few seconds tick off the timer.

"The telescope is ready to turn, sir." Pam was awaiting his orders.

Frank looked at Daniel. "You ready for this?"

"Are you kidding me right now?"

"You heard him, go for it."

The view on the screen shifted as stars drifted across the screen. They watched with bated breath. Suddenly something strange came into view. Rather than a metallic spaceship, they saw Earth but it seemed different. The oceans were still a deep blue, and white clouds swirled along the ball's surface, yet where green swaths of trees adorned the land on Earth this planet had a bizarre mixture of fall colors all weaved together. There seemed to be three separate landmasses on the side facing the sun. Here on the far side of the sun, completely hidden away from human eyes, floated Earth's true twin. Born to forever chase its sibling, the two were locked in an eternal dance.

"What the...?" Frank couldn't believe his eyes. The whole room was a buzz. He could barely hear his own thoughts over the commotion. Everyone seemed to be experiencing varying levels of disbelief. "Everyone, please quiet down for a moment."

All his efforts were in vain, but he couldn't blame them for their bewilderment. He, himself, had no idea how exactly to handle the situation. He took to the front of the room and shouted out at the top of his lungs, "Attention." No one paid him any mind.

"Everyone shut up for a sec!" A deep authoritative voice commanded. It managed to supersede all the chatter. Silence fell over the room.

"Thank you, Daniel. Now I know this is the most...the greatest find...well ever. But we need to remember why we're looking here in the first place. We're looking for our crew from the Phoenix VII."

He pointed to the screen. "According to their last signal, this is where they should be. I want to find out everything we can about this planet.

Forward all the data we collect onto Julie and then take an hour to get this out of your system so we can all get back to work. There could be lives at stake. For now, I have to ask you not to tell anyone outside of this group."

The keyboards sprang to life. There was a series of hurried clicks and people started exiting the room one by one. Frank stayed behind just to stare at the image. He was completely perplexed by the prospect of another possible life-bearing planet. Just then a small object passed by the planet. *Could it be the ship?* Frank rushed over to the nearest computer and pulled up the feed. It just so happened that NASA recorded all their satellite feeds. He pulled up the video and backed it up. There it was again. He slowed the playback down to a tenth of the speed. It tracked across the planet and lit up in the sun.

"Shit." He slammed his fist against the keyboard. "A fucking asteroid? Really?" He looked down at the broken keyboard. "Damn it." He would have to take care of that later. Right now, his attention needed to be dedicated solely to the newly discovered planet.

"Sir, are you alright?" Julie asked from the back of the room.

Frank had forgotten she was still there. "Yeah, sorry you had to see that."

"It's alright. There's been a lot of pressure on you."

"Thanks, but I still shouldn't break stuff like that."

"It's fine, really. I'll have them send in a replacement right away."

"I'd appreciate that if you have all the data you can forward it to me and go ahead and take a break with everyone else."

"Info's already sent."

"Great. I'll see you in a bit."

Once she was gone. He pulled up all the information the satellite had compiled. Most of it was raw unprocessed data at this point. He uploaded it to his zip drive and headed off to the conference room. A few phone calls later and every top scientist on base was on their way. With that part done, he now had the hard task of reaching the President. The phone rang and rang.

"You've reached the office of President Graham. Can you please tell me who's calling?"

"This is Frank Bruner. Head of NASA."

"And what is the nature of your call?"

"We're getting ready to have a meeting on the findings from the midpoint relay satellite."

"I'm sorry but your satellite pictures are going to have to wait until the president is free."

"I need to talk to him now." Frank was getting frustrated. This conversation was going nowhere.

"Sir I'm afraid you'll just have to wait."

"Listen, just tell him who's calling. I'll take the heat if he gets mad." That had to be enough to get through.

"Fine, please hold. But I can't promise he'll take the call."

"Thank you." Frank held the phone closely. He couldn't wait until that snarky receptionist had to come on the phone and apologize. The other end picked back up.

"Sorry about that, sir. The president said he would gladly take your call."

A smirk crossed over Frank's face. It was so grand. He felt as though the receptionist could feel it on the other end of the line. "Glad to hear it."

"President Graham here. I'm all ears, Frank."

"Great, I'm going to patch you through to the conference call system." He pushed a button and the speaker in the center of the table took over. "Let me know if you can hear me."

"I can."

"Great. The others are just now arriving; we will start in just a minute."

"I'll hold on."

The others took their seats, unaware of what they were all in store for. "Everyone comfortable?"

They all nodded.

"I'll go ahead and start. Just a little bit ago, NASA received their first video from the Midpoint Relay Satellite. Our initial hopes were to find the Phoenix VII intact and establish a relay. Instead we found something completely unexpected. It appears that there is another planet in our solar system. It lies in our orbit on the far side of the sun. It appears that an asteroid orbits the planet. There seems to be liquid water on the planet's surface. Other than that, not much more is known at this time. Mr. President, I will send you everything I have so you can take a look."

"Are you saying we found a new planet that could support life?"

"Yes. And judging from the last location of the signal from the ship, and not seeing any signs of them orbiting the planet, we have to assume they are safe on the planet's surface. I would like your help to figure out as much as we can about this new finding."

The speaker box interrupted, "Let me know what kind of funding you need. This finding could change everything."

"Agreed. We will need to discuss future plans. I was hoping to open up a discussion about sending a rescue mission."

"That would take several years to even get the plans made up," one of the scientists said.

"Exactly why we need to discuss it now. If we have any hope of getting them back alive, we need to get things underway." Frank had to give it his all. "These are our people. We owe it to them. Besides, we don't have to worry about contaminating the planet. If they are on its surface it's too late to do anything. Just think of everything we could learn. There may even be life on that planet."

"Let me see the data once you get more information and we can discuss it at a later date."

"Thank you, Mr. President. Now any questions?"

The voices all intermingled as they hurried to please their inquisitive minds. Frank knew he didn't have all the answers they were seeking, but he would do his best. This discovery would be one that without a doubt would forever alter the future of human history.

Epilogue

The sun shone down upon a barren red landscape. The red dust was the only remnants of the once beautiful and lush ribbon forest that adorned the land. Rusted skeletal fragments, scattered throughout, were all that remained of the once glorious Phoenix that had delivered the aliens to an otherwise undisturbed planet. A yellow barrier surrounded the red wasteland, spreading its fingers out to expand the destruction. Anything that dared to come into contact with the yellow moss would find nothing but death.

There was, however, one spot that managed to stave off the cold touch of death. A large swath of land remained in pristine condition. The moss had ceased to exist along its borders. The cause, a strange blue plant that covered the ground with an interwoven series of vines. Here, life could be seen and heard carrying on undisturbed. The gel backs scurried through the ribbon branches collecting pieces of food. Their orange nests thrived amongst the ribbon trees. The echoes of the lost crew's voices rang out sporadically, forming an incohesive conversation being had between the mimics. Their ghosts would forever haunt the forest that took their lives.

A pack of spikers surrounded their tunnels. The sunbeams streaming through the ribbons above, casting intricate shadows along the forest floor. The largest amongst them kept guard. It watched the pups chase each other around. Occasionally stopping to let out a high pitch squeal. The little spikes quivering with excitement.

The forest held within its protection, another secret. A series of nine worn rocks, placed deliberately, the remains of etchings barely visible on the surface. Time had not been kind to the crude memorial. The blue net plants had taken over, indifferent to the memorial's significance. A weathered toy Warneg Hero kept watch over the stones. Its color had long faded away. Just a few feet away, an empty lean-to with a rotten roof and a stone ring where a fire pit had once been, made up a now-abandoned campsite. Beside the lean-to, the antenna remained ever vigilant, pointing to the sky. Its efforts were in vain, for the battery cells had run dry, now only filled with dust.

A hungry beast swung from ribbon branch to ribbon branch through the tangled forest towards the abandoned sight searching for food. Its six limbs allowed for flawless transfers. It caught the scent of food on the far side of the camp. Seeing no easy way to cross, the creature clambered onto a sturdy branch. It extended the loose skin on its sides into wing-like extensions. In a single bound, the creature went flying into the air. It slowly glided through the air following the scent. The source was just ahead. It threw out its limbs and grabbed ahold of a passing branch. The wing-like structures deflated and the creature descended the ribbon tree climbing onto a lower branch. It found what it was hunting for. A strip of twisted cloth was hanging down from a lower branch holding up the decayed remains of Trent's body. Bits of sinew just barely held the spine together. The bones were covered in scraps of flesh. Loose, tattered cloth draped over its shoulders. In the breast pocket a water stained bit of paper that sat neatly folded. On the ground the limbs laid in a pile of bones littered with teeth marks. The creature descended the rope and began gnawing at the vertebrae. It removed what little sustenance the body could provide, casting used bones into the pile beneath it. An explosive sound overhead caused the creature to flee in terror.

The source of the ground shaking sound was flying overhead. A large spaceship had pierced through the planet's thin atmospheric veil. In doing so the sheer speed ruptured the sound barrier. A noise only heard once before on this alien world. A red-hot glow encapsulated the front of a ship on its descent to the surface. A large American flag and the words USA adorned the outer hull.

What will the Ship find when it lands on the planet?
Is Earth prepared for the truth?
Find out when the story continues in

Avernus book 2

What They Left Behind

Until then, here's a little glimpse of what's to come

Kaylen

Eight miles per second; that is the estimated speed at impact when the ground was gashed open. The land exploded outward leaving behind a hole nearly a mile wide and deep enough to hide the statue of liberty if one felt so inclined. Its sides were sheer cliffs with only two possible routes to traverse them. Soft dirt and new growth littered the inside of the crater. In the very center rested several large metal beams and sheets, remnants of a once glorious shuttle now torn and twisted. Sunlight glinted off its surface. Somewhere amongst the scrap heap lay the secret to the crash, locked within a metal box. It was up to Kaylen and her crew to find it and return it to the base camp for analysis. She stared out at the scene before her. "NASA, we've successfully reached the wreckage. Requesting permission to head in."

"Permission granted," a gravelly voice responded.

"Rodger. Okay Bryce you go ahead and wrap around the left side. I'll head to the right. Dan you take center. Keep your radios on."

"Gotcha," Bryce said as he took off.

Kaylen headed towards her route, but in her peripheral she noticed Dan hadn't moved. She switched over to the private com channel. "Yo, Dan you alright?"

"Yeah sorry, it just looks a bit tight in there."

"I tell you what, we can switch roles. I'll head into the middle and search. How does that sound?"

"Thanks. Sorry to make you do that."

Kaylen gave him a nudge with her forearm to reassure him. "Hey, don't worry about it. We're a team, which means we look after each other. Now get your ass over there."

His laughter in response was a good sign. Now it was up to her to charge headfirst into the wreckage. It started off simple. The way was blocked by some low hanging metal beams crossed with others jetting from the ground. She placed her hands on top of the first beam and swung her legs up to the side. It was just like rock climbing. She hopped to the next beam and under the next that led her to one handing out over a small opening on the ground. She leaped down and walked past a large metal panel, but then came face to face with a twisted maze. If she was going to make it through the narrow passages she would have to get down on all fours. Luckily, the spacesuits were more form-fitting than their ancestors and the oxygen tanks were no longer large cylinders, but rather thin boxes that weighed just over five pounds. She crawled through the corridor, guided by the light atop her helmet, and the small pinpricks of light that dotted the passage, being careful not to catch her suit on any of the sharp metal edges. Exposed wires hung from the mangled ceiling above her like roots branching into a cave. By the looks of it this had once been a hallway. Up ahead a wall blocked her way through, forcing Kaylen into a side room.

The room itself seemed to have remained mostly intact. There was enough space for Kaylen to stand up once again. She swept through the darkness with her light. Bits of broken machinery were strewn about. "Guess this is as good a place as any to start looking," she told herself. "Let's see, if I were going to hide something in this room where would I put it?"

"Did you say you found a room," Dan asked over the com.

"Oh, sorry I forgot you guys could hear me." She flipped over a metal sheet hoping to find something of use in her search. "Yeah I found a room full of broken machines. It seemed like just as good a place as any to find the box."

"Well glad someone's having good luck," Bryce joked. "There ain't shit out here. But better you in there than me,"

"Yeah you'd be freaking out in here. And trying to drag your sorry ass out would be impossible." Her words were followed by an uncontrollable guffaw.

"Just let us know if you find anything." Dan seemed annoyed by the whole exchange.

"Can do." She let the conversation go, shut off her mic, and returned her focus to the worst game of Where's Waldo ever. For all her flipping of metal panels, and moving around crates, her search remained fruitless. By now she had rearranged almost the entire room, in fact the only thing she hadn't touched was the electric box on the wall. It hadn't occurred to her to look there. "Enh why not give it a try." She clambered over to the wall and inspected the panel. It seemed to still be intact. There was no lock holding it closed which was a good sign. "Let's see. Usually there's a latch." She felt along the edges and felt her hand hit something along the base of the box. A quick flip and the latch disengaged. The panel opened and there sat the black box she was searching for.

"Hey, guys I found it" she said, but no response came back. She started to work her way back towards the narrowed hallway that she had crawled through initially. "Did you guys hear me?" still nothing. "What gives," she asked as she entered the tunnel. "You guys playing a …" she suddenly realized what had happened. The mic was still off from earlier. "Goddammit." A double tap on the side of her helmet let out a beep that echoed in her ears to signal she was live. "Am I coming through?"

"Yeah we hear you." Dan's replied. "Hadn't heard from you in a while. Bryce and I Thought you might have run off."

"Nope. right here. Well wherever here is. It's kind of crazy in here." She was trying to remember the path she climbed along to get to the tunnel system.

"Yeah see that's why I went near the outside of the wreck. Less chance of getting lost. Kind of like you." Bryce seemed to be downplaying that he had been too scared to go into the middle of the wreck.

Kaylen shrugged it off. She had more important things on her mind. "Crap, I got off-topic. The reason I was trying to contact you guys was that I found the box."

Her companions both spoke at once in a muddled congratulations.

"I'll meet you guys outside the wreckage on the East side."

Bryce responded first. "Okay on my way."

It took Dan a bit longer, but soon he agreed to the plan too.

As Kaylen made her way back through the collapsed beams and destroyed rooms it reminded her of being a kid. All those hours spent on the playground climbing through tubes, scaling the side of the jungle gym, and her daring attempts to walk along the top of the railing came flooding back to her. It made her feel giddy. A low beam forced her to crawl army style to get past. Coming out the other end she ran into a slanted wall that she could just as easily walk around but her brain was dead set on having some fun. She placed the small box inside the pack on her suit and lined herself up with the wall. Her hands pushed her body forward and she took off in a full sprint. The weight of the suit could be felt inhibiting her movement just enough to cause her to doubt herself, but it was too little too late. The distance was short and before she had time to adjust to the misstep the wall was directly in front of her. *No time to hesitate*, she convinced herself and placed her first foot on the metal sheet. Using her momentum, she managed to take several steps up before gravity pulled her forward. She reached out and clung onto the ledge. The textured gloves gave her enough grip to pull herself up onto the top ledge. The view was spectacular, she took a second to just sit and look around the site and at the crater's ledge in the distance. It all felt so alien. As she sat there watching the world seemingly sitting still around her, the sight of a green object moving between the rubble reminded her that she had somewhere to be. If her guess was right, that was Dan on his way to the meetup.

"Welp, time to get moving. Now, how to get down." She stared below her at the soft dirt. "Looks like I can make the jump."

"What are you talking about?" Dan seemed highly invested in her dilemma.

"Oh nothing. Just talking to myself." She decided she should keep her thoughts to herself for now. *I don't want to risk tearing the suit, and it's a bit bulky so tucking and rolling seems like a bad idea. I guess I could climb back down the way I came up.* She looked back and realized that it just didn't seem fun enough so instead she found the rubble holding up the wall and decided to climb down it. She lowered herself down and searched for a foothold. Her foot rested on a small ledge, just big enough for the ball of her foot. She grabbed on to a piece of rubble further down the wall. Her next step rested on a metal pole. She shifted her weight but the pole gave way beneath her, sending her body falling. The only thing that saved her was her firm grip. Dangling there, she found a new foothold and stepped down, and then hopped off. Once her feet hit the ground she headed back, this time making sure to not take in any more detours or unnecessary stops.

Kaylen emerged to find Dan awaiting her patiently. "Hey you beat me."

"Guess you're just slow."

Without a word she pulled the black box from her pack and presented it on open palms.

"Well I'll be."

"Yeah now who beat who. Hey, speaking of beating each other have you seen or heard from Bryce?" Kaylen looked around in hopes of seeing his green suit poking out. Maybe he was just hiding. She ran around and searched the nearby wreckage. No sign of him anywhere.

"Now that you mention it the last time, I heard from him was when you were telling us about the box." Dan's face showed more concern than his voice let on.

The best option Kaylen could come up with was to head in his direction and hope they found him. "Let's go take a look. He might be lost. Dude doesn't have a great sense of direction." Walking side by side, the pair set out to find their companion. Under normal circumstances one would just call out for their friend and listen for a response, but these conditions were anything but normal. "Bryce, come in." Nothing. "Olly, Olly, oxen free." Kaylen kept her eyes sharp. She spotted a bright green patch and headed towards it only to realize it was a plant. She gave it a swift kick while ranting, "Stupid fucking bush."

Up ahead, a beam of light moved along the ground. At first, she thought it was the wind, but it wasn't moving in a regular pattern. There was no way it could be Dan since he was off to her left. "I think I found him," she hollered over the headset forgetting that it would come out directly into Dan's ears. She could apologize later. The beam didn't seem to change its erratic movement. If Bryce was under there was no way he could hear them. She hurried around the bend and found him trapped under a fallen sheet of wire mesh and a steel beam. "Dan get your ass over here." On command, he appeared in front of her. One look at him was all it took to get him to start lifting the beam. She pulled the wire mesh aside and reached her hand in. Bryce was still conscious. The green glove locked into hers and she used the weight of her boots to help her pull him out. His body broke free just in time to see the mess come crashing down. Dan had lost his grip on the beam. The collapse threw a cloud of dust into the air.

Steven Webb was born in Chandler, Arizona in 1989. He grew up in Phoenix where his imagination flourished while reading indoors to escape the long hot summers. His love of animals then took him to Colorado where he studied animal biology at Colorado State University all with the dream of one day becoming a Veterinarian. It was at this school that he first envisioned the concept for this book. He fell in love with the state and all of its beauty, making it hard for him to leave. Realizing that moving back home was the change he needed, he packed up and move into an apartment with his dog, Lunette. Being able to live on his own and the change of scenery inspired him to finally set to work on his first book when he wasn't busy helping foster group home children though his job at OCJ Kids.

www.ingramcontent.com/pod-product-compliance
Lightning Source LLC
LaVergne TN
LVHW021654060526
838200LV00050B/2355